PRAISE FOR

Winner of the Warwickshire Secondary Book Award 2019, the Great Reads 'Most Read' 2018 Senior Award and the Sussex Coast Schools Amazing Book Award 2019

'S.T.A.G.S. is a pacey and well-plotted young adult story that champions outsiders and questions out-dated viewpoints in a constantly evolving world.'

CultureFly

'M. A. Bennett is brilliant at keeping the reader in suspense.'

Book Murmuration

'M. A. Bennett reinvigorates the boarding-school thriller . . . This is a darkly compelling examination of the allure of privilege, and the unscrupulous means by which it preserves itself.'

Guardian

'S.T.A.G.S. is a thrilling and thoroughly enjoyable YA novel with dark undertones. A fun mystery thriller that sheds light on issues surrounding class and society. Highly recommend.'

Book Bag

'A gorgeous and compelling romp.'

Irish Times

T.I.G.E.R.S.

BOOKS BY M. A. BENNETT

S.T.A.G.S.
D.O.G.S.
F.O.X.E.S.
T.I.G.E.R.S.

The Island

T.I.G.E.R.S.

M. A. BENNETT

First published in Great Britain in 2021 by
HOT KEY BOOKS
4th Floor, Victoria House, Bloomsbury Square
London WC1B 4DA
Owned by Bonnier Books
Sveavägen 56, Stockholm, Sweden
www.hotkeybooks.com

A CIP catalogue record for this book is available from the British Library.

ISBN: 978-1-4714-0868-7
Also available as an ebook and in audio

1

This book is typeset using Atomik ePublisher
Printed and bound in Great Britain by Clays Ltd, Elcograf S.p.A.

Hot Key Books is an imprint of Bonnier Books UK
www.bonnierbooks.co.uk

To Ina,
who was my grandmother

Thou art of the Jungle and not of the Jungle . . .
But I love thee . . .

Rudyard Kipling, *The Second Jungle Book*

PART I
Trust in Me

1

It was seven o'clock of a very cold evening when I set out for my meeting with the Abbot.

I snuck out of the front door of Lightfoot House into the shock of the January cold. I crossed the Garden Quad, then went down the Hundred Steps – slippery with frost – past Honorius House and Oswald House, past the illuminated windows of the library and into the gothic dark of the chapel. All the way the letter fluttered in my hand in the bitter breeze. As if there hadn't been enough drama, what with the fire at Longcross Hall and the death of its lord, Rollo de Warlencourt, the letter which I now clutched had told me that there was *another* secret society, *besides* the Order of the Stag. The letter had shockingly revealed that rebels against the Establishment had been watching the Order since the time of the Gunpowder Plot, tracking them for centuries. Rebels known as the FOXES. Their leader – their own Grand Master – known as Reynard, had written to recruit me. And I was pretty sure I was going to meet one of his agents right now.

The meeting was to be at seven o'clock in the chapel

because everyone else would be in the Refectory at Commons – the evening meal. I didn't tell anyone I was going to meet Abbot Ridley. Not Shafeen, even though he was my boyfriend. Not Nel, even though she was my best friend. And not Ty, the outsider who'd become an insider; the one who knew much more about this than any of us. Apart from maybe Abbot Nathaniel Ridley, headmaster of STAGS and all-round nice guy, who, I was convinced, was up to his handsome neck in it. It was the Abbot, after all, who had directed me to check my post. He'd known the letter was coming.

He was there before me, in the front pew, sitting poker straight, with the cowl of his habit drawn right up. From the angle of his head, he seemed to be looking up at the window, the one that showed St Aidan and the white stag. The chapel was dark, lit only by the pinprick light of candles, but moonlight flooded through the window, its silver hue unchanged by the white flanks of the stag.

As I walked down the aisle – I'm not going to lie – I had the strongest feeling that there would be someone else beneath that hood. It hadn't occurred to me until that very moment that I might be in danger. But as I slid into the pew beside the cowled figure, it raised a pale hand and lowered the hood to reveal the ruffled curls of the Abbot.

I knew just what to say, don't you worry. There was no wondering where to start. I waved the letter under his nose. 'OK,' I said. 'I did what you asked. I checked the post. *Now* show me.'

He didn't waste time asking me what I meant. It was truth

4

time and we both knew it. The gaslighting days were over. He turned over his long left hand, the fingers splayed, and showed me the pad of his thumb. There, in the moonlight, I could see the smooth scar tissue in the shape of a perfect little M. I looked at it for a moment. Without hesitation, I pressed my own branded thumb to his.

He didn't draw away but returned the pressure. We looked at each other and smiled a grim smile. Our dynamic had changed forever. The brand gave us an undoubted bond. I knew we couldn't be the only people in the world who'd been tried by the Dark Order of the Grand Stag, but right now that's how it felt: just us two Manslayers, sitting together in a pool of moonlight in the STAGS chapel. We were no longer headteacher and pupil. I spoke to him now as an equal.

'So – you're one of the FOXES?'

He said nothing.

'First rule of the Fox Club, eh?' I said. 'You don't talk about it?'

'Something like that.'

'And I take it that you being here at STAGS isn't an accident?'

'No. The school was identified as, shall we say, the epicentre of the problem. This was clearly where the "prey" for the death hunts were being sourced.'

That was one way of putting it, I thought. All those poor kids who had thought they were being invited to a lovely country-house weekend, being pursued through the green fields of England. 'Then,' he continued, 'when Gideon Villiers had to "disappear", I was fed in.'

He'd lost me. 'Sorry, who?'

'The Old Abbot. Gideon Villiers.'

'Ah.' I'd never known his full name. In the game book of 1969, when all the old friars and Shafeen's dad had been Rollo's guests at Longcross, he'd been written in the book only as the Grand Master. That, of course, reminded me that the Grand Master of the DOGS had an opposite number in the FOXES. The mysterious sender of the letter I now held. A thought occurred. 'Are *you* Reynard?'

He smiled again. 'That I can tell you. No.'

'Then who is?'

He was silent.

I sighed. 'All right, let's try another one. Is Ty involved in this?'

'Let's just say that, when we discovered where her . . . interests lie, she was invited to join our number.'

'So you've been in this together?'

'You might say that.' He tapped the letter where it lay in my hand. 'And you? Have you thought about Reynard's offer?'

'I'll answer you that if you answer me another. Did you murder Rollo de Warlencourt?'

He looked at me as if I'd asked a trick question.

'He died in the fire at Longcross,' he said slowly.

I shook my head, keeping my eyes on him all the time. 'Nope. He was poisoned.'

'What?'

I gauged his reaction carefully, but the shock on his face seemed genuine.

'But you did kill someone, right? That's why you have the brand.'

He shifted a little in the pew. 'Not deliberately. It was a long time ago, in a country far, far away.'

I appreciated the *Star Wars* reference – he did look pretty Jedi at that moment.

'Who was it?'

'That's another of the things I can't tell you. For your own protection.'

'Was he one of the Order of the Stag?'

'Yes.'

'Aren't you going to ask me the same question?'

'But I know who you killed,' he said. 'Henry de Warlencourt, formerly of this parish.'

Hearing Henry's name like that, and from the Abbot, was a shock. 'But he's alive.'

'I know that too.' He seemed to know an awful lot. 'Some people believe in reincarnation, you know.'

I was sceptical. 'Are any of those people in this chapel?'

He pointed. 'Him.' There was a crucifix over the altar, where a polished wooden Christ hung neatly, seeming politely not to notice that he was nailed hand and foot. 'He made a comeback after three days.'

'You're not, surely, comparing Henry de Warlencourt to Jesus Christ?' I said. 'Because I think even Henry would say that was a stretch.'

'I never met Henry. But no, from all I hear, it's not a comparison that I'd make.'

I *almost* sprang to Henry's defence. He had, after all, saved Ty from the fire at Longcross. But maybe if the Abbot didn't know about the poisoning, he didn't know about Henry and

Ty. Only Shafeen, Nel and I had seen him before he'd vanished into the ashes like in *Avengers: Infinity War*. If the Abbot could keep secrets, so could I.

'I merely meant,' he clarified, 'that many world religions believe in reincarnation. Hinduism in particular.'

'Now you sound like you teach religious studies,' I observed.

'Habit,' he said, and it was hard to tell if he was punning on his outfit or not.

I studied him. 'Do you really believe that Henry came back?'

'I think it more likely he never went away.'

There was something I suddenly had to know. 'The person you killed. He . . . she?'

'He.'

That was somehow better, but if you asked me, I wouldn't have been able to explain why. 'Did you *mean* for him to die?'

He seemed to give this some thought. 'If I were to think of a word for it, it would be that I was a Manslaughterer.'

I smiled to myself, remembering. 'I don't think that's a word.' Then another thought occurred. 'Are you even an English teacher?'

'I used to be.'

Before he'd joined the FOXES, presumably. 'Did you know that Esmé Stuart was a man?' I remembered when he'd muddled the gender of Ben Jonson's friend and patron. It was the first time I'd suspected that the shiny new Abbot might not be all that he seemed.

'Not at first. I did later.'

I *knew* I'd been right about that.

'I suppose it was a kind of . . . shibboleth,' he confessed. 'And I failed the test.'

'What's a . . . shi-shi— *what* did you say?'

'A shibboleth,' he said. 'A word, or a question, that's a test.' He nodded to the school bible, open on the lectern as it always was. 'In the book of Judges, the residents of Gilead would challenge strangers to say the word shibboleth.' He was doing that explaining teacher thing again. 'The Ephraimites couldn't say the word properly, so they were found out.'

'Ah, OK,' I said. 'Like at the end of *The Great Escape*, when the German officer says *good luck* to the British prisoners and they say *thank you*, giving themselves away as English.'

'If you like.'

'What happened to them? The Eph-Eph—'

'. . . Ephraimites . . .'

'. . . If they couldn't say the word?'

He looked at me directly. 'What happened to those prisoners in *The Great Escape*?'

'They were put to death,' I said soberly.

'Then there's your answer.'

'Well then, you got off lightly,' I said, trying to make a joke of it. 'I didn't do that to you.'

'No, but you found me out.'

I fiddled with the carving of the pew in front of me. 'And why didn't you know the . . . shibboleth? Why didn't you know Esmé Stuart was a man?'

'Let's just say I was insufficiently briefed.'

'By whom?'

He was silent again.

'All right. Let me change the subject. Blowing up Longcross, the full-on *Baader Meinhof Complex* thing. Was that a FOXES plan? Because I have to tell you, I'd have severe reservations about joining a group that had just tried to blow up me and my friends. You guys couldn't have known we would get out in time. Even Ty, one of your own, would have been collateral damage. So you tell me, *Abbot Ridley –*' I gave his title a biting emphasis – '*did* you plan to kill us all? Or did Bates the Bitter Butler go rogue?'

This made him squirm a bit. 'I can't say.'

'Because you don't know? Or because you won't tell?'

'I'm afraid,' he said regretfully, 'that I can't even tell you that. All I can say is that you were never intended as targets.'

I stood up, frustrated. 'This is useless.'

'Where are you going?' He sounded, for the first time since I'd known him, a bit panicked.

'Lightfoot,' I said over my shoulder as I strode down the aisle. Then I stopped. Sighed heavily. Turned back. 'You know, this is not how I thought this would go.' I slapped my hand down on one of the carved wooden terminals of the pews. 'I thought this was going to be a truth fest. Cards on the table. If you want me to join your little rebel alliance then I'm going to need *all* the information. But you're *still* keeping secrets. And if you won't help me, I'll go to someone else.'

'What will you do?' he said warily.

I regressed to primary school. 'Tell.'

'Tell who?'

'The authorities,' I said. 'The governors.'

He got to his feet and met me halfway up the aisle, as if

we were going to get married or something. 'Listen . . . if I'm keeping things back, it's for a reason, I promise. If you "tell", as you call it, I would be fired. And you and your friends would be in *much* more danger than you are now.' He held out his hand to me in a pleading gesture and I saw again the thumb, and the M burned into it.

It was the brand that held me. We were on the same side – had to be. '*Are* we in danger?'

'Not at the moment. I'm protecting you. But I have to be here to do it. We – the FOXES, that is – have to preserve this . . . equilibrium.'

That, at least, sounded plausible. 'So what do *we* do?'

'The hardest thing of all,' he said. 'Leave it alone. *Watch the wall.*'

'Watch the *wall*?'

'Don't you know your Rudyard Kipling?'

'Just *The Jungle Book* really.'

'Book or film?' he asked.

'Film,' I said shamefacedly. 'I told you it was truth time.'

He smiled for the first time. 'Well, when he wasn't writing *The Jungle Book* he wrote a poem called "A Smuggler's Song", about smugglers in the West Country. There's a line in it where a mother cautions her daughter to turn a blind eye to the smugglers' activities. She says: *Watch the wall, my darling, while the gentlemen go by.*'

'I guess you are an English teacher after all.' We stood there, in a standoff, now more like a scene from *The Gunfighter* than *Four Weddings and a Funeral*. 'So *now* what do we do?'

'You should probably revise for your exams.'

'About *this*.'

There was that lopsided Harrison Ford smile again. 'I'll keep you posted.'

It was a weirdly archaic expression, which fitted with his habit and the surroundings and this whole batshit medieval set-up. The white stag and St Aidan still watched over us both from the stained-glass window.

'Ironic, really,' said the Abbot, following my gaze.

'What is?'

'St Aidan. His power was to protect his disciples from fire.'

I nodded at the saintly face as I turned to go. 'Perhaps he did.'

I was nearly at the door when he called after me.

'Greer. If it's any consolation, I don't think *you* are in any danger at all.'

2

After all that, I ambushed Shafeen and Nel on the way out of Commons.

I marched them off to the Paulinus well, because even though it was fricking freezing, it was the place where we always discussed important stuff. Set as it was right in the middle of the green quadrangle, you could see any would-be eavesdroppers approaching from miles away. The first thing I did, of course, was to share Reynard's letter with them. They read it together, one dark head and one blonde head bent over the paper, and I watched their eyes widen as they absorbed the fact that there was a centuries-old secret society working *against* the DOGS.

Straight away Shafeen noticed something I hadn't. 'This is the same seal, and the same writing.'

'As what?' I asked.

'As the Monteagle Letter. The letter I got at Cumberland Place. The letter that warned us not to go to Longcross. It had the same fox seal, and the same writing.'

'So the Abbot was telling the truth when he said we weren't supposed to be targets,' I blurted out. Then, of course, I had to explain all about my meeting with Abbot Ridley in the chapel.

'So this letter is from the Abbot?' asked Nel, the girl with the one-track mind. She'd had a crush on the Abbot since day one.

'He said not,' I assured her. 'But he wouldn't tell me who Reynard is. The Abbot's definitely one of the FOXES, but I don't think he's at the top of the organisation. And he kept going on about being briefed and stuff. I don't know if he's even a teacher, but he gives a pretty good impression of being one.'

The idea of him being some sort of *Man from U.N.C.L.E.* undercover agent obviously increased the Abbot's glamour in Nel's eyes. She had an interesting take on the whole thing. 'Well, that suits me if he's not really a teacher,' she said archly.

There was no need to ask her what she meant. 'You're not seriously planning to take that whole crush thing to the next level, are you?' I said despairingly.

'Why not?' she asked, wide-eyed. 'It's not against the law. Not now, anyway.'

'Hmm, I dunno,' I said doubtfully. 'He's still supposedly in a position of power over you, and that makes it a bit . . . well . . . *icky.*'

'Leaving aside Nel's love life for a moment,' said Shafeen, 'I think him clamming up like that is a good thing. We're obviously not required to do anything just yet, even if we choose to join the FOXES. Like I said last term, we can't spend all our time Sherlocking. We've got grades to get. Nel and I have got our Oxford interviews. This way we can concentrate on our own thing and wait for him to make a move, and be ready to support him all the way.'

'You've changed your tune,' I said, a bit sharply. Shafeen had never had much time for the Abbot before. 'You would run with the fox then, not ride with the hounds?'

'A hundred per cent,' he said.

'Nel?'

She nodded in agreement. 'Nathaniel Ridley, *contra mundum*.'

I must've looked blank.

'Against the world.'

So we watched the wall, and term just carried on as if nothing had happened. A couple of times I tried to talk to Ty privately, but she wasn't having it – in company she was as friendly as ever, but even so she was always able to avoid any alone time with me – as slippery as one of those silvery fishes in Longmere. The one time I did catch her alone, she was crossing Bede's Piece one evening. I saw her footsteps falter as she came towards me, but it was too late for her to avoid my path. I tried to talk about the FOXES then – what were they planning? And when? Ty just shook her head and said, 'Seen anything of Henry lately?'

'No, of *course* not,' I said. 'You?'

She gave me a weirdly hostile look, and I thought then how odd it was being friends with someone who trusted me as little as Ty did. She made as if to walk past.

I grabbed the sleeve of her Tudor coat. 'Ty,' I said, 'what happened at Longcross, with Henry? That night when you talked to him?'

She looked at me with her head on one side. She smiled, almost in her old way. 'We got on like a house on fire.'

15

Then I was alone in the middle of the playing fields, the night growing dark around me.

When I'd told Ty that I hadn't seen Henry, that was *almost* the truth. Shafeen, Nel and I had scoured the Internet for any clues as to his whereabouts. By night, with our curtains closed and doors locked, we'd take out our Saros smartphones and look for him. All those creepy fan sites were there, and the faceless Facebook pages, and the threads of conspiracy weaving all through Twitter. There were thousands of posts paying tribute to Henry's beauty, and his style; plenty of pictures of his house, and his horses, and his clothes – what I call Privilege Porn. Oxbridge dining societies would still have moonlit black-tie dinners in his name, and YouTube nutters would jump off stupidly high waterfalls in what they called the De Warlencourt Challenge. And yet no one, but *no one*, was suggesting that Henry was still alive. No one had an inkling that Henry was still lurking somewhere on Google Earth. There hadn't been a single sighting, and his de Warlencourt features hadn't been captured in any photographs.

Except one.

It was a grainy photo of the fire-ravaged facade of Long-cross, which we'd found on the *Daily Mail* Online. It was a creepy enough photo, with the windows like empty eye sockets, the glass burned and cracked and blasted from the heat of the inferno. Bruised eye sockets too, charred and blackened all around from the flames. I'd been the one to see it first – I'd pinched and enlarged the picture until it was hopelessly pixelated. But there, I was sure, was a face at one of the windows.

'That's *him*,' I said.

The others looked over my shoulder. We were on Shafeen's bed in Honorius, curtains open so the moon could see in. Nel peered closely. 'That could be anyone.'

'With blond hair,' I said.

Shafeen peered. 'Could be a hard hat. That's a workman, trust me.'

'No. It's him. I can tell by his face,' I insisted.

'I dunno,' said Nel doubtfully. 'I mean, it *could* be. But . . .'

'But what?'

'Not being funny,' she said reluctantly, 'but you could be projecting. It's like the Man in the Moon.'

'What?? Explain,' I demanded.

'Well, you know how people see a face on the moon's surface? But there's nothing really there. I mean, there is *something*. But not a face. Just seas and craters and stuff.'

I stared at the picture, the hollows that could be eyes, the slash of a mouth. The seas and craters of – a face?

'All right,' said Shafeen. 'Suppose it *is* him. What's he staring at?'

I didn't reply. I knew for a fact that was Henry in the window. I could tell by the way he was standing, the way he was staring.

And I had the oddest feeling he was staring at *me*.

3

I didn't say anything to the others, but back in my own room I fired up Instagram and sent the picture to **mrs_de_warlencourt**.

You never knew – she might have been able to confirm my suspicions that Henry was still living in the shell of his ancestral home. But the account lay dormant. I wasn't sure, weirdly, if I missed **mrs_de_warlencourt** or Ty more, and that was mad since they were the same person. But something was keeping me and Ty apart, and his name was Henry. That beautiful sisterhood we'd formed in my hospital room had stalled. Henry was the reason Ty couldn't trust me.

As for the three OG friends, we spoke way more about Rollo's death than Henry's resurrection. Shafeen and I went over and over that deathbed scene that we'd witnessed. It wasn't so much the doctor's revelation that Rollo had been poisoned that consumed us (although we did indulge in some *Knives Out* guessing games about whodunnit), but that last, cryptic apology that Rollo had spoken to Aadhish Jadeja, via his son. Shafeen dwelled on that a lot.

'Why was it so important to him?' he wondered aloud. 'Of all the people in that house, the one person he wanted to say goodbye to was me, because he thought I was my father. Why did he need to see him? Why did he need to say what he said?'

'Hmm,' I mused. 'It was his Rosebud moment.'

'Rosebud?'

'*Citizen Kane*. When Kane dies he says one single word: *Rosebud*. No one has a clue what he's talking about. And the whole of the rest of the film is finding out what the hell he meant.'

'Well,' said Shafeen, 'Rollo said considerably more than one word. But we still don't know what the hell he meant.'

'Yes,' I agreed. 'All that *Kiss me, Hardy* stuff – I mean, what was all that about? And the apology?'

'It's deathbed confession stuff, isn't it?' said Shafeen, clearly still affected by what he had seen. 'As a good Catholic it's the last chance saloon, the final moment to repent of any sins before shuffling off this mortal coil. And what he'd done to my father was clearly top of his shit list.'

'True,' I said, 'but what about what he'd done *with* him. Think about it. Rollo's exact words were: "But I'm not sorry for what we did *together*." That sounds like they *both* hunted – or shot or fished – someone *else*.'

And there I always hit a roadblock. Shafeen simply couldn't bring himself to believe that his father had done anything wrong back in that Justitium weekend in 1969. 'You could always ask him,' I said simply.

'I will,' he said. 'At Easter. I haven't even told him Rollo's dead.'

'You haven't?' I was surprised. 'Why not?'

'My parents know about the fire and everything,' he said.

19

'But I wanted to break the news about Rollo myself. I'm going to India at Easter and that's only a few weeks away.'

'Why in person?'

He looked at me very directly. 'You were there, Greer. You know how . . . weird it all was. Rollo's death is all caught up in what he said about my father. I just feel like it's something I want to tell him myself.'

Fair enough. Then a thought struck. 'Maybe,' I would say, if I dared, 'if your dad did . . . join in all their reindeer games, as it were, he was sort of *forced* to? You know, he maybe had to play along with the death hunts, otherwise he'd be the victim himself?'

'No,' Shafeen would say. 'Not Father. He would never do that in a million years.'

And I'd shut the hell up. But the facts were there. A dying man had spoken.

What we did together.

Rollo's Rosebud moment was pretty damning for Aadhish.

So the FOXES were at bay, hiding in the undergrowth for now. Cass and Louis, Henry's twin cousins, went about their business, untroubled by any rumblings of revolution. Neither one of them, it seemed, had seen Henry in the fire, but Cass happily believed him alive, and Louis – as he was still Lord Longcross, following the death of Uncle Rollo – happily believed him dead. The new lordling was merely marking time until he could leave school and take over the estate. Nothing more was said about Rollo's untimely death. The word poison was never mentioned – according to the press, he'd died in the fire.

The Earl of Longcross was gone, his body was ash and there would be no prospect of a post-mortem. Shafeen, perversely, seemed happier since he had seen the living, breathing Henry de Warlencourt. He knew very well that I thought of Henry, that I wondered what he was doing and that I'd found him a changed character. But it was almost as if he could deal with a living rival better than a dead one. I got the sense that he thought this was more like a fair fight. And there, at the head of it all, the Abbot stayed in his post, watching and waiting.

But soon the DOGS and the FOXES and all the other creatures of the forest had to take second place to something else. The Probitiones loomed – the STAGS equivalent of A levels – and straight after Christmas and all the drama of the fire and Rollo's death, we had to cram for our mocks. All of us had to work hard, and our exams consumed our days. Even when they were over, we were into the last big push of revision, before the real deal in the summer. I was accepted into Oxford, followed by Shafeen and then Nel, and it almost seemed as if we'd all be leaving the school without any more drama. And we would have, if it hadn't been for one thing that happened just before the Easter holidays.

One Savage intrusion into our Medieval world.

It was a phone call.

4

When I was summoned to the Abbot's study, two days before half-term, I knew something big had happened.

As I followed the Year 10 kid who had come to get me from my history class to the gatehouse I thought: *Here we go. The game's afoot. He's going to keep me posted, as he said he would.*

So when I walked into the dark-wood study and saw Shafeen sitting at the Abbot's desk with the old-fashioned phone receiver in his hand, I was shocked. The Abbot was standing over him, one hand on his shoulder, looking down at Shafeen with an unreadable expression. As I walked forward Shafeen lifted his head to look at me – his face was grey. I went straight over and stood by him.

'What's happened?' I asked the Abbot. He just shook his head. And that's when I knew it was serious.

As if I'd taken over his sentry duty, the Abbot gave up his place and retreated to the window. Nervily, I just waited with one hand on Shafeen's shoulder as he talked into the phone. I stared, almost unseeing, at the collage of things in frames behind the Abbot's desk. A master's degree certificate from the University of Oxford. A younger version of the Abbot in graduation gear standing with two tall, good-looking parents outside the Sheldonian Theatre. A slightly older, gap-year-aged Nathaniel Ridley (wearing an orange-and-black stripy tie that made him look like an overgrown schoolboy) on some sort of safari in a hot place. And all the time Shafeen's voice was there in the background, speaking Hindi to the person on the other end of the phone. I felt it under my hand, rather than heard it; that beautiful, frightening, alien language.

Eventually Shafeen replaced the phone receiver onto its old-fashioned stand, so carefully, as if he might shatter it. 'That was my mother.' He didn't seem able to say any more, as if the switch from one language to another had temporarily glitched his brain.

I looked at the Abbot. He said softly, 'I received a phone call from a hospital in Jaipur. Prince Aadhish has suffered a heart attack. I informed Shafeen myself, then invited him to call his mother. But I thought he would like you here.'

Instantly my memory flipped back to the term before, when Abbot Ridley had received a phone call, on that same ancient rotary phone, about the Old Abbot's 'death'. I said hesitantly, 'The prince. He's not . . . not . . . ?'

'No,' said Ridley. 'Not dead. He is stable but has not yet recovered consciousness. In view of his condition, and the fact that we are only two days from the Easter break, I think it best that Shafeen goes home without delay.'

Shafeen got up, slightly unsteadily. He looked dazed. 'Yes. Yes, of course. I'll see if I can get a seat on an earlier flight.'

He didn't look in any condition to do anything. As I watched

23

him struggle to even work the door handle I made up my mind. I wasn't going to let him face this alone.

'Better see if you can get two,' I said. 'I'm coming with you.'

He turned, still dazed. 'Coming where?'

I caught his hand and gave it a little waggle. 'Where d'you think? To India.'

PART 2

Colonel Hathi's March

5

Of course, it wasn't as simple as all that.

I had to make things right with my dad (easy – he was going to be filming for most of spring), get some jabs (harder – and quite painful, if I'm honest) and get a visa for India (hardest – the Abbot had to pull some serious STAGS strings at the Foreign Office). But the short version is that three days later Shafeen and I were landing at Jaipur International Airport.

It had been in my mind to invite Nel – we'd always been a three – but this was Shafeen's thing really and I was there to support him as his girlfriend. This wasn't Glastonbury – I couldn't just invite her along. Nel actually didn't seem to mind – as her parents were overseas too, she was staying at school for this sixth-form half-term Revision School they were doing. Although that sounded absolutely deadly to me, she seemed quite content – I was pretty sure she saw it as an opportunity to get closer to the Abbot, now that she knew he wasn't, in a conventional sense, a teacher. At any other time this would have been a worry, but at that moment I had no bandwidth for anyone but Shafeen.

That remembered heat, like opening the door of an oven,

hit me as soon as we left the plane. I'd been to India once, visiting with Shafeen the summer before, but had forgotten, after our polite English sunshine, how fierce the sun could be.

After the hubbub and crowds of baggage claim, the Jadejas' driver, Hari, was a welcome sight.

His slick appearance, with crisp, white shirt and sunglasses, and the long, black car that was waiting for us reminded me just how rich Shafeen was.

Henry rich.

Shafeen had paid for my plane ticket without hesitation, and now his driver helped us politely into the car, which was so air-conditioned that goosebumps immediately stood up on my arms. I sipped ice-cool bottled water as Hari smoothly answered Shafeen's questions over his shoulder while at the same time negotiating Jaipur's mental traffic. I looked at the back of Hari's sleek head. He must have his own life, his own family, like the driver guy in *Parasite*, but he had given his life to the Jadeja family. The parallels between the Jadejas and the de Warlencourts were complete. A handsome older dad. A much younger mum. An only son and heir – the image of his father. And now, here, the Jadejas' version of Bates, the faithful family servant. I just hoped Hari was a bit more faithful than Bates had turned out to be.

Apart from Hari's polite greeting to me – *a pleasure to see you again, memsahib* – master and servant spoke, for the moment, in Hindi, which gave me a moment to look about me and absorb the sights and sounds of Jaipur. I remembered this feeling from last year, that there was almost too much to take in, so I zeroed in on details – a stone arch above the traffic; a magnificent horned cow sauntering down the street; a young girl riding a bicycle, her black hair flying out like a flag.

And then something that didn't fit – a golden flash in the corner of my eye. I turned my head and stared, but he had gone. His presence imprinted itself on my eyes like a photograph. In the midst of that strange city, someone familiar – someone with blond hair, and, below it, the seas and craters of a face.

Imagination.

It had to be.

I turned my face from the window and clasped Shafeen's hand. 'How is your dad?'

'We're going straight to see him now,' he replied tensely. 'We're nearly at the hospital.'

6

The hospital in Jaipur was state of the art.

In contrast to the India outside of stone and wood and history, this was a bang-up-to-date modern India of metal, glass and science. A harassed-looking but polite doctor directed us down a spotlessly clean corridor to a private room. 'Will your mother be here?' I asked Shafeen.

He shook his head. 'Hari said she was here all night and until lunchtime. They sent her home to sleep.'

Shafeen went in first and I followed.

And there he was.

Aadhish Jadeja, the boy from the book.

He lay on the snowy sheets, hooked up to machines that beeped and hissed and whistled. He looked smaller than the tall man I remembered from last year. That smiling, handsome chap who'd towered over me, in his beautifully tailored English clothes with his beautifully tailored English accent, was now laid low. He had a ventilator mask over his mouth, tubes coming out of his nose fixed with Elastoplast and one of those pulse-counter things on his finger. With his sunken face and white hair, he now looked every one of his sixty-eight years. I put my hand on his son's shoulder. The last time we'd seen a man this age on a bed like this, he'd never got back up.

Shafeen sat by the bed and held his father's hand. 'Father?' he whispered in a voice so intimate that I felt like I shouldn't be there. I almost turned to go, but I could see Shafeen willing him to wake, hoping against hope that his presence would be the one missing element of his father's recovery. His expression was so raw and vulnerable, I knew I had to wait with him for as long as it took . . . I was actually looking around for a chair when Shafeen unexpectedly got back up. 'Let's go,' he said. 'He isn't here anyway.' Then, avoiding the tubes and plasters, he kissed the one clear patch of his father's cheek.

I was reminded, again, of Rollo, and how Shafeen had kissed him goodbye.

And I hoped against hope that Aadhish would wake up.

7

When I'd been to Shafeen's house (or, more accurately, his palace) the year before, it had taken a good long while to drive out of the city into the hills. I settled myself in for a long haul.

So I was pretty surprised when, after about five minutes of driving through the *Fury Road* traffic, we stopped in front of a grand building. Shafeen got out, so I did too.

'What's this?' I asked.

'Our house,' he replied.

'I thought your house was in the hills, where we stayed last year.'

'It is our home in the summer, when it's much cooler in the hills. But my parents mostly stay in the city during the rest of the year. My father's on the board at the bank, and it would be one hell of a commute from the mountains.'

It was a small joke, but it was a joke all the same, and it was good to hear him sounding more cheerful. I looked up at the grand apricot frontage of the mansion, with its elegant columns and frilly arched windows. I still couldn't quite get my head around the idea of having two houses. I thought again of the parallels with the de Warlencourts. As if he'd heard my thoughts, Shafeen remarked: 'You might say, if the hill palace is our Longcross, this is our Cumberland Place.'

Just as Cumberland Place was, in its way, easily as grand as Longcross, this city house was just as grand as the Aravalli Palace in the mountains. The wooden door was beautifully ornate and gave on to a cool atrium of white stone with a plashing fountain in the middle. The fountain had a wide marble bowl, with an enamelled peacock perched on top. As we walked through the courtyard, he regarded us with his beady jewelled eye.

As soon as we were in the house proper, things seemed a little more normal. Shafeen used his keys and then chucked them on a side table as we entered, just like I might do at home. But this wasn't like any home I had ever known. The narrow hall opened out into a wide, airy room, with white arches holding up the ceiling and open veranda doors leading out into a long, green garden. Everywhere there were bronze bowls, exquisite rugs and painted vases. It looked palatial and perfect. In fact, the only slightly scruffy thing about it was a pale square of wall above the table where Shafeen had thrown his keys, which was a few shades lighter than the paint on the rest of the wall. Because it was the only imperfect thing in the place, I was curious. 'What used to be there?'

Shafeen glanced up. 'A picture,' he said. 'Actually, a photograph.'

'Who took it down?'

'I did.'

'Why?'

'Because I didn't like it,' he said shortly.

33

'Was it of you?' I said sympathetically. I'd done the same in my house – there was a school photo of me from Year 10, when I'd had a very ill-advised peroxide-blonde dye job. My dad hung it on the wall just to troll me, and I kept taking it down. 'Did you have buck teeth? Bowl haircut?'

He looked slightly surprised. 'No,' he said. 'No, it wasn't of me.'

On an ordinary day I would have prodded more, but this wasn't the moment to be even more annoying than usual.

I followed Shafeen into the beautiful, airy room. My instinct was to walk right into the garden, but on the veranda I realised that we were not alone.

8

A woman was stretched out on a fancy ornamental couch, her beringed hands folded neatly under her cheek.

Her wrists were shackled in stacks of thin gold bangles. She was wearing a coral-coloured sari and bright drop earrings of gilded filigree, which fell across her cheek and pillow. Just above her nostril was a tiny diamond stud, and the plaited rope of her silver-shot black hair fell almost to the floor. She slept neatly and silently, with the almost imperceptible breathing of the truly knackered. Shafeen smiled for the first time in I don't know how long. He sat beside the figure and gently shook her shoulder.

'Mother.'

Princess Himani woke at once. 'Aadhish?'

Man, Shafeen got mistaken for his father a *lot*. But this time I got it. His mother had obviously been dreaming of her husband and had woken to find his younger self before her. 'It's Shafeen, Mother. We just arrived.' Tears started into her dark eyes at once, and she hugged her son so tightly I thought he would break. Covering his face with kisses, she murmured little endearments in Hindi. I didn't understand a single word, but I guessed what they must mean; tender, secret, toddler words meant for her only son since the cradle. For the second time that day I felt like I was intruding on a private moment. But I needn't have worried. She sat up straight and smoothed her sari over her knees, then held out her braceleted arms to me. I stooped to hug her and kissed her powdery cheek. She smelled of something nice and floral and comforting – a mum smell that I didn't even know I remembered. 'Greer,' she said, smiling and holding both my hands in hers. 'I'm so glad you could be with my *priy*. I mean, my darling.'

'You can call me *priy* – *he's* not here,' said Shafeen drily. 'What did the doctor say about him?'

There was clearly only one *him* in the house – the prince.

'Just what I told you on the phone. He had a heart attack, and he hasn't regained consciousness.'

'But he's not . . . damaged?'

'No. No other organ failure. And the heart itself is recovering well.' She attempted a smile through the tears – a charming smile, like her son's. 'He just won't wake up. They are trying all kinds of things to bring him round. Injections, drugs, you know.'

She waved her arm and her gold bangles clashed again. 'They say he will recover, and that it's just a matter of time, but it's just about finding the right trigger to bring him round. They can't explain it. Perhaps your father is right about Indian doctors.'

'*Mother.*' Shafeen put his forehead in his hands.

'What? You know what he would say. Your father always says they are very nice, but he never really trusts them. Not like the ones in England.'

36

'And if I qualify in medicine? Will he trust me? *I'll* be an Indian doctor.'

She patted his cheek. 'Of course he will,' she said. 'Because you have had a proper *British* education.'

'I give up,' he said. But he smiled.

The princess turned her head. 'Where's Hari?'

'Parking the car.'

'Tell the boy to bring tea, then.'

'For God's sake, Mother, it's not the Raj. "The boy" is called Prem, and he's about forty.'

The princess ignored him. '*You'd* like tea, Greer, I am sure?'

My stomach wasn't really sure what time it was. I didn't know if it wanted breakfast or a Big Mac, but it definitely wanted something. 'Lovely,' I said.

'I'm going to splash some water on my face. You two young people wait on the veranda. I won't be long.'

Shafeen and I settled ourselves in some chairs at a little white table a bit further along the veranda overlooking the garden. Even in the shade it was pretty hot. The lawn was wide and green and enclosed in this ornamental wall, with decorative tiles set along it at intervals. A peacock, looking like he'd just come alive and hopped down from the fountain, strolled across the lawn, and Shafeen gave him no more attention than he would a pigeon. I stretched out my legs, which were still a bit air-travel wobbly. We'd had some pretty swanky airline seats, but being in one position for ten hours is not kind to the limbs. 'Do you think there will be food?' I asked. 'I'm starving.'

'It's the jet lag,' he said. 'And don't worry. Mother doesn't mean tea in a mug. She means "proper" tea – English-vicarage-

37

at-four-o'clock tea. Cucumber sandwiches, cakes – the lot. Tea fit for the Queen of England. Or a princess, at least.'

'I always wondered,' I said, 'why princess? Why the royal titles?' I stretched my arms above my head. 'It was one of the first things I ever heard about you. At STAGS, I mean. That your father was an Indian prince. Before I even knew you.'

'I bet it was,' he said. 'Rank is the only currency that matters in that place.'

'Not wealth?'

'No.' He squinted up at the sun. 'Look how they treated Nel. It has to be the "right kind of money". No, my rank is just fine; I'd be the "right sort" if it wasn't for one thing.'

I knew what he meant, but he said it without bitterness. I got the feeling he didn't want to be part of the club any more anyway. He was over that now. And certainly, sitting here under the Indian sun, STAGS, the Abbot and the FOXES all seemed a million miles away. 'So how come the prince and princess thing?'

'The princely states were part of the old India,' he said. 'When the British came they allowed the rulers to remain on their thrones so long as they acknowledged the British as their overlords. Really the princes were maharajahs and maharanis – like my grandparents were – or nawabs, the traditional Indian ranks.'

'Jesus. It's like that tortuous conversation in the House of Lords all over again.' I remembered trying to disentangle the differences between marquises and earls and dukes.

'Yes. Basically the simple version is that all those princely states went away after the British buggered off in 1947 and there was Partition – you know, the division of India and Pakistan. All those princely states became the new state of India. Palaces were turned into hotels. Maharajahs became hotel managers, but their titles remained. To remind them of a time when they were once kings.' There was a distant look in his dark eyes, harking back to that time of princes and palaces.

'Why didn't your parents keep to the Indian titles?'

'My father chose to style himself as a prince because it sounded more . . . British.' Now he looked at me, his gaze back in the present again. 'It's my father's way,' he said. 'Always anglicising. Always deferring to the Crown. *I am your mother and your father,* the British used to say. Father thinks the Raj was the best thing ever to happen to India.'

'And you don't.'

He looked away. '*God*, no.'

His answer was so definite, almost hostile, that I didn't like to ask why. But there was something I did want to ask. 'Don't get mad,' I said, 'but what actually *is* the Raj?'

'Was,' he corrected. 'Not is.'

'Was then. I've been in India about five minutes and I've already heard that word three times. I mean, I know a *bit*. I've seen *A Passage to India.*'

'You mean a film by a white man about India?' He sounded quite fierce.

'Well, yes, I suppose so.'

'Have you ever seen any Bollywood movies?'

I thought about this. 'I don't *think* so, no,' I admitted. 'Unless you count *Slumdog Millionaire.*'

'I certainly don't,' he said sternly. 'That's just another movie about India by a white guy.' He shook his head. 'You know, it's pretty funny if you think about it. You're always going on about movies, but you've never seen an Indian one.'

'*Jungle Book?*'

'Now you're just being funny.'

I didn't mind Shafeen telling me off. If he was getting all heated at me, he wasn't worrying about his dad. I got him back on track. 'So. The Raj then.'

He took a breath. 'From 1858 to 1947 the British ruled India. So Queen Victoria was our sovereign too. Queen of the United Kingdom of Great Britain and Ireland and Empress of India.'

'How come?'

'The British had made inroads into the country for centuries through trade – the East India Company was an enormously powerful network of merchants. The Indians rebelled against them in 1857, and that's when the British cracked down. The Crown took over, essentially to protect Britain's trading interests. There were rich pickings here, fortunes to be made. India was known as the jewel in the Empire's crown.' He stretched out his legs to match mine. 'When the British came they brought a way of life with them, and for some people that never really went away. When my father thinks of the Raj he thinks of tiffin and polo and drinks at the club. That's why it's all "mother" and "father" and *The Times* newspaper with breakfast and tea at four.'

'And what do you think of?' I asked.

He was silent for a moment. Then he said, as if he was telling a story, 'On 13th April 1919, hundreds of Indian families crowded

40

into the Jallianwala Bagh gardens in the town of Amritsar.' He shot a look at me to see if I registered any recognition, but my mind was a blank. 'As they flooded into the walled garden, the British army blocked off the entrances behind them.'

The peacock cried out a warning. I had a sudden premonition that I wasn't going to like this story.

'With absolutely no notice, the army opened fire on the people gathered. They concentrated their aim on those who were desperately trying to escape. They fired 1,650 rounds of ammunition into the crowd; 1,000 people died, and 1,500 were injured.'

I couldn't speak.

'Remember, this was just one year after the First World War. Hundreds of thousands of Indians had fought shoulder to shoulder with the British. But that didn't count on that day. They were all mown down.'

I found just one word. '*Why?*'

'The British thought it was the beginning of an uprising – the 1857 rebellion all over again.'

'And I'm guessing it wasn't?'

'It was a religious festival. The Sikh festival of Baisakhi. There were women there, Greer. Children.'

I didn't know what to say.

'There's one bit I can never get out of my head. People were trapped, desperate to get away. They were clawing their way up the walls to escape the gunfire. And in the middle of the gardens there was a well, Greer. Just like the Paulinus well. Our well, where we gather to chat shit, and where Henry and his posse used to smoke.'

I thought of that well in the middle of the green and pleasant quad of STAGS. It seemed a million miles away.

Shafeen bit his lip. 'In that well in the Jallianwala gardens, they found 120 bodies – 120 people had jumped into the well, in desperation, to avoid the gunfire.'

The horror silenced me once more.

'The dead were left there overnight, where they'd fallen, because their families weren't allowed into the gardens to collect them. The British imposed a curfew to prevent another "illegal gathering".'

Finally I found my voice. 'What happened to the guys who did it?'

Shafeen snorted humourlessly. 'Nothing. The man who gave the order, one General Dyer, was widely praised for his actions. Lots of people thought he did the right thing. Rudyard Kipling was quoted as saying Dyer had done his duty to the Crown.'

'Rudyard Kipling as in the guy who wrote *The Jungle Book*?'

'The very same.'

I didn't know what to say. I felt, in some weird way, that I should apologise for my people, but that would have sounded mad.

'So,' he said, 'you asked what I think of when I think of the Raj. *That's* what I think of. Amritsar.'

I went silent. Then a thought occurred. 'The picture in the hall,' I said. 'The one you took down. What was it of?'

'The Queen of England,' he said.

Then his mother came back.

9

As soon as the princess sat down with us, a man dressed in a long white coat and a white turban came over.

He was bearing a tray set with a china teapot and three fine china teacups, just like the ones we had used at Cumberland Place at tea with the countess. As Shafeen's mother picked up the teapot and performed the international action of pouring tea, I studied her properly. Again I clocked the comparison between her and Caroline de Warlencourt. She too was beautiful, with no more than a few fine lines mapping her face. She, like Caro, had a much older husband. If Aadhish and Rollo were together at Longcross in 1969 they were both heading for seventy. But I wouldn't put Caro and the Princess Himani at more than fifty or so. That meant both mums had become mums at a normal sort of age, but the dads had become dads much later in life. Why? Had Rollo, as Caro had once hinted, been playing the field before settling down to produce a son and heir? Had Aadhish done the same?

The man in white came back with an amazing silver cake stand stacked with tiny fancy cakes and sandwiches, just as you might see in a swanky English hotel. There was a folded newspaper on the table in front of us, and Shafeen moved it helpfully so the cake stand could be set down. 'Father still gets *The Times* from London, I see.' He gave the corner of the paper a contemptuous flick.

'Whenever he can,' said his mother, pouring another cup collectedly. 'Although they are sometimes a good few weeks behind. This is the one he was reading on the morning he . . . he . . .' Suddenly her face crumpled and she put down the teapot with a crash.

I said comfortingly, 'I'm sure he'll be back home soon to finish it.' I took the teapot from her and started pouring the tea myself.

As I did so, Shafeen said gently, 'Mother. What happened that day? Did you see him have the attack?'

'Me? He wasn't here, *priy*.'

'Was he at the bank?'

'No. He'd had his breakfast, here at this table. He'd eaten his white toast and his marmalade from Fortnum & Mason, and read his *Times* newspaper, just like he always did. It was just like any other day.' Then she frowned, and the fine lines deepened. 'Except . . .'

'Except?' prompted Shafeen.

'Except he didn't finish,' she said. 'He didn't have his second cup of tea, like he always does. And he didn't finish the paper. Usually he reads it cover to cover. When I came down –' She turned to me. 'I rise much later, my dear – his toast was still on his plate, half eaten, and his tea was still in his cup, half drunk.'

I set down the teapot, job done. 'And where had he gone? To work?'

'Well, I thought so. But it turned out he hadn't gone to the bank. He'd gone to the Tiger Club.'

'The Tiger Club?' Shafeen sounded gobsmacked.

'Wait,' I said. 'What's the Tiger Club?'

'It's an exclusive club, up in the hills,' he answered. 'It was founded in 1859 in the days of . . . you guessed it . . . the Raj.'

'Is it like the STAGS Club?' I asked.

'Not really,' he said. 'For a start, it's in the country, not the town. It's all green lawns and colonnades and cool fountains.' He was doing that thing where what he was saying seemed nice, but he was clearly disapproving.

'Oh, it's a marvellous place, Greer,' said the princess, just as obviously approving. 'There's a library, a dining room and even an ice-cream parlour.'

'You've been?' I asked.

'Many times,' she said. 'Aadhish is a member, of course. And Aadhish's father, the maharajah Kasim Jadeja, Shafi's grandfather, was the first Indian member.'

'Tell her when,' said Shafeen sardonically.

'1959 they started to admit Indians,' she said, with no trace of bitterness.

Her son was not so forgiving. 'So to recap: *one hundred years* after it opened, *in India*, the Tiger Club admitted Indians.'

'And what do people do there? I mean, why do people want to join?'

'Gentlemanly pursuits,' said Shafeen bitingly. 'Not indoor ones like the STAGS Club – not so much chess and fencing. It's all polo and swimming and croquet. And, of course, their USP – the Tiger Hunt.'

'You're joking.'

'I'm not,' he said. 'They don't hunt any more, of course. Now it's all safaris for members and their honoured guests. But that's what it was set up for. You can't escape the hunt, wherever you go, Greer.'

'Shafi's grandfather Kasim used to go on the hunts. In 1961 he went on one with the Queen of England and Prince Philip,' boasted the princess proudly. 'We have a –'

'So what was Father doing at the club that day?' interrupted Shafeen abruptly.

'I've no idea. But he went straight there – left his breakfast, as I said, and had Hari drive him up there. He told Hari to go home and that he would call for him later, and then the next thing I heard was that he was in the hospital. He'd had a heart attack at the club, and they'd called an ambulance.'

'Big of them,' said Shafeen. I wasn't sure why he was being so vicious – I could understand him not loving the Tiger Club if they were connected to the detested Raj, but it sounded to me like they'd done the right thing by his dad.

'Speaking of the hospital, I ought to get back.' She swapped her plait from one shoulder to the other, as if it was a device to change the subject. 'So, children. For dinner – what would you like? How about roast beef and Yorkshire pudding? Or would you prefer roast chicken?'

I looked from mother to son. I remembered last year at the other house the menu had seemed pretty British, but I'd assumed that was just for my benefit. 'Oh. I mean – don't change the menu on my account. I mean, I don't need to "eat English", as it were.'

The princess looked a little surprised. 'My dear, that's what we usually eat. It's what Aadhish likes.'

Shafeen gave me a look that said *told you*, but other than that he wasn't really helping me out. I said, 'If you don't mind . . . I mean . . . if there's a *choice*, and it isn't any trouble, what I'd really like to try is some Indian food. You know, traditional Rajasthani dishes and stuff . . .' I trailed off.

But the princess actually looked pretty pleased with what I'd said. 'Well, that might be a nice change. *Priy?*'

'I'm happy,' said Shafeen, and he looked it.

'There then. That's settled.' She squinted up at the white sun, which had moved behind a shady tree as we'd been talking. 'I must get back to the hospital. I won't tell Aadhish about the dinner.'

Realising belatedly that this was a joke of sorts, I smiled. 'And I expect, Greer, you'd like to lie down in your room?'

As soon as she said that, I suddenly realised how tired I was. The jet lag was really kicking in. 'Actually, I would *really* like that.'

Hari, who had reappeared, showed me to my room with his ever-present smile. At that moment I couldn't have told you what the room looked like, only that it had a bed in it. I closed the shutters against the fierce sun, and the cry of the peacock was the last thing I heard before I slept.

10

Rested and dressed, I went down to dinner and the first thing I saw in the dining room was the tiger-skin rug.

I'd only seen a tiger-skin rug once before and that was at Longcross. I remembered that one being a bit bigger and paler. I knew absolutely zero about tigers at this point, but I would say at a guess that the one at Longcross was a male and this was a female. This gal was magnificent – her pelt a searing turmeric colour and her stripes inky black. A queen among tigers. Her jaws were wide, showing sharp, white teeth, her snout creased in a snarl and her glass eyes stared in absolute rage that anyone would dare to end her life.

I don't know why but I bobbed a little curtsy to her. 'Your Majesty.' As it happened, I was wearing just the right thing for curtsying – a long, flowing turquoise dress sewn with little gold peacock feathers. I don't need to tell you that the dress wasn't mine. Obvs I had nothing with me for a winter term at STAGS that would double up for a boiling-hot April in Jaipur. Someone had left it out for me while I slept. Once again, I was reminded of Longcross.

Shafeen came out of the dark to greet me. He gave me

a cool kiss on the cheek, but his eyes were warm. 'Did you sleep?'

'Yes. It was amazing. You?'

'No.' He didn't expand on that. I didn't know whether it was worrying about his father that had kept him awake, or whether he was used to the journey and jet lag.

He looked lovely in an open-necked white shirt, and trousers held up with what looked like a school tie, striped in orange and black like the tiger. His dark hair was all ruffled from the shower and his feet were bare. Sometimes I'd see him as if it was for the first time and couldn't quite believe how lucky I was. 'I see you've met Melati.' He nodded down at the tiger affectionately. 'My father loves her.'

I noticed how everything came back to Aadhish but was heartened to hear Shafeen speak of him in the present tense. It was strangely hopeful.

Once we'd politely skirted the tiger – I saw that Shafeen deliberately avoided treading on her and I copied him – I noticed the rest of the room. It had those lovely frilly interior arches that were a feature throughout the whole house, but this room was covered in mosaics. The mosaics were of flowers in vases and birds in skies, but it wasn't so much the designs that were special, more the colours. The whole place looked like it was set with jewels.

There was not a dinner table as such, but a sunken surface surrounded by fat silken cushions. Shafeen's mother was reclining on one of them.

I greeted the princess, and once again noticed her lovely floral scent. 'I love your perfume,' I said. 'What is it?'

'It's Guerlain L'Heure Bleue,' she said. 'Aadhish buys it for me, so I wear it for him. Always the same one.'

'Tell her why,' said Shafeen, half amused, half exasperated.

'Because it is the scent worn by the Queen of England herself,' said Himani. 'It's her favourite perfume.'

I sat down on one of the cushions. 'You don't have a table,' I blurted out like an idiot.

They both smiled smiles that were uncannily similar.

'We do,' said the princess. 'But we are giving you the authentic experience. Don't expect cutlery either.'

What followed was one of the most delicious meals that I can remember. We had chapattis and curries, samosas and pakoras, and sweet mango lassi to drink. I copied the Jadejas and ate with my hands – they managed it neatly and I made a right old mess, but no one seemed to care. The food was full of flavour and colour and heat, and I properly stuffed myself. The jetlag and the sleep had made me ravenous, and I really found it hard to stop eating. This meal could not have been more different to the genteel tea on the veranda, with the polite cucumber sandwiches and the tower of cakes. I certainly knew which I preferred.

And it seemed that the princess, in a much more refined way, felt the same. She sat back on her cushion, laid her ringed hands on her knees and ceased to look worried for the first time since she'd woken from the couch.

I smiled at her. 'Was it good?'

She smiled back. 'I haven't eaten like that for *years*. I used to have all this in my father's house before I was married. Shafeen's father won't touch it. He says he last had curry in England, funnily enough.'

'Yes, he had it at Longcross.' I nodded to Shafeen. 'Don't you remember? When we were at the STAGS Club, Rollo said your father insisted on curry when he went to stay for the weekend in 1969.'

Shafeen turned to his mother. 'Did Father ever tell you about his school days? At STAGS?'

'No. I just remember that when it was time for you to go to school he insisted you went there. There was never any question of you staying here. *A proper British education*, he said.'

'What about a weekend at a place called Longcross, back in 1969? Did he ever talk about that?'

'That was well before I knew him, of course. But I never heard of the place until you stayed there.'

'What about a school . . . friend called Rollo?'

She shook her head and her earrings flew about her cheeks like gilded hummingbirds. 'No. Never.'

'That's so *weird*,' I said to Shafeen. 'Your dad clearly meant so much to Rollo; odd that he would never mention him.'

'Is it? He never mentioned Rollo to me either. Or STAGS, or Longcross. Until I went to school I'd never even heard the name de Warlencourt.'

Himani sat up suddenly. 'De Warlencourt? I know de Warlencourt.'

'You do?'

'Of course,' she said. 'That name is almost as connected to this place as ours is.'

I pointed to the sunken table, as it was in the centre of the room. 'To this house?'

'To India. To Jaipur. To the Tiger Club.'

'*How?*' Shafeen sounded nonplussed.

'They were presidents of the club for *years*. Didn't you know that?'

'*No.*'

'Oh, yes,' she said. 'Josiah de Warlencourt was the founding president in 1859. Then there was his son Edwin.' She counted these dead de Warlencourts off on her ringed fingers. 'Then Robert de Warlencourt. Then *his* son Montgomery was president after him.'

'Wait,' I said, exchanging a glance with Shafeen. '*Monty* de Warlencourt?'

I remembered, as I could tell Shafeen did, that night at the drinks party in Louis's rooms in Honorius. We'd spotted the elephant's-foot bin and wondered who had killed the unfortunate creature. Cass had told us that it was the twins' (and Henry's) grandfather *Montgomery de Warlencourt. Colonel in the British Army, magistrate at Jaipur during the Raj and all-round shit.*

I left out the shit bit, and asked, 'Colonel in the British Army and magistrate at Jaipur?'

'That's him, yes,' said the princess. 'He died a few years ago.'

I remembered that too – when Cass had been telling Shafeen about going to Jaipur she said they'd all gone out there for Monty's funeral.

'He was president of the club for a long time,' Himani went on. 'He was there when Shafeen's grandfather was admitted.'

Prem came over to clear all the detritus away, but the princess didn't pause. Here there seemed to be no secrets from the staff, as there had been in Cumberland Place.

'Monty was the chief magistrate for the whole Rajput area. He and Kasim – Shafeen's grandfather – had their differences. Kasim was forever defending the Indians who had ended up in court, facing Monty's harsh sentencing. But in the end it was Monty who forced through Kasim's membership to the club. I never understood why, as they never seemed to get along together. But maybe they were friends after all. Anyway, it always seems to be one of that family who holds the presidency of the Tiger Club.'

Prem came back with a silver dish full of brightly coloured sweetmeats and set them down before us.

'And who is president now?' I asked.

'I've no idea,' she said. 'But whoever it is, they deserve our thanks – they got Aadhish to hospital in good time.'

Shafeen took one of the tiny puddings, carried it almost to his lips, then put it down on his plate.

'Mother. When we were at Longcross at Christmas, you know that there was that fire?'

'I know. Thank the gods you were safe.' I noticed the plural. 'Your father felt responsible for that.'

'For the *fire*?' asked Shafeen. 'How?'

'Not for the fire. For you being there. When he heard about the fire, he said he knew he should have stopped you going.'

I remembered the difficult phone call Shafeen had made at Cumberland Place, telling his father that he wouldn't be home for Christmas.

'Yes,' said Shafeen. 'He said I was putting my hand in the tiger's mouth. I was only able to convince him by saying I was going to help a girl who was in trouble.'

'Ty?' I asked.

He nodded. 'Ty. I actually told him that I was going to rescue a damsel in distress. That's the sort of chivalrous, archaic language he understands.'

'So what did he say to that?'

'He said, *Well, my boy, in some circumstances a gentleman has to put his hand in the tiger's mouth.*'

'And this damsel in distress,' put in his mother. 'She was rescued?'

'Yes. But, as it turned out, not by me.' Shafeen did not go into detail. I could see it was difficult for him, even now, to cast Henry in the role of hero. 'But while we were there someone else died. He was called Rollo de Warlencourt. He was the lord of the manor.'

'He died in the fire, this man?'

'No, no – from a . . . riding accident.' I could hear the hesitation in his voice. I could sense that he wanted to tell the truth, but not the whole truth. 'He was a . . . friend of Father's. They'd been at STAGS together, and they'd spent a weekend at Longcross in the autumn of 1969.' Shafeen leaned forward where he sat. 'At the end he thought I *was* Father. He called me by his name. And he said he wasn't sorry for that weekend in 1969, for "what they'd done together". Do you know what he might have meant?'

She shook her head. 'No.' Her dark eyes, so like her son's, took on this glossy, faraway look. 'All I can tell you is that Aadhish Jadeja is the most honourable man I have ever met. He would never, *ever* do anything wrong.'

Her face slackened again and I thought she might cry.

54

I put my hands over hers. 'He'll be all right,' I said, although I was far from sure of it. Rollo hadn't been.

'I hope so.' She attempted a smile. 'I've been praying every day.'

'At All Saints?' Shafeen asked.

'Wait,' I asked. 'What's All Saints?'

'The English church in Jaipur,' he replied. 'It's where Father always took us. Every Sunday. Religiously, you might say.'

'No,' his mother said in answer to his question. 'I haven't been to the church. I'm not talking to Jesus at the moment.' She spoke of JC as if she'd fallen out with a friend. 'I've been talking to Durga.'

I looked at Shafeen, my explainer-in-chief.

'Durga is a sort of protective mother goddess,' he said. 'Very warlike. She's no pushover. She's got ten arms, sort of like a human Swiss army knife.'

'Handy,' I said.

'She fights the battle of good over evil,' said the princess.

'She defeated a buffalo-headed demon called Mahishasura,' supplied Shafeen.

'OK then.'

He smiled at me. 'You sound sceptical.'

'No,' I said at once. 'I was actually thinking it's no stranger than St Aidan turning a white stag invisible.'

'I've been going to the Shila Devi temple at the Amber Fort,' confessed the princess, 'where I used to go as a girl.' She looked almost warily at Shafeen. 'Do you disapprove?

He spread his hands wide. 'Why on *earth* would I disapprove?'

'Because you were raised a Christian. You're at a Church of England school.'

'It sounds eminently sensible to me,' he said. 'Talk to Durga, talk to Vishnu, talk to Shiva. Talk to Lord Krishna himself. Whatever helps you. Whatever helps *him*.'

'I'm glad you said that. Because while you still approve of me, I must tell you something else.' She patted his hand with hers. 'Don't tell your father, but I've been going to an astrologer.'

Shafeen pressed his lips together so they disappeared into a line.

'He's a well-respected Vedic practitioner called Guru Kalyan.'

'*Guru Kalyan.*' Shafeen's voice dripped with scorn.

'And he did your father's astrological charts. So now what do you say?'

I could see Shafeen was struggling with this one. He shrugged. 'Like I said, if it helps . . .'

'But . . . ?' she probed, her voice rising in a question.

He cracked. 'But I think it's all a crock of shit.'

She laughed fondly and stroked his cheek. 'There! Sometimes, *priy*, you are the image of your father. You play the Indian, but sometimes you are British to the core. You know, here in your homeland astrology is a respected science. They teach it at the university.'

'The second part of that statement may be true,' said Shafeen. 'The first is most certainly not. And I bet you didn't find this crackpot at the university, did you?'

She didn't quite meet his eyes.

'Mother?'

'He lives in Jhalana kacchi basti.'

'For God's *sake*.' Shafeen didn't specify which god. 'That's hardly safe.'

56

'What's a kacchi basti?' I chimed in.

'A slum,' he said briefly, to get me off the line before returning to his mother. 'Did you go on your own?'

'No, of *course* not,' she said. 'Hari drove me.'

'Hari should know better.' Curiosity fought with disapproval; curiosity won. 'So, what was it like?'

'Interesting. Guru Kalyan looked a hundred years old. His beard reached down to his feet. He practises in a sort of cave in the rocks there, where there is a hole in the ceiling so he can read the moon. He has stars and signs painted all over the inside of the cave. It was really quite striking.'

'Everything you're saying points to a respected man of science,' said Shafeen drily. 'Go on then. What did this great guru say?'

'He studied your father's nakshatras – his lunar mansions. Apparently those are the divisions of the night sky, dictated by the moon, in which we may read the fate of the subject.'

'And?' asked Shafeen.

The princess looked about her and lowered her voice dramatically. Night had fallen outside and the moon, hearing its name, eavesdropped beyond the arches of this golden cavern of a room – as if we were in a cave ourselves. 'He said your father had seen a ghost. And it was the ghost who gave him a heart attack.'

This statement gave me a real shiver – just like they say, the feeling of a chill travelling down my spine. I pictured the guru in his painted cave, reading Aadhish's fate in the face of the moon.

But Shafeen looked at his mother, then at me, his gaze loaded with scepticism. 'What else?'

'He said that I shouldn't worry. He said your father will recover because he has unfinished business. And the key to his recovery is to find out what that business is.'

Shafeen put his head in his hands in mock despair. His mother reached across and lifted his chin, waggling her son's head from side to side.

'Shafeen feels the push and pull,' she said to me. 'His mother and his father are like two magnets. He's an Indian boy with an English education. He has an Indian mother who is Indian at heart, and an Indian father who is British to the core. If that makes any sense.'

'Sure,' I said. 'You're Merchant. He's Ivory.'

I didn't have to explain. 'Precisely, my dear.' She caressed her son. 'Poor *priy*. Poor darling.'

Shafeen kissed the hand that stroked his cheek and smiled resignedly. I sensed this was not the first time he'd heard this speech. He lifted his head and sat back on his cushion.

'So, my mother. So, my *maan*. What do we do now?'

'I will keep on praying,' she replied. 'And you know what, *priy*? You could pray too.'

11

I couldn't sleep that night.

At about midnight I went out onto my balcony. The air was still warm and I looked out over the garden, feeling the cool night breeze and listening to the alien sounds of India's insect population. Then I heard another sound and looked across to the balcony next to mine. There was Shafeen, doing the same thing.

'Hi.'

I moved to the side of the balcony so I faced him and not the garden. He did the same.

'Can't sleep?'

'No.'

'Like Romeo and Juliet,' I said.

'Juliet and Juliet more like,' he quipped. 'We're both on a balcony.'

We joined hands across the divide.

'I know something we could do,' he said.

And suddenly I was cool with it. Suddenly I felt that this was the right time. Here there were no ghosts of Henry de Warlencourt. He'd never set foot in this place. Nor was I troubled by the ghosts of my younger self as I had been at home – by my toy tiger staring at me from the bedside table. Shafeen needed this. To sleep with someone for the first time for comfort was a terrible reason, but if he was ready, I was too.

'Get dressed then,' he said.

That surprised me – it was kind of the opposite of what I'd expected him to say. As I went back into my room to find some clothes I reflected that I was, in fact, an idiot. This wasn't about me. I might be ready, but now he wasn't. Of *course* he wasn't in the right headspace to do anything with me right now, with his dad in a hospital bed. He clearly had something else in mind.

When he answered his door he was already dressed. He slipped out of his room, closing the door behind him, and we crept downstairs, through the front door and into the midnight streets. We walked away from the house into places that were narrower and darker and busier.

'Is it safe?' I said, going all *Marathon Man*.

'Yes,' he said. 'Perfectly. And also no, not at all. Isn't that wonderful?'

I took his hand and we walked for a while, taking in every strange sight and sound. Then, among all the unfamiliarity, something that was familiar; something I would have recognised anywhere in the world.

A neon sign, a white hoarding with lettering on it and a snaking queue of people.

A cinema.

I whistled. 'That's a pretty long queue.'

'Cinema is another one of the religions here,' he said. 'You can pretty much watch films 24/7.'

I read the title on the hoarding out loud. '*JUNOON*,' I said. 'What's it about?'

'You'll see,' he said.

The film was amazing. It was about this guy who is bitten by a cursed tiger and turns into a tiger on every full-moon night. It was like *An American Werewolf in London* on steroids, or *Ladyhawke* on crack. It must have been made in the eighties or nineties because of the big hair and the shoulder pads, and the tiger effects didn't exactly hold up to today's standards, but it was a fabulous slice of schlocky horror, perfect for a late-night screening.

We walked back through the warm streets, drunk with the ridiculous brilliance of the film. It happened to be a full moon and we amused ourselves by jumping out and roaring at each other as though we were in *Junoon*. Shafeen looked happier than he had since the phone call in the Abbot's office. And, of course, by the time I got back to my room I was shattered and slept immediately, untroubled by any stripy faces in my dreams.

PART 3

The Bare Necessities

12

'What are we going to do today?'

It was just Shafeen and me at breakfast. The dining table was back in place, with chairs set around it. We were back in our Western clothes and the breakfast was as English as it could be. There was no sign of Princess Himani. As she'd mentioned, she liked a lie-in. But her perfume, the Guerlain L'Heure Bleue, lingered deliciously in the air.

As if he sensed her presence too, Shafeen said, 'For possibly the first time ever, I'm going to take my mother's advice.' But he smiled. 'She told me to pray, and I'm going to pray. So, if you don't mind, we're going to visit a temple.'

'Are you kidding? I'd *love* that.'

'It's a pretty good one, as temples go. It's the one Mother went to – the Shila Devi Mandir at the Amber Fort.'

Hari drove us. It was a beautiful day, and the whole of Jaipur seemed to be out on the roads in various vehicles. Hari had to nose the big car carefully through the traffic, visibly enjoying himself more once we were on the open road out of the city.

The Amber Fort was more like a palace – a huge sandstone

structure on top of a hill. Although it was still quite early, the fort was packed. It looked like an interesting place, but Shafeen wasn't stopping to sightsee. He led me unerringly to a distant courtyard to join a crowd of people waiting at some silver doors.

We had to wait for a little while, shuffling forward until it was our turn to stand at the doors. They were beautifully wrought, each panel featuring a different deity. 'Where's Durga?' I asked.

He pointed. 'There she is.'

I looked closely. There was the goddess, with an ornate headdress, her ten arms fanned out about her body. She was riding what looked like a small bear or an enormous cat. 'Is that a lion?'

'Did I not say?' said Shafeen. 'She's always depicted riding a tiger.'

'*Lions and tigers and bears, oh my*,' I quoted softly, and followed him into the temple.

When we went forward to the shrine itself I hung back a bit. In the fragrant dimness I could see the shrine of the goddess, draped with jewel-coloured fabrics, her dark face and almond eyes gazing on her faithful. Shafeen bowed to the idol. As he prayed I could see how much he loved his father. He was critical of him, sure, but he absolutely adored him. I closed my eyes and prayed too. I'm not proud of my prayer, but it went like this: 'Durga,' I said, 'please wake up Aadhish Jadeja. Please ride your tiger to the hospital and wake him up. Please put all of your ten arms around him. Amen. I mean, thank you.'

When we came out of the shrine, Shafeen looked more downcast than uplifted.

'Did it help?'

'Not really. I just feel so . . . *helpless*.'

I put my arm around him, wishing that *I* had ten to hold him with. 'You won't always feel like that.'

'Won't I?' he said listlessly.

'Well, put it this way,' I said. 'Why do you want to be a doctor?'

'It was that or open a corner shop.'

'Ha ha.' I gave him a stern look. 'Seriously. It's so you can help people like your dad, right?'

'Something like that.' He didn't seem to want to discuss it further. 'Come on. Hari's waiting.'

13

We drove back into the city, and as we neared the centre I saw a series of strange white structures that I'd never seen before, set high on a hill.

I pointed. 'What's that?'

'Jantar Mantar,' said Shafeen. 'It's an observatory, built in the eighteenth century by Maharajah Jai Singh. D'you want to see?'

'Aren't we going to see your father?'

'He won't notice if we're a little late,' he said with black humour. 'Besides, it's to do with him.'

We got out of the car and Hari, after a short exchange in Hindi with Shafeen, drove away.

'Where's he going?' I said, a bit nervously.

'He's going to pick up Mother and take her to the hospital.'

We walked among the white structures in the baking heat. Close up, I could see that they were not standing stones, like Stonehenge, but steps and platforms that led nowhere – staircases to the sky. There was a huge triangular structure and a vast sundial, like an ornament from a giant's garden. 'What's this place got to do with your dad?' I asked.

'He watched the moon landing here,' he replied. 'In 1969.'

It seemed a world away – and it was. 'The same year he was at Longcross?'

'Yes. It would have been . . . well, let's see: the moon landing was in July, and he was at Longcross for Michaelmas Justitium. So about three months after.' He squinted up at the steps. 'Come on.'

He climbed the stairway to heaven and I followed him. At the top we sat down together in the fierce sun. It was so still – there was no wind to topple us, and the traffic in the city had diminished to a bee's hum.

'The moon landing wasn't broadcast live on TV in India,' said Shafeen. 'So they came up here. Someone had a radio tuned to an American station, and as the landing was happening they just looked at the moon from here.'

I looked up, just as the young Aadhish must have. There was a slight ghost of a noonday moon hanging high in the blue sky. Had Aadhish tried to see, among all those seas and craters, the fly-speck of a man?

I peered at it until my eyes watered, so I had to look down. The city was just as awe-inspiring as the sky. All those dwellings, the rosy-pink palaces, the jammed traffic. Earth under the heavens I'd been gazing at. The work of man under the work of God. Or, in India, gods. Everything was so . . . *different*. We sat and looked at the view in silence for a long, long time. Then I articulated what I'd been feeling all morning. 'I don't know anything about this country,' I said, almost desperately.

Shafeen said, 'Neither do I.' He whipped a stone down the hillside in frustration and the view swallowed it. 'It's ultimately unknowable.'

I looked at him with admiration. That was kind of what I'd been meaning to say; he just said it much better than I did. 'That sounds really wise,' I said.

He stood. 'No, it's not. It's one of those things that sounds profound, but it isn't really.' He turned his back to me and talked to the city. 'I mean it. Sometimes I feel like a stranger here. They sent me to STAGS when I was eight. *Eight*, Greer. Same as Henry. Sure, I came home every holiday, and sure, I have some pretty strong childhood memories, but really STAGS was my home. I think that's why I got so drawn into their world. STAGS colonised me. Ultimately I only ever wanted to be part of it. I really don't know where I belong.'

I didn't know what to say to this. I thought he would sit back down, but he didn't – there was something restless about him, like a pacing tiger. He turned and hauled me to my feet.

'Where are we going?'

'To the hospital.'

'Is Hari back?'

'No. I told him we'd walk. It's really close. Come on.'

It was pretty hot, but I'm glad we did walk. Because that's when I got to know Jaipur. Not all of it, of course; as Shafeen had suggested, I'm not sure anyone ever could. It was a place of millions of little bits of light, hundreds of facets, like a diamond.

A kid sitting in a gutter, under the shade of a tree. Another kid selling mango juice from a barrow, in reused bottles whose faded labels boasted familiar globalised names like Fanta and Coke. Jaipur was selling cubes of bamboo from a stainless-steel bowl. Jaipur was a rose-pink palace, big as a cathedral. But Jaipur was also a crammed side street, with hundreds of hollow-cheeked people just sitting on their thresholds, hands outstretched to beg.

Shafeen said, 'You asked me why I wanted to be a doctor.' He nodded to the crowded alley. 'That's why. These people have nothing. Not even the bare necessities of life.'

'Is there a health service in India?'

He shook his head. 'No,' he said. 'There are some terrific hospitals. But you can only stay if you can pay.'

Soon we were at the shining hospital where none of those people in the side street would ever go. We walked the spotless corridors to Aadhish's private room, and this time the princess was at her husband's side. She'd got hold of a recent *Times* from London and was reading it to him as we entered. It was very odd hearing her talk about the stock market or the royal family to her sleeping husband. Shafeen stooped to kiss her and she stopped reading to greet us. I looked at Shafeen's father as closely as I could from the distance I'd kept. He wore his hair long like Shafeen did, but since it was pulled back by a surgical cap, I noticed for the first time that one of his earlobes was curiously ragged, as if part of it had been bitten off. Despite the tubes, he looked like he was sleeping, but not entirely peacefully. There was a pair of little wrinkles between his eyebrows, as if he was troubled by something. I couldn't help thinking that, despite Shafeen's scepticism, the guru the princess had visited might have had it right – Aadhish *did* look like he had unfinished business.

After a moment or two Shafeen got up to go. I could tell he was uncomfortable seeing his father this way. 'Will you come?' he said to his mother. She shook her head. 'No,' she said. 'My place is here with him. You children go home and have your lunch.' And she took up the newspaper again.

Shafeen kissed her goodbye, then straightened up and hesitated. 'Do you think he can hear you?'

'Oh yes,' she said gently. 'I know he can.'

14

It was still boiling hot, so we had lunch in the shade on the veranda table where we had had tea the day before.

The *Times* newspaper from the morning of Aadhish's collapse still lay on the table. It was as if no one had had the heart to take it away. I watched Prem, the serving guy, place the cutlery reverently around it, as if it were a holy text. Perhaps the English language in which it was printed, and the centuries-old masthead design of a lion and unicorn, held some sort of mystical power for him, as it did for his master. Shafeen, by contrast, grabbed the paper out of his way, tearing it slightly, and dumped it on the floor, making it easier for the guy to put down the platters from his tray. The food was club sandwiches and fruit salad, such as you might get in a West End hotel. There was nothing on the table that you could have identified as Indian. Shafeen's dark eyes flicked over the platters. 'Prem, are there any samosas?'

'In the kitchen, yes, sahib.'

'Could you bring them, please?'

'Yes, sahib. At once.' Prem stood to attention and saluted Shafeen, as if he were in the British Army. Once Prem had retreated, Shafeen rolled his eyes. 'There's another one. Stuck in the rigid ways of the Raj, just like Father.'

I asked, 'Why is your dad like he is?'

'How d'you mean?'

I nodded at the *Times* newspaper, where it had landed on the white decking of the veranda. 'So . . . *wedded* to the idea of the English gentleman. I mean, when you think of his experiences in England . . . educated at STAGS, a guest at Longcross. I mean, think of how things were for you. You were practically the only person of colour there until Ty came along. Can you remember what the Medievals used to call you?'

'I'm not likely to forget that,' he said ruefully.

'Well, imagine how much harder it must have been for your father. He was there in the *sixties*, for God's sake. When Rollo and his Medievals took him to Longcross, he was shot, just like you were. We know that from the game book. So why is he so crazy about everything English?'

'I don't know, Greer.' He sounded irritated. 'I just don't know.'

Prem brought the samosas, and I studied Shafeen as he helped himself, pointedly leaving aside all the Western food. Something had changed in him since the temple. It was hard to describe. Not an awakening to India or anything spiritual like that, but rather a . . . a hardening against all things British. Including, perhaps, me? Shafeen's whole attitude was summed up in his reaction to the newspaper. Yesterday he'd given it a contemptuous flick with his finger. Today he'd torn it and dumped it on the floor.

He ate in silence and seemed disinclined to talk. But you know me by now – I can never leave anything alone. 'Do you think it's weird that your dad never mentioned the de Warlencourts to your mum in . . . how long have they been married?'

'Twenty-one years,' he said shortly.

'And in all that time he never mentioned the family? Even though they were so involved in that . . . Tiger Club, which is just up the road?'

'But they married well after my father knew Rollo. They met thirty years after that 1969 Justitium.'

I ploughed on. 'But even when you went to STAGS? And then Longcross? And even when Henry fake-died? Not to mention his family name? Not to say, *I knew the boy's father once, you know . . .*'

'Stop interrogating me, Greer,' he said testily. 'I can't explain it.'

I thought I could. I thought it was all to do with The Secret. I thought that whatever had happened at Longcross in 1969 was so bad that even to *mention* the de Warlencourt name was too painful for Aadhish. And yet that didn't explain why he was so adamant that his son should go to STAGS and repeat the cycle over again. It was pretty confusing. But with Shafeen in what I now called 'tiger mode', I thought it best not to antagonise him.

I framed my next question carefully, as I really, really didn't want to offend. 'Did your dad . . . *choose* your mother?'

He drew his brows together in a look I knew well. 'What do you mean?'

I thought this was a bit unfair. He knew what I meant. He just wanted me to say it. Once again, I got the feeling we were now on different sides. 'Was the marriage . . . arranged?'

'Not this one, no. My father married very late – he could choose for himself. After all, he was nearly fifty.'

There it was again: that parallel with Rollo. The late marriage, the young wife, the one son and heir.

'I believe he *was* meant for someone,' Shafeen conceded, 'when he was younger. My grandparents had found a wife for him – a young woman of good family.'

'What happened?'

'I don't know, but the match was never made. This was when he was my age, or a bit older.'

Just after he'd been to Longcross.

'He met my mother much later. She'd been to the university; she had a job. He always told me, *Don't marry an idiot.*'

'Guess *we're* not getting married then.'

That made him smile, and suddenly the old Shafeen was back. He put his elbows on the table, put his chin on his hands and studied me affectionately.

I was encouraged and, not willing to push my luck further, I changed the subject completely. 'What shall we do this afternoon?' I echoed my breakfast-time question. 'Do you want to visit your father again?'

'No.'

He didn't explain – didn't have to. As far as he was concerned, that wasn't his father in the bed. 'Tourist things then. Show me the sights.'

'Yes, memsahib.' He put his palms together in a namaste and bowed obediently. But the gesture wasn't loaded. The antagonism had gone, and I knew a joke when I saw one.

'You should really see the Palace of the Winds. It's pretty interesting. It's the big pink building we passed in the car – would you like that?'

'Yes, great.'

'I'll give Hari a shout.'

As he pushed his chair back the legs caught on the newspaper. He looked down at *The Times* for a long moment and I thought he might trample it underfoot. But instead he picked it up and shook it out, remembering perhaps that it was precious to his father. He made to chuck the paper back on the table among the glasses and plates, but then checked himself as a headline caught his eye.

His expression made me go cold, despite the heat. 'What?'

He turned the paper to face me. Above the main headline, which was something about the economy, there were a couple of smaller headlines. The one he pointed to read:

PEER DIES IN TRAGIC RIDING ACCIDENT
Story page 8

And there was a small picture of Rollo, looking very handsome and smiling his charming smile.

My heart thudded painfully.

'Turn to page eight,' I urged.

He flipped the pages with shaking hands. There, on page eight, was a much bigger picture of Rollo, at about the age Shafeen was now, in his full STAGS uniform of white cravat, black Tudor coat and deer-leather belt, all worn over the blood-red stockings. The caption made Shafeen catch his breath – *Rollo de Warlencourt, pictured in 1969*. But it was Rollo's face that made me catch mine.

He looked *exactly* like Henry.

We huddled close to read together: *Lord Rollo de Warlencourt, 13th Earl of Longcross, died on Boxing Day following a fall from his horse,* it began. Then there was all this CV guff about his birth, his education at STAGS and his time in the army, Foreign Office and House of Lords. Then the last paragraph said:

Lord Longcross's death comes just a year after the death by drowning of his only son and heir, Henry de Warlencourt, and on the day of the earl's demise there was a serious fire at his ancestral seat, Longcross Hall in Northumberland. The late earl can indeed be said to have been the unlucky number thirteen of his line.

I exchanged a horrified look with Shafeen. 'So your dad was reading *this*,' I said.

He nodded.

'It must have had a profound effect on him,' I said slowly. 'He left half his breakfast and went straight to the Tiger Club.'

'Yes,' Shafeen agreed, as if in a dream.

'But *why?*'

In answer, he got up from his chair. 'Let me call Hari,' he said urgently, and hurried off.

I sat back in my chair, goosebumps forming on my skin.

There was no need for me to wonder where we were going that afternoon.

I knew.

We were going to the Tiger Club.

15

The Tiger Club was much bigger than I'd imagined.

I thought it would be a small, low building, like those clubhouses you see in films like *White Mischief* and *A Passage to India*. I'd expected a glorified golf club. But this was quite different to that – all pillared porticoes and frilled archways, splashing fountains and clipped green lawns. It was like a white palace.

It had been a longish drive from the city into the cooler hills, and Hari dropped us at the front steps of the club. 'Stick around,' said Shafeen, as if he were in a different kind of movie altogether. 'We won't be long.'

As we got out of the car I looked again at what Shafeen was wearing. He'd told me after lunch that we'd need to wear formal dress to be admitted to the club, so I'd put on one of the dresses that had, Longcross-style, found its way into my wardrobe. This one was a white linen tea dress, with a kind of spriggy pattern on it, and it wouldn't have looked out of place in a Merchant Ivory movie.

Shafeen, however, had surprised me. When I'd met him at the car, he was wearing an outfit I'd never seen before. He had on a silk jacket with a faint shadow of a paisley pattern on it, with no collar and buttons down the front. The jacket – which was more of a coat and went down to his knees – was tied with a sash of the same material, with a soft gold fringe on the ends. He wore it over a pair of loose cream-coloured trousers. It was a coral-red colour, not designed to blend into the background. He looked, of course, absolutely gorgeous, and back at his home in Jaipur he'd fitted in just fine, looking absolutely *right*. Here, in front of the steps of the Tiger Club, he stood out like a tiger in the snow. It made me slightly uncomfortable to think that in my English tea dress I fitted in better than he did. I saw a few members come down the steps. They were wearing light trousers and blazers even in the heat, and both wore an identical tie of black and orange stripes. I recognised it. It was the one Shafeen had used to tie up his trousers the previous evening. Then, to eat dinner in his own house, he had dressed like the quintessential English gentleman. Here, at the Tiger Club, he'd gone full-on Indian prince. The club members reached the bottom of the steps. They glanced at me and nodded politely but stared, in that discreet British way, at Shafeen.

And then I knew that, of course, he'd done it on purpose.

As we walked up to the door I had a sudden qualm. 'Do you think they'll let you in?' I remembered the cringeworthy moment at the STAGS Club in London when he'd been forced to put on the club tie. He obviously *did* own a club tie in this instance, but had pointedly left it at home.

His lips twisted in a humourless smile. 'I'd like to see them try to stop me.'

But they didn't try. Our entry into the club was as smooth as it could be. In fact, it was unexpectedly smooth.

There was a man wearing the club tie standing by the doorway. He was tall, standing ramrod straight, and sported an impressive gingery moustache. He stepped forward as we entered.

'Mr Jadeja, isn't it?' he said, holding out his hand. 'Colonel Sebastian Moran, undersecretary of the Tiger Club. Might I enquire after your father?'

Shafeen, obviously a bit freaked by this, took the hand in a bit of a daze. 'He is stable, thank you. We're told his recovery is just a matter of time.'

I stole a glance at Shafeen. Had he been here before? How many times, if this guy recognised him so readily?

The colonel smiled. 'I'm jolly glad to hear it. We were so distressed when he fell ill on these very premises. I assure you we acted as swiftly as we could.'

This was not what I'd expected at all. I'd expected Shafeen to be belittled, even cowed, in this environment. But this guy was really pushing the boat out, being mega polite and deferential. He even seemed a bit afraid. Then it clicked. He was probably worried about his precious club being sued.

Shafeen said, 'Can you tell me a bit about what happened last Wednesday?'

The colonel pressed his hands together as if in prayer – a very English prayer, rather than a namaste. 'I regret that I wasn't here that day. But if you'll allow me, I'll fetch our club secretary. He'll be able to furnish you with a little more detail. Always better to talk to the organ grinder rather than the monkey, what?' By which I figured that he meant we ought to talk to his boss. He picked up a phone at his little desk, which I could swear was made of ivory, and made a whispered call.

While he was phoning I looked around. We were in a long sort of hallway that opened out right to the back of the building. Through a distant arch I could see palm trees swaying in the breeze and misty blue mountains beyond. The passageway reminded me of a school: there was a polished teak floor instead of carpet, and on the walls there were a whole load of framed photographs, like when you see all the year groups of classes gone by. When the colonel had replaced the receiver he marched back over to us. 'Could I offer you some refreshment while you wait?'

Shafeen looked at me. 'Greer?'

'Sure,' I said, shrugging in a manner which I was pretty sure the colonel would deem unladylike. But he merely indicated the archway to the outside and said, 'If you'd like to wait on the veranda, the secretary will be with you shortly.'

Once he'd gone, Shafeen turned to me. 'What do you think?'

'Well, the place is great, of course,' I said. 'But I've seen nothing that explains why your father rushed up here the minute he found out about Rollo's death.'

He nodded thoughtfully. 'Unless he just came up here because this place has such a connection with the de Warlencourts. Maybe Rollo came here himself once?'

'But if he *hated* Rollo,' I argued, 'and his obituary just brought back terrible memories of 1969, then why seek the family out?'

We wandered towards the daylight, but I couldn't help

looking at all the photos on the wall as I went. They were all in black and white, all in gilded frames, and they told a story of a world gone by.

They imprinted themselves on my mind like film stills – all snapshots of scenes lost in time, featuring actors wholly unfamiliar to me.

Except one.

One of the pictures replicated itself in a flash of memory.

I had seen it before.

'Shafeen,' I said, low-voiced and urgent, never moving my eyes from the picture. 'Come here.'

He turned back and we looked at the picture together.

It was of a blond guy, with an impressive bristling moustache, wearing a white regimental uniform covered in medals. At his shoulder stood a turbaned boy, cooling the guy with an enormous feather fan.

'Who is it?' Shafeen asked.

'Well, I don't need to tell you the family name, do I?' The resemblance was there for all to see.

'No. I can see it's a de Warlencourt. But who? It can't be Rollo, unless he was a time traveller.' He pointed to the frame. 'It says 1935.'

'That,' I said, 'is good old Monty de Warlencourt himself. That's the exact same picture I saw in Louis's bedroom in Honorius, d'you remember? The night that Cass threw up.'

He peered closer. '*Colonel* Monty to you. Look at the number of stripes on his shoulder.'

Another colonel. I looked into Monty's eyes as he arrogantly stared down the lens. In common with all the de Warlencourt men, he seemed to have no doubt of his place in the world, nor of his importance in it. His direct gaze gave me a sudden thought. 'Do you think your dad had his attack when he saw this picture? It might have been a bit of a shock to see a reminder of Rollo staring at him. Monty was Rollo's dad after all.'

'I don't know,' he said doubtfully. 'I mean, he's not *that* much like Rollo.'

Shafeen was right. Colonel Monty had a certain resemblance to all of them – Rollo, Henry and Louis – in that strange way families have; the same genetic material, jumbled up to give a slightly different combination of features. But he was no more like Rollo than the rest.

'And by that logic,' said Shafeen, 'if he was going to keel over in front of a picture, why come all the way up here to do it? Why not do it on our veranda at breakfast, when he saw an *actual* picture of Rollo in *The Times*?'

'You're right,' I conceded, and we left Colonel Monty hanging and wandered out onto the veranda. It was lovely and airy out there, and there were comfortable chairs and tables set in the shade, but Shafeen seemed too edgy to sit. He did his tiger pacing thing while I stood and looked out at the view. I half expected to see a stripy form emerge from the undergrowth, his pace matching Shafeen's, but the only wildlife to be seen flew high above the mountains. Strange birds wheeled and dipped on the thermals in their own hypnotic rhythm. They must have been massive, to be visible at this distance.

'What are those big birds?'

Shafeen stopped pacing and stood by me to look. 'Vultures.'

'Really?'

'Yes,' he said, squinting against the sun. 'They're scavengers. If they are circling like that it means something has killed something else far below. Somewhere the hunter's found the hunted.'

'Lovely,' I said.

'Yes. They feed on dead flesh,' he said with a certain amount of relish. 'Contrary to what Walt Disney would have us believe, they don't hop around singing Beatles songs. They are not nice birds.'

'Well,' I said, looking at them stooping and circling in their strange, slow dance, 'it's not necessarily that they are not *nice*. It's in their nature.' There really could not have been a better cue line for what came next.

'Hallo.'

We turned to see a figure emerging from the clubhouse.

It was Henry.

16

He strode easily towards us, one hand in his trouser pocket, like some Burberry model.

He was wearing a light cream suit and the club tie – that distinctive black-and-orange stripe – knotted at his throat. He fitted in perfectly; more than that, he looked like he ran the place. And then I realised. He *did* run the place. 'You're the secretary of the Tiger Club?' I blurted, by way of a greeting.

'Yes.'

'Since *when*?'

'Since 1st January. I had a rather . . . trying Christmas.'

By the dry, clipped way he said that, you'd think he'd lost his wallet, not his father and his ancestral home.

'But . . . you're only eighteen.'

'Yes,' he said. 'And according to regulations, that's the minimum age.' He smiled his familiar, shit-eating grin. 'Of course, to be brutally frank and candid, it's all about having the right name. Having a de Warlencourt at the helm is a bit of a tradition here.'

'So we've been hearing.'

'The place is mostly run by Colonel Moran, the chap who

greeted you. Terror for big game is the colonel. He once crawled down a storm drain after a wounded man-eating tiger.'

Shafeen stared at Henry all the way through this exchange with the hostility I'd seen so many times before. The one time I'd seen a softening was when Shafeen had taken Ty from Henry's arms on the night of the fire. Now he looked hawkish and hostile, like one of those high-flying birds. 'Why the hell did you come all the way out here?'

Henry regarded him. 'Let's have a drink. It's a bit of a long story.'

He indicated a nearby table and pulled out my chair for me, earning himself a filthy look from Shafeen. Both of them waited, in a kind of chivalric stand-off, for me to sit down before they did. Henry settled himself easily in a chair and I remembered well that cat-like grace that made him seem at home anywhere. Shafeen, in his national dress, sat straight and stiff. You'd have thought this was Henry's country, not his.

Henry raised a lazy hand. 'Bearer!'

A guy came over, and he was the first Indian guy I'd seen in the place. He was wearing, unbelievably, the same outfit that the feather-fan servant had been wearing in the picture of Monty de Warlencourt. Head-to-toe white, with a turban, complete with a tiger-orange jewel nestled in its snowy folds.

'*Burra peg*,' commanded Henry, without a please or a thank-you. I didn't understand what he'd said, but Shafeen clued me in.

'Still using the old Raj vocab, eh?' said Shafeen sharply.

'If it ain't broke,' said Henry outrageously, 'don't fix it.' But then I caught a wicked glint in those blue eyes and knew he was deliberately baiting Shafeen.

Even Shafeen smiled bitterly, and, as the drinks came – something clear on ice, with a slice of lime – he thanked the bearer ostentatiously in Hindi. He and the bearer shared a look.

Shafeen took a sniff of his drink. 'Bit early for gin and tonic, isn't it?'

Henry handed me a glass, then raised his.

'My father always used to drink to the Siege of Gibraltar,' he said.

'Why on earth?' I asked.

'Gibraltar was attacked so many times that the British navy felt they could make the toast at any time of day,' said Henry, 'safe in the knowledge that, at that moment, Gibraltar was always under siege. It means –' he looked pointedly at Shafeen – 'that it's never too early for a drink.' He took a gulp. 'Trust me, if you ever find someone who drinks to the Siege of Gibraltar, it means they are the right sort. It's kind of a code.'

'I'd rather drink to my *father's* health.' Shafeen's toast dropped into the conversation like a stone.

If the two of them had been playing poker, which they kind of were, Shafeen had played his ace. Even Henry looked discomfited. He sat a little straighter, and straightened his face too. 'Yes, of course. How is he?'

'We'll get to him in a minute. First, answer the question. Why did you come all the way out here?'

Henry leaned back in his chair, completely at ease. He took out a cigarette case, such as you might see in *Rebecca*. He offered the cigarettes around and then, when we refused, lit one himself. It was while he was carrying out this elegant action that I first noticed his hands.

They were completely scarred – a desert of pinched, burned flesh, healed shiny and tight. A lump rose in my throat. So this had been the price of saving Ty from the fire.

He caught me staring. 'Bit of a mess, eh?' he said. 'Luckily they don't entirely spoil my beauty.'

I looked away swiftly and could feel my cheeks heating up. I concentrated instead on the object he'd set down on the table. It was one of those fancy silver lighters on which you flip up the top and then spin the little wheel to get a flame. I could see it had something etched on the side. A lion and a unicorn, and some sort of coat of arms.

I risked a look back at his face as he took a drag on his cigarette. I'd never seen him smoke before. I knew he did, knew all the Medievals did, because we used to see their fag butts jammed in the wire mesh of the Paulinus well. 'Terrible habit,' Henry acknowledged. 'But I started again after Christmas. Stress, I suppose.' He blew a plume of smoke at the peerless view of golden plains and the misty blue mountains towering behind like an incredible piece of CGI in a film. 'You asked an interesting question,' he said to Shafeen. 'Why *did* I come all the way out here?' He picked a fragment of tobacco from his tongue with those damaged fingers. 'Let me ask you one in return. Do you know the story of the Tiger, the Brahmin and the Fox?'

'Everyone in India knows it,' said Shafeen. 'You learn it at your mother's knee.'

'*I* don't know it,' I said.

They both started telling the story at once, like a couple at a dinner party trotting out a well-worn anecdote, then stopped, and Henry sat back in his chair. 'You tell it, darling,' he mocked with a gracious flourish of his cigarette.

Shafeen frowned and spoke to the landscape. 'Once there was a Brahmin – sort of a holy man – walking down a road. He saw a tiger in a trap. The tiger pleaded very eloquently for his freedom, promising that he would not eat the Brahmin if he was released. The Brahmin set the tiger free, and the tiger immediately goes back on his promise and states his intention to eat the Brahmin. The Brahmin appeals to a passing fox to judge the case. The fox claims not to understand what has happened and asks to see the trap. The fox is shown the mechanism but claims he still doesn't understand and asks the tiger to show him how it works. The tiger gets back inside the trap to demonstrate and the fox shuts him in.'

'Precisely,' said Henry. 'We know there are FOXES at play. Now we just need to work out,' he said, glancing at Shafeen, 'who is the tiger and who is the Brahmin.'

So he knew. Henry knew about the rival order of anti-establishment rebels out to get him and his kind.

'Foxes in fairy-tales always win,' Henry went on. 'Always. Think of Chicken Licken, the Gingerbread Man. They are cunning and cruel and always one step ahead of the game.'

He started faffing about with the lime in his glass, pushing it down into the G&T and watching it bob back up. 'The FOXES tried to take out our entire Boxing Day guestlist, and they succeeded in taking out my father. I just didn't fancy them taking *me* out.'

90

'I don't think that was them,' I said, without thinking.

'Which bit?' asked Henry.

I ignored Shafeen's warning look. 'Your father. I don't think the FOXES killed him.'

He turned his very blue gaze on me. 'What makes you say that?'

I looked away. Henry could always make me tell him things when he looked at me like that, and I didn't want to give the Abbot away. Besides, despite Henry telling me the 'fox in a box' story, and taking me to the Red Mass, and saving Ty's life, I still couldn't be 100 per cent sure he was now one of the good guys. 'Instinct.'

He looked back at the view again and took a drink before speaking. 'Well, despite my well-developed respect for your instinct, *darling* Greer –' I sensed Shafeen bristle at the endearment – 'I didn't want to take the chance.'

'So you ran away,' said Shafeen bluntly.

Now Henry turned his blue gaze on Shafeen. 'How interesting that *you* would say that, old chap.' He smiled pleasantly. 'I'd rather characterise it as giving myself a chance to regroup.'

'Well, as concerned as we are for your welfare,' said Shafeen sarcastically, 'I have a few questions about my father.'

Henry straightened up once again, stubbed out his cigarette and immediately lit another one. 'Of course.'

'Were you here that day?'

'Yes, I called the ambulance. He'd sent his driver away.'

Shafeen thawed a fraction. 'I suppose I should thank you for that.'

'Yes,' said Henry, with a ghost of a smile. 'I suppose you should.'

But Shafeen said nothing.

I jumped into the silence. 'Where was he? When he collapsed?'

Henry swivelled around in his chair. He indicated the hallway we'd just come from. 'Just there. In the passageway.'

'You saw him go down?'

'Yes.'

'How did he look?' Shafeen's voice broke a little.

Sounding more sympathetic than I'd ever heard him, Henry said, 'To be quite frank, old chap, he looked like he'd seen a ghost.'

This struck me – it was just what the guru had told Princess Himani.

'I just about caught him before he hit the deck,' Henry continued. 'Then we put a cushion under his head. I checked he was breathing, stuck him in the recovery position and waited for the experts.'

Finally Shafeen said it. 'Thank you.'

Henry inclined his head. 'You're welcome. How is he?'

'Still unconscious. They're hopeful he'll pull through but can't be sure.'

Henry's mouth twitched a little in sympathy. 'Believe it or not, I know what you're going through.'

'Really?' said Shafeen scornfully. 'I doubt that.'

'As I have just lost my own father, I call that an ungallant remark.'

Now it was Shafeen's turn to be chastened. 'You're right, I'm sorry.'

'And I didn't get to say goodbye to mine. You did.'

'Who told you that?'

'Our faithful family doctor, of course,' said Henry. 'He's been with us for generations. He even helped my mother give birth to me. So he was happy to fill me in about that tender little scene. *Kiss me, Hardy*.' Henry flicked his ash viciously into the ashtray, but it was hard to gauge, from the lightness of his tone, how much that had actually hurt him.

'OK,' said Shafeen, shifting a little uncomfortably in his chair. 'You know what went down. So we might as well talk about the apology. The deathbed confession, I mean. Your father said he was sorry for what he did that Justitium, the autumn half-term of 1969.'

'No,' I interrupted. It was time for truth telling. 'He said he was *not* sorry for what they did *together*.'

Shafeen sighed faintly, but he didn't disagree. 'Do you know what he . . . they might have done together?'

Henry shrugged. 'Not a clue.'

Shafeen said, 'Do you think they might have gone huntin' shootin' and fishin'? Like you did?'

The blue eyes flickered. 'It's possible. It's a long-established family tradition. Or rather, it *was*.' He stubbed out his cigarette in the chunky glass ashtray with an air of finality.

I was inclined to go a bit softer on him than Shafeen, since he had, in fact, saved Ty's life – and perhaps Aadhish's too. 'So your father never mentioned that Justitium weekend? Never told you what happened?'

Henry unhurriedly lit another cigarette and breathed out the answer with the smoke. 'No.' He looked from me to Shafeen.

'The way I see it, since my father *most* inconsiderately shuffled off this mortal coil on Boxing Day, the only person who can tell you what happened is *your* father.'

I took a tiny sip of my gin and tonic. 'There's a suggestion,' I persisted, 'that there might be unfinished business.'

I looked at Shafeen, and he picked up his cue. 'My mother went to see a . . . a guru. A Vedic astrologer. It was he who said that my father had unfinished business.'

'A moon reader, eh?' said Henry. 'Hmm.' I expected him to laugh or pour scorn on the idea. He did neither. He stretched out his long legs in front of him and said, 'You know, before I came out here, I would have said that was all rot.'

'And now?' I asked.

'Now I don't know.' He gazed beyond us at the view. 'This place changes you.'

'For Christ's sake.' Shafeen put his glass down sharply on the table. 'This is not your spiritual retreat. It doesn't exist for you to have some sort of awakening. This is *my country*.'

I'd never heard him speak so passionately about India when he was in England. He looked out to the mountains, the birds above and the trees below, where tigers may hide. 'God, nothing changes, does it? Take what you want and leave the rest.'

Henry regarded him. 'Ah, yes. The naughty British Raj.' He tutted, as if at a wayward child, and flicked a glance at me. 'Been filling you in, has he? Britain bad, India good? That's it, isn't it?'

I couldn't deny it.

'Did he tell you all the Evil Empire's Greatest Hits?' He

leaned forward and stage-whispered, 'Did he tell you about Amritsar?'

I don't know what my face did in reply to that, but Henry read it immediately.

'He did, didn't he!' he crowed.

'Don't do that!' Shafeen snapped.

'Do what?'

'Use Amritsar to make a cheap point.'

Henry flicked more ash. 'Why not? *You* did.'

'Hardly. I think it was an abomination.'

'I too. But are you *quite* sure you didn't use it to demonstrate to your girlfriend how mean and nasty the Raj was?'

'I'm not just someone's –' I began hotly. But I might as well not have been there. This was between those two.

'Yes. I'm absolutely sure,' Shafeen said over me.

Henry sat back and laughed to himself softly.

Shafeen let a silence fall. Then he said, quite calmly, 'What do you want from me, Henry?'

'Balance,' said Henry equably. 'Just balance.'

'What does that mean?'

Henry breathed in smoke. 'An acknowledgement that, alongside the undoubted and manifold evils of the British occupation of India, marched some good.'

'Like?'

'Roads. Railways. Education. Trade. A legal system.'

'We heard all this from your father.'

Henry looked at me. 'Did your boyfriend tell you about the caste system? You think the British class system is bad? My Christ.'

'You're clutching at straws now,' said Shafeen.

'All right then.' Henry exhaled smoke perilously close to Shafeen's face. 'What about suttee?'

Shafeen's expression went suddenly still.

'Did you tell her about that?' probed Henry. 'Did you tell Greer what would have happened to your mother if your father died, if the British hadn't come along?'

For a moment they looked at each other, eye to eye, like two cats about to pounce. I was transported back, suddenly, to that first time at Longcross, when Shafeen had told his story about being the tiger's son. This time Henry moved first. He got up from his chair, whereas Shafeen seemed frozen to his seat.

'Well, I must get on. Let me call your driver for you.'

It all seemed very abrupt. I wasn't sure how much the secretary of the Tiger Club had to do, but it very much felt like we were being thrown out.

Henry softened the blow. 'Don't be strangers, will you? And don't leave it too long. I'm only here for a few more days.' He looked up to the fierce blue sky. 'It will be getting too hot for me soon.'

I wondered if he meant literally or metaphorically. He stooped to stub out his cigarette in the ashtray right in front of the immobile Shafeen. 'We're going out to see the tigers tomorrow if you fancy it. Elephants, beaters – the lot. You are both cordially invited, as my guests.'

'A hunt?' I said, as Shafeen seemed to be temporarily out of action.

'We don't hunt any more,' he said, almost regretfully. 'Not like the old days. It's more of a safari now. And after that I'll probably toddle back to dear old Blighty. I'm sure things will have cooled down by now. I mean, the home fires can't still be burning, can they?'

With that devastating exit line, he skipped off to find Hari. I gave Shafeen a little shake. 'Are you OK?'

He seemed to come out of his trance and smiled weakly. 'Yes. Yes, I'm fine.' He got to his feet and smoothed down his coat.

'What did he say? What was all that about your mum?'

'Nothing,' he said. 'It's nothing.'

Henry was waiting for us at the top of the steps and Hari at the bottom in the car.

Henry offered his ruined hand to shake and Shafeen took it rather limply – he still didn't seem quite himself. And before I could dodge him, Henry kissed me on both cheeks.

'Think about the tiger safari,' he said. 'It will be the last one for a while because the mating season starts. I'll be gone after that.'

He stood in the portico at the top of the steps to watch us get into the car, hands in his pockets, in an unassailable position of authority. But just as Hari was about to drive off he took his hands out of his pockets, trotted easily down the steps and leaned in at Shafeen's open window, his scarred fingers on the car door and his stag signet ring clinking on the metal. 'Look, if it helps, I would say don't underestimate the power of what you heard.'

'What do you mean?'

'Only that I never heard my father apologise for anything in his life.' Henry paused. 'He certainly never apologised to *me*.'

17

Back in the car Shafeen was silent, staring out of the window, his profile unreadable.

I was desperate for him to explain what Henry had said about his mother. But Henry had also touched on something that I'd vaguely heard about before, which I thought would be safer ground.

'What did Henry mean by the caste system?'

I saw Hari look briefly into the mirror, directly at us, before his eyes returned to the road.

After an uncomfortable pause Shafeen said, rather stiffly, 'It's the way in which Hindu society has traditionally been divided. Different social strata.'

I thought of what Henry had said. 'Like the class system?'

'If you like. It has Brahmins at the top, and Dalits – the "untouchables" – at the bottom.'

'So you – the Jadejas – are Brahmins?'

'Yes.'

I remembered. 'Like the man in the story, yes? The Brahmin, the Tiger and the Fox.'

'Sort of. He was a holy man – Brahmins were traditionally

priests, teachers, intellectuals. Then there are Kshatriyas, the warriors and rulers. Next come Vaishyas, who are farmers, traders and merchants. Then Shudras, the labourers. Hari's a Shudra.'

I glanced at the driver in the rear-view mirror. As ever, he had his sunglasses on and it was hard to read his expression. I knew Hari didn't have much English, but he knew his name all right and had looked up at the sound of it. Shafeen said something in Hindi, obviously explaining what we'd been talking about, and for a moment I wondered if Hari minded being breezily categorised like that; in some ways Shafeen could be as high-handed as Henry. But Hari was nodding fervently, and then said to me in halting English, 'Caste good. If no caste, no society. No good. Finish.'

I smiled politely and nodded myself, and then said to Shafeen, 'And who did you say were at the bottom?'

'The Dalits,' he said. 'They do the most menial jobs: sweeping streets, cleaning toilets. They are also known as the "untouchables".'

The only *Untouchables* I knew about were from the Kevin Costner movie. But this was hardly that. This sounded brutal. A dreadful, degrading name for what sounded like a dreadful, degrading life. Perhaps Henry had a point. No society was perfect.

'Do you know any untouchables?'

'Of course. Prem.'

By a weird coincidence Prem was the first person we saw back at the house, smoking happily on the front porch. He stood up as we walked past, giving his odd Britisher salute, deferring to his Brahmin master.

And then it struck me, the answer to the riddle: if Abbot Ridley was the fox, and Shafeen was the Brahmin, then it was Henry who was the tiger in the trap.

18

Shafeen opened the front door for me, as he always did, but when he closed it behind his back he leaned heavily on it and closed his eyes too.

I could see then that he'd been holding it together in the car, in front of Hari, but now Hari had gone to put the car away he could crumble. When he opened his eyes they were wet. 'I don't know what to do, Greer. I genuinely don't know what to do now. What can I do? We went to the hospital. We went to the temple. We tried science, we tried religion. We even went to the Tiger Club. Where do I go now? How can I help Father?'

I ushered him to a divan near the door. He pushed the heels of his palms into his eye sockets, as if forcing the tears back in. I put my arm around him. 'I don't know,' I said, in answer to his question. But as we sat there, I thought about our days in India: the skin of Melati lying flattened in the dining room; the ridiculous genius of the guy in *Junoon* turning into a tiger at the full moon; Durga riding her tiger into battle against a demon and the strange Raj hangover that was the Tiger Club, preserved in tiger-coloured amber, like the nugget the bearer wore in his white turban. 'All I can tell you is: it has something to do with tigers.'

At that, he abruptly escaped the circle of my arm and got up. He wrenched open a drawer in the carved chest that stood by the front door and pulled something out. It was a picture – or, more accurately, a photograph.

It was a big photo, about A3 in size, and as he held it up before him something clicked into place like a piece of a jigsaw. It was the exact same size and shape as the pale square of wall above his head. This, then, was the picture he had taken down.

I got up, walked over to him and joined him in gazing at the photograph he held in his hands.

It was black and white, and gilt framed, just like the ones in the Tiger Club. It showed a group of people, both men and women, standing together, but my eye was drawn not to them, but to the magnificent tiger that lay stretched on the ground in front of them, clearly very dead. An Indian boy of maybe ten or eleven had his foot on its neck. Shafeen pointed to the boy. 'That's him. That's my father.' I looked at the other people around the boy – all adults. A quick scan of them gave me a massive shock. One of the women, standing just to the right of the boy, was very, very familiar. 'Is that . . . is that the *queen*?'

'Yes,' he said.

'So that –' I pointed to a tall man on the far right of the picture – 'must be Prince Philip.'

'Yup. And look. That, I realise now, is our old friend Monty.' He pointed to a tall, blond moustachioed guy – unmistakably him.

'You didn't know that was him until now?'

'No. Remember, I never laid eyes on him until today. I didn't see the picture in Louis's room. I didn't ever go in there.' He looked back at the picture. 'This is the maharajah, my grandfather.' He pointed to a smiling man who very much resembled Shafeen's father as he was now. 'And the maharani, my grandmother.' The maharani was a very striking woman, rivalling even the Queen of England in beauty and poise.

'Wow,' I said. 'What a glamour puss.'

'Don't forget the ultimate glamour puss.' He pointed to the tiger. 'That's Melati. She went on to be our rug.'

'Jeez. But your father loved her, you said.'

'Always.'

'But didn't he shoot her?'

'He was there, yes. But he was only . . .' He did a quick calculation: '1961, he would have been eleven.'

I could see why he'd taken the picture down. It was such a club, such an elite of predators. And even the expression on the boy's face was complicated. So serious and . . . oddly triumphant. But now Shafeen stroked the small, fierce features. 'If only he was here to tell me what to do.'

Maybe that was the answer. 'If he *was* here, what would he say?'

'He would say . . .' He stopped, then looked at me, eyes wide. 'He would say, *Sometimes you have to put your hand in the tiger's mouth.*'

'Melati,' I said.

Shafeen shoved the photograph back in the drawer and took off into the house. I followed him to the dining room. We sank down onto the floor at the head of the tiger-skin rug, just as we had knelt to pray before Durga the day before.

I looked at Shafeen – this strange, crazy part had to be done by him. Slowly, carefully, he slid long, brown fingers between the sharp, white teeth and pushed his hand down the tiger's throat. What he felt there made his expression change. The hand withdrew, holding a little book the size of a diary. It was bound in faded orange leather and tied up with a thin strip of the same skin. Shaking, Shafeen unwrapped the tie from the book and opened the cover. I leaned in and read over his shoulder. The writing on the first page, although spidery and ink-blotted, was quite clear.

It said:

Longcross Hall
24th October
1969

We looked at each other, wide-eyed. 'A diary,' I said. 'It's a diary.'

'It's *his* diary,' said Shafeen.

'Let's have a read then,' I said, impatient.

'Not here,' he said. 'Somewhere quiet where we won't be disturbed. The roof terrace.'

It was an enormous act of will to wait while Shafeen gathered lamps and cushions and things to eat. It can't have been more than five minutes but it felt like five hours. At last we were settled on a comfortable divan on the roof of the house. There was a peerless view of Jaipur but I had eyes for nothing but that little orange book. 'Come on then,' I urged.

And Shafeen opened his father's diary, and we started to read.

PART 4

I Wanna Be
Like You

Friday, 24th October 1969

<u>Afternoon</u>

I have three names.

Aadhish, which is my name.

Hardy, which is what I call myself.

And Mowgli, which is what <u>they</u> call me.

The Abbot, who takes us for theology, says God has three names too – Father, Son and Holy Ghost. They talk about God a lot at STAGS, probably because the school is named after a saint. I told the Abbot about the Indian goddess Durga who rides a tiger. But he told me to *stop talking nonsense, boy*.

The Mowgli thing started two years ago, in 1967, when *The Jungle Book* came out at the cinema. I do not blame Mr Walt Disney. I do not think Mr Walt Disney knew, when he decided to make *The Jungle Book*, that he would be making life hell for the only Indian boy in an English public school. But ever since the film came out, <u>they</u> started calling me Mowgli.

<u>They</u> are the Medievals. Three girls and three boys who are the prefects of the school. They hate me. Or rather, I thought

they did. When I am writing this I am very happy, because it turns out they do *not* hate me. I have been invited to spend the autumn term Justitium weekend at Longcross Hall, the home of one of them – Rollo de Warlencourt. And because I am embarking on something <u>Momentous</u>, I thought I would write a diary of the weekend. Well, more of an account, really – I will try to include <u>Dialogue</u> and <u>Feelings</u> like Mr Kipling, so that anyone who reads this will know how IT happened – how I became a <u>Proper English Gentleman</u>. Also, I have no one to talk to, and have never had anyone to talk to since I started at STAGS. So I am going to talk to <u>you</u>.

Because this is definitely the beginning of something. This is what my father meant by acceptance. He said that once I was accepted, I would be <u>in</u>. The name Hardy was my father's idea. He said it was a good English name, and it sounded a bit like Aadhish, so he registered me at the school under that name. It was his idea too to send me to STAGS in the first place, so that I should endeavour to become a Proper English Gentleman. Ever since we went on a tiger hunt with the Queen of England herself, he has been obsessed with the idea of my being an English gentleman. And I think The Invitation – which was pushed under my door last night – is the start of that.

I have been waiting for years for such an invitation. I heard rumours at school – not directly, for no one has ever confided in me; just stories of legendary country-house weekends, of hunting, shooting and fishing, of lavish dinners and luscious lunches. But I was always excluded, always marginalised. Until this: my eighteenth year and my last autumn at school.

The Invitation changed everything. It was addressed to Hardy, not Mowgli, so I know it was for real and not one of their 'japes'. And once I had it, I was not about to refuse – no, indeed. I followed every instruction to the letter. That commanding piece of card became my holy text. It told me to take the train from school to a station called Alnwick, where there would be a car waiting to take me to the house. I do not know how the others were getting there, but I was relieved to have the train carriage to myself. Even though I am now technically a man, I still would struggle to carry on a polite conversation with three English young ladies and gentlemen. Especially those ones.

When I saw the sign saying ALNWICK I got my suitcase down from the luggage rack above my head. Father made sure that I had all the proper equipment for school – he'd taken me to London himself when we'd come over for the beginning of term. I wanted to go to Carnaby Street and see all the shops that people call *groovy*. But we'd spent the morning instead in the outfitters of St James's – what you might call the Medieval part of London, not the Savage part. I was measured and trimmed and brushed and pushed and pulled, getting all the right clothes and shoes. And my suitcase. I was very proud of my suitcase. It was a proper English gentleman's suitcase in caramel-coloured leather. The vendor called it a weekend suitcase, for 'when you go away with your chums'. That was when I was eleven. For the seven years I have been at STAGS I have never once taken the suitcase down from my wardrobe. My trunk has been used every holiday, to pack up my clothes for India, but my weekend case sat, year in, year out, waiting in tissue paper.

It was only when I got off the train and the driver took it from my hand that I saw that my lovely English suitcase had been chalked with a design. Two sweeps of white with little branches coming off them.

Deer antlers.

I wonder what they mean.

Evening

If I was lucky to have the train carriage to myself, I certainly paid for it when I had to walk into the entrance hall of Longcross on my own.

They were all there, all the Medievals, gathered around the fire. These were the six people who had dubbed me 'Mowgli' and kept the nickname going for two years, fuelling the fire whenever anyone showed signs of forgetting to call me that. It felt like they were waiting for <u>me</u>.

It was not until that moment that I found out who was actually going to be there for the weekend. And it was really most peculiar, because outside of themselves – that is, those three young ladies and young men who ruled the school – I seemed to be the only other guest.

I looked around the room at them all. Francesca Mowbray, with wild red curly hair and freckles. Serena Styles, her hair smooth and blonde. Miranda Petrie, dark-haired and serious. (I have observed over my seven years at STAGS that all the names of well-to-do young English ladies seem to end in A.) Then the boys. Gideon Villiers, fair and tall; an expert sportsman. Charles Skelton, bookish, bespectacled and scarily intelligent.

And, at the centre of them all, Rollo de Warlencourt, flanked by faithful Labradors as if he were a painting. Fair like Gideon but blonder and taller and bluer of eye; the friendliest of all; the most frightening of all; the very model of a modern English gentleman.

I feel I know Rollo de Warlencourt better than I know myself. I certainly look at him more than I look at my own reflection, know his face better than my own. I watch him constantly – have watched him for seven years. My father knew Rollo's father back in Jaipur, and it was Rollo's father who suggested I attend STAGS. 'Colonel Monty's boy goes to the school,' said my father. 'If you want to know how to behave, just copy him.' I've taken this very much to heart. And although Rollo has barely noticed me in all that time, I've done little else but notice *him*.

Rollo was the only one to greet me, but I didn't interpret this as friendship so much as the duty of the host to his guest. 'Hardy, old chap.' His host's manners obviously demanded the use of my adopted name for once. 'Glad you could come. Train all right?'

'Perfectly, thank you.'

'Drink?'

He nodded to the butler, who stepped forward. I knew the answer to this one, thanks to my Saturdays at the Tiger Club. Gin and tonic. I did not say please. One does not.

Drink in hand, I glanced at Rollo in an effort to copy his stance. Like him, I rested one hand on the fireplace, drink in the other hand, but I'm not sure I quite pulled it off. Wholly uncomfortable, I nodded at the rest, and they eyed me back.

Some smiled, some didn't, but all of them looked happy to see me. Not in a friendly way exactly, but in a sort of . . . hungry way.

Perhaps they had been waiting for me in order to dine, but they were all still in their travel clothes. The thought of food made my stomach growl like a tiger. It had been a long time since lunch, and ever since I reached my full height – I am taller than any of them apart from Rollo – I seem to want to eat all the time. I thought of samosas and raab and ghevar but knew there would be nothing like that here.

I've been thinking long and hard about the correct things to say at a country-house weekend for all the years I've known that weekends like this were happening without me being invited. I have practised what I would say in front of the small looking glass in my room at STAGS, and mouthed English platitudes to myself at night. My mother has been my guide in all this; she taught me a very valuable secret, which is that in English society everything you say is either U (good) or non-U (bad). U is the right way to say things – but if you slip and accidentally say something non-U, you will be found out and scorned and shunned, and people will laugh at you behind their hands.

Luckily Rollo took the lead. 'A toast,' he said. 'To the Siege of Gibraltar.'

As everyone raised their glasses, heartily repeating the toast, I made my first mistake. 'I had no idea Gibraltar was besieged, currently.' I tried to keep abreast of current events and could have spoken, with tolerable knowledge, about the Vietnam War or the Cuban Missile Crisis. But it was news to me that that particular British territory was in dispute.

'It's not,' said Charles, the walking encyclopaedia.

I saw them all exchanging smiles with each other and my face grew hot. I stood there awkwardly, uncomfortably silent and regretting my chosen position by the fireplace. I supposed I ought to make conversation, but I was not at all sure what to say, or even if it was good form for the guest to introduce a topic. One thing my father told me was <u>on no account</u> to talk about India. 'Not if you want to be accepted. Remember, they ruled over us for 300 years,' he said. 'The English gentlemen do not care about maharajahs, temples and tigers. To them, an Indian king is lower than the man who sweeps the streets in England.' So I had to rely on my mother's advice. One phrase she taught me floated into my head. It seemed suitable, so I deployed it now. 'Do we dress for dinner?'

Rollo said, 'Of course. But we aren't dining here. I've had a bit of a wheeze. We're having a moon party.'

I looked at the others, at a loss. This was something my mother had not taught me. 'Ah, yes,' I said. After the Gibraltar thing I thought it better to feign knowledge. 'Of course. A moon party. Yes. Yes.' I nodded my head sagely.

The others smiled at each other again, in a way that seemed to entirely exclude me. Serena put her head on one side. 'You don't know what that is, do you?' she said pleasantly.

'Probably doesn't even know that man walked on the moon,' snorted Gideon. 'Maybe the news didn't reach India. No television sets, eh, Mowgli?'

This, of all things, stung me. I love the moon landing and everything about it. I have knowledge of it that I think would rival even Charles's and was anxious to display it. 'Of course

I know. *Apollo 11*. 20th July. Mr Neil Armstrong, Mr Buzz Aldrin and Mr Michael Collins.' It was three months ago now, but the excitement still hasn't died down. It is all the nation can talk about. In fact, all the world can talk about – India was just as obsessed when I went home for the summer.

'That's right,' said Rollo. 'So we thought we'd celebrate *man's great achievement*.' Something in his voice was a little off – as if he did not think the achievement that great.

I felt a little uneasy, and decided it was safer to drop any pretence at knowledge. 'What happens at a moon party?'

Rollo drained his drink. 'Get your monkey suit on, old chap, and you'll see.' He glanced out of the mullioned windows. 'There's a lovely moon tonight.'

'It's called a hunter's moon,' said Charles, who always has the facts at his fingertips. 'First full moon after the harvest.'

'Perfect,' said Rollo, looking at me intently. 'It's almost as if it were meant.'

It turns out that the term 'monkey suit' was not, in fact, a racial slur, but merely a colloquial term for a dinner jacket. When I came back downstairs all the boys were dressed just like me. So it was in full black tie that I found myself walking through a dark forest, called, apparently, Longwood, with the others – the boys in their black tie, the girls in coloured taffeta under fur coats. I had no idea where we were going but dared not ask. For all I knew this was a normal occurrence for the English upper classes, to set out on a late-October night by moonlight. There were no torches, and dark clouds kept scudding across the face of the moon so that the figures ahead of me flickered like a cinefilm. It was an odd procession. Rollo led the advance party, and we were followed by a line of servants in black livery with white gloves, bearing hampers and baskets and bottles. One of them carried a gramophone for playing records, and when I looked back I could see the moon shining on the big brass bell. No one said anything to me on the walk except Gideon, who caught me up just as we were about to plunge into the trees.

'You must be used to the jungle, eh, Mowgli?'

'I do not live in –' I began, but he pushed past me into the dark.

We were out of the forest and into the open, and our well-dressed convoy walked up a little hill, silver in the moonlight, to a round building with a cupola on top. The cupola reminded me with a pang of India. There were lights on in the building, streaming out into the night, changing the grass from silver to gold. Our strange procession reached this temple, and two servants opened the double doors to let us in. Rollo led the way, and, bringing up the rear, I could see the interior was set with a round table, like Camelot. The table was a treasure trove of silver plate and crystal laid out for a dinner fit for a king.

Rollo stood behind his chair. 'Ladies and gentlemen, welcome to the folly. A fitting place, I feel, to mark the moon landing.' I looked up and saw that the folly had been decorated with shooting stars and planets and spherical white-paper lanterns revolving silently over our heads, their insides lit by candles. At least four servants stood around the edges in the shadowy dark beyond the reach of the candlelight. The three footmen I could see by their white gloves, and the only maid by the white lace on her cap. We were sitting boy/girl, so I was flanked by Serena and Miranda.

As we sat down, and the servants brought us soup and red wine, I tried to interpret our host's welcoming remark. Folly, I knew, meant foolishness or a mistake. 'Does he not like the moon landing?' I asked Serena, low-voiced. 'It does not sound as if he likes it.'

'None of us do.'

I was surprised. To me, the moon landing seems to be the foremost achievement of mankind – the zenith of science and pinnacle of accomplishment. 'Why ever not?'

'Because it's so *Savage*, darling.' I have never received an endearment before that sounded less fond. 'This isn't a celebration; it's a wake.'

'To trample on the face of the moon! And Americans too!' added Francesca. '*Ghastly*.'

'Did you watch it, Mowgli?' asked Miranda.

'Yes. That is, in a manner of speaking.'

'On television?' she probed.

'No.'

'He doesn't have one. I told you,' crowed Gideon from the other side of the table. Now everyone was listening and I was in what my father would call a no-win situation. If I confessed to a television – and we do in fact have a small one in the Aravalli Palace – I would be seen as Savage. If I claimed not to have one, I would be seen as a *literal* savage, i.e., a primitive. Actually the truth is somewhere in the middle. India has a national television channel, but it only broadcasts for two hours a day, and therefore did not carry the moon landings live.

'I did not watch it on our television set. I watched it at . . .' Damn it all, I had checkmated myself. I had to mention India now '. . . at Jantar Mantar.'

They all snorted like the horses in our stables at home. Then they began to chant *JantarMantarJantarMantarJantarMantar*, mimicking the accent I haven't quite managed to shift in seven years. I could not remember the part where my mother had said it was U to ceaselessly mock your guest. But I am so used to mockery that I looked down and patiently crumbled my bread roll between my fingers, waiting for them to stop. At length, they did. 'What on earth is Jantar Mantar?'

'It's an observatory.'

'Telescopes and electronic instruments?' asked Charles pertly.

'No,' I said. Having broken my father's golden rule and spoken about my home, I did not want to go into detail. 'It dates from 1734. It is a series of astronomical structures. Staircases to the sky.'

That night of the 20th July was magical. My cousins and I went up to the observatory with our transistor and listened to the landings on All India Radio. We watched the moon from the top of the ghostly white structures. We looked at the moon's surface, with the seas and craters, and strained to see the pinprick shadow of the LEM, and the two mosquito-sized men crawling about on the surface. I was in love with the science that had taken them so far. It was a modern miracle. But I was not about to say that to these jackals.

Alone among all of them, Rollo looked interested. 'Staircases to the sky, Mowgli. It has a certain poetry to it.'

He took a long drink. 'That's what's gone now,' he said. 'The poetry.'

'What do you mean?' I asked.

He got to his feet unsteadily and held out his glass as if to make a toast. He lifted it to the full moon, which peered in at the window. *'Queen and huntress, chaste and fair, / Now the sun is laid to sleep, / Seated in thy silver chair, / State in wonted manner keep'.*

I shifted a little. I was not used to people declaiming poetry outside of English literature lessons. But I had to admit that Rollo spoke the lines well, like Mr Michael York, and there was a real yearning in his voice.

Then know-it-all Charles spoiled the moment. *'Cynthia's Revels*, by Ben Jonson,' said he.

'Precisely, Charlie,' said Rollo, giving his friend an odd, intense look when he uttered the name of the poet, and pointing a wavering finger at his face. I wondered how many G&Ts Rollo had had while they were all waiting for me. 'But she is not chaste any more, is she, the moon?' he said savagely. 'Those dirty Americans have crawled all over her. Laid their filthy boots in her silver dust. Penetrated her with their flag. Despoiled her and taken her booty home in their phallic rocket ship.'

In all the endless flag-waving coverage of the newspaper and television news – even fashion articles about moonboots and metallic dresses, and how to make moon meringues and baked Alaska – I had never heard this perspective before. On the one hand, it sounded deranged. But on the other, it sounded oddly . . . chivalrous. And very, very, British.

But I did not agree that there was no poetry to the moon landings. Yes, I loved the science of it, the equations and the instruments and the pure maths. But that did not mean there was no romance to this moment of history. Maybe the wine gave me courage, for I said, 'Perhaps the old words are replaced by the new. Think of what Mr Armstrong said when his foot touched the moon. *One small step for man, one giant leap for mankind.*' I heard those words just a few short weeks ago, crackling through the radio, and in that moment my heart swelled. 'Was that not poetry? Will those lines not be remembered for as long as your Mr Jonson's?'

They all looked at me as if one of the Labradors had learned to speak.

Then Gideon started to laugh. 'He jolly well ruined it by what he said next though,' he said. 'Bloody funny, that. You have to hand that to the Yanks.'

'What *are* you talking about, Gidders?' asked Rollo, as he collapsed back in his chair, raking his blond hair back from his forehead.

'You *must* have heard about this,' said Gideon. 'Right after the *one small step* bit, he said: *Good luck, Mr Gorsky.*'

'Gorsky? Sounds like a bloody Commie,' said Charles.

Miranda said, 'Who's Mr Gorsky?'

'Well,' said Gideon, glad to have the attention of the room. I sensed he liked being the leader, even though he could never really outrank his friend Rollo, Lord of the Manor. He leaned forward in the candlelight and pressed his hands together like a namaste. 'Apparently, when Neil Armstrong was a kid he was playing in his back garden and he heard his neighbours arguing. They were a Jewish couple called the Gorskys, and he went to the fence to listen. The wife was screaming at her husband, *I'll give you a blow job the day that kid next door walks on the moon!* So of course when Armstrong *does* walk on the moon, the second thing he says is, *Good luck, Mr Gorsky.*'

There was a silence in which everyone looked at Rollo. He looked very stern for a moment, and then his beautiful face split into a grin. An infectious laugh burst out of him and he laughed until I thought he would cry. Of course, that set them all off, as if they'd been given permission. I did not laugh, because I did not understand the joke.

Gideon must have spotted my serious face. 'Didn't you know that one, Mowgli?'

'No,' I said soberly.

Serena put her chin on her hand and leaned towards me, her eyes unfocused. 'You do know what a blow job *is*, don't you, Mowgli?' she asked sweetly.

'Of course,' I lied.

'What is it then?'

I was silent, staring at my empty soup plate. I could have kicked myself. After the moon-party slip, it would have been much safer just to admit the things I didn't know. The maid's hand came into my view and I could see every detail as if it were magnified: slender fingers; bitten nails; a freckle on the thumb. She whisked away the plate and I wished I could vanish so easily. I whispered unhappily, 'I don't know.'

'What's that?' Serena cocked a hand behind her ear.

They were all looking at me. I had to say it louder. '*I don't know.*'

Serena sat back, satisfied with my humiliation. But Gideon hadn't finished with me yet. He watched me like a cat as the footmen and the maid brought round the main course – some sort of poultry in a creamy sauce. 'A blow job, my dear brown friend, is when you put your . . . there are ladies present so I'll say your *pocket rocket* in someone's mouth, and have a jolly nice time until blast off.' He watched me closely; they all did, including Rollo with his cool, blue gaze.

I did not know what to do under such scrutiny.

I thought of Ritu. That time I met her – the only time – at the Chatterjees' party. She was sitting modestly below the fairy lights and the mango blossom like a goddess in a shrine. Like an idol, she was literally weighed down with gold – on both arms, on her headdress and from her nose to her ear. When she smiled at me the chain from her nose to her ear had relaxed into a bow, smiling too. I imagined for a moment asking such a thing – this *blow job* – of that goddess and felt my stomach churn.

'Well,' said Gideon, clearly enjoying himself. 'This is a weekend for new experiences. Maybe you could try it.'

The maid, the owner of the bitten nails and the freckled thumb, was placing his plate in front of him at that moment.

'You'll give our Indian friend a blow job, won't you, sweetheart?' From where I was sitting I could see that he slid his hand up the back of her thigh, under her skirt, and placed it between her legs.

Her hand flicked upwards in reflex and she tipped the entire contents of the plate into his lap. 'Jesus *Christ*. You stupid little *bitch*,' spluttered Gideon, jumping to his feet.

The others started laughing again. And I could hear Rollo saying, 'I reckon you asked for that, Gidders.' The maid, sobbing, wrenched open the double doors and fled. Unable to bear the laughter, I pushed back my chair and followed her into the cold.

Night

Outside it was as bright as day – the hunter's moon shining her hardest. I caught up with the maid at the bottom of the hill. She was sitting on a stone bench, doubled over, shivering. It was very cold, but I was sure it was not the winter that shook her. I took off my jacket and put it around her shoulders. She looked up and for the first time I saw the face below the white lace cap.

The first thought I had was that she was very pretty.

The second was that hiring a girl who looked like that to work this weekend was like getting a rabbit to work for wolves.

'Are you all right?'

I sat down beside her, but not near enough to frighten her. The stone was freezing under my seat, and the wind whistled through my dinner shirt.

'Yes.'

She didn't sound all right. 'I'm Hardy.'

'I thought your name was Mowgli. That's what they were calling you in there.' She jerked her head towards the folly.

'No.'

'Why'd they call you that then?'

'It is from a film. Well. A book first, by Mr Rudyard Kipling. Then a film by Mr Walt Disney.'

'I know *that*,' she said scornfully, and I formed the impression that on any other day she might have laughed. 'I go to the pictures. Five shilings at the Newcastle Odeon. I seen *The Jungle Book* four times.'

'So you know where the name comes from then.'

'Yes. I know.' She breathed out a long sigh. 'My name's Ina.'

Her accent was strange and unfamiliar but pleasing to the ear.

'I am delighted to make your acquaintance, Miss Ina.'

She merely sniffed in reply.

Gideon's actions had nothing to do with me, but I felt unaccountably as if I should apologise.

'I am sorry for what happened to you in there. It was not – it *is* not gentlemanlike behaviour.'

She was silent for a moment and then said, 'No one's ever spoken to me like that before.'

I was not sure what she meant. 'In there? Or out here?'

She snorted. '*They* speak to me like that all the time. No. I meant out here. Now. With you.'

'Then I am sorry for that too.'

She did not seem inclined to talk, but I could not just leave her.

'Did they hire you for the weekend?'

'No, man. I been here for more'n a year.'

I was surprised. She seemed very young to be in service for England. 'How old are you?'

'Just turned sixteen.'

So she was two years younger than I, but while I was learning Latin verbs, she was waiting on Neanderthals like Gideon. 'Where do you live?'

She looked surprised. 'At the Hall.'

'So you live at Longcross? In the house?'

'Yes.'

I thought of another way to ask the question. 'Where are you from?'

'Washington.'

'Ah.' That explained the strange accent. 'The United States.'

Her laugh, through the tears, sounded more like a gulp. 'No, man. Washington in County Durham. Mebbe an hour down the road.'

'Where are your parents?'

'Still there. With me brothers and me sister.'

'So who looks after you?'

'There's Mrs Nicky. Mrs Nicholson, the housekeeper.'

'Is she a . . . pleasant lady? Could you tell her about . . . about this?'

'Haway!' she exclaimed, a word I had never heard and did not understand. 'She'd most probably give *me* a thrashing for being forward.'

I began to get the idea. This young lady, no older than a schoolgirl, had been sent away from a very crowded home to make money, and was expected to tolerate overtures such as these without complaint, for there was no one to confide in anyway. It was no worse than what happened in India, but something about her plight still touched me.

'I have to go back in there.'

'Surely not tonight,' I said. 'Can you not go back to the house?' The grand structure in the distance, lit at every window by pinpricks of light, now seemed like a haven. 'There are four footmen attending the party, and only one course and brandy to go.'

'If I don't, I'll be dismissed.'

The statement, uttered so matter-of-factly, was hard to argue with.

I looked down the silver hill into the black wood. I'd rather take my chances in that dark jungle than do what she had to do. And what I had to do. 'I have to go back too.'

'Why? I thought fancy young fellers could do whatever they want.'

'Not this one.'

'Then why?'

'It does not matter. The stakes are much higher for you. My problems are nothing to yours.'

'Why?'

She was certainly persistent, this Miss Ina. 'Because . . . because I have something to learn. It is the culmination of years of hoping and striving and waiting and false starts. So I cannot give up now.'

'Like the astronauts,' she said.

I looked up at the moon, and the moon looked down at me. 'I suppose if the astronauts could walk up there, I can walk back in here.'

'They weren't alone though,' she said. 'There were three of them.'

'Two,' I said. 'Mr Michael Collins stayed in the craft.'

'OK,' she said. 'So we'll be the two that moonwalked.'

She held out her hand to me. I shook it. 'Do you want to be Armstrong or Aldrin?'

I did not want to be Mr Armstrong, after that agonising Mr Gorsky conversation. The silver of his reputation had forever tarnished a little for me. 'I will be Mr Aldrin,' I said.

'OK. I'll be Armstrong.' She got up. 'Come on. Time to make contact.'

We walked up the little hill to the folly. I entered the glass doors first; she slipped in in my shadow. As I sat down and a footman replaced my napkin on my lap, Rollo hissed, 'Where have you been?'

It was the first time I had ever seen the charm slip. He looked angry and anxious all at once.

'I went to the aid of a lady in distress.' Suddenly I felt stronger, as if I was on solid ground. 'Any gentleman should do the same without hesitation.'

I had been hunting long enough to know when something was wounded. His eyes flickered. 'Hardly a lady.'

I thought he was wrong about that. I watched Ina as she quickly and efficiently cleared the plates, even from Gideon's place. To look at her you would not know that anything untoward had happened – she was so poised and self-possessed. I admired her very much in that moment. But as I watched Ina, Rollo was watching me. Then I realised. He was <u>jealous</u>. He wanted Ina for himself.

When I returned to the house I went up the stairs and almost bumped into Ina coming down the passageway outside our rooms. My day was over, but she was carrying brass cans of hot water for washing.

I would have offered to carry them, but I did not want to make things worse for her. But I did, as she passed, murmur, 'Goodnight, Armstrong.'

She gave the ghost of a smile. 'Goodnight, Aldrin.'

As I went into my room I wanted so much to collapse fully dressed onto the four-poster bed. But I knew I had to write this – to record the first day of my <u>transformation</u>. So this is a full account of what happened on my first evening at Longcross Hall. Goodnight.

I suppose that won't do. It's not enough to end like that. All the writers I admire end their chapters with some sort of homily – a conclusion drawn or a lesson learned. So for tonight mine is this:

I realise I have made a friend at Longcross Hall, but not at all the one I had expected.

I realise too that I have acquired yet another name.

Sleep well,

Aldrin x

'Those arrogant *shits*!' exclaimed Shafeen hotly, flinging the book away from us and sitting up. 'How *dare* they treat him like that?'

He looked out over the rooftops at the lights of Jaipur. '*Christ*. And to think that prick Gideon Villiers grew up to be the Old Abbot. I remember when he was our headmaster we all thought he was Santa Claus. I guess he was always a monster.'

I sat up too and stroked his arm. 'Yes, but what you're missing is how lovely your *father* was. Look at how he came to Ina's rescue.'

'He shouldn't have had to,' said Shafeen grimly. 'Talk about history repeating itself – or rather, foreshadowing itself. Rollo's *exactly* like Henry.'

'And your father's exactly like you,' I said, picking up the diary again and finding our place. 'Settle down. I want to know what happened.'

And together, we started reading again.

Saturday, 25th October 1969

<u>Morning</u>

What happened today is almost <u>unbelievable</u>. I'm shaking so much I can hardly write. But I'm going to really try to set this all down as it happened. The biggest challenge will be to write each part of the day without leaping ahead to the terror that came later.

I must remember that I actually woke feeling quite optimistic. Although the Medievals were foul to me last night, meeting Ina was a comfort, and her courage gave <u>me</u> the courage to try my best to listen and learn and mould myself into an English gentleman.

We had breakfast in an attractive smallish dining room, painted a pale gold colour and lit by weak winter sun. Our breakfast waited on the sideboard, beneath great silver domes. Behind the sideboard was a vast portrait of Queen Elizabeth. The first Queen Elizabeth, I mean; not the one I met when I was eleven. On the gilded frame was a carved legend, which said: *Either a hunter or the hunted be.* It seemed like sound advice.

There were no footmen in attendance, as we were all to help ourselves. I did see Ina though, coming round with a coffee pot – silver too to match the domes. She looked neat and composed and, apart from faint violet shadows under her eyes, no worse for her ordeal of the night before. As I took my place between Miranda and Serena I saw with relief that all the Medievals were dressed in casual country clothes. I was relieved too that I was not required to make conversation. Rollo held forth, telling us of the morning's plans.

'An easy start,' he declared. 'Just a bit of cubbing this morning.'

The Medievals all gave a pleased cheer, but my mouth went dry around my toast and marmalade. I had no idea what cubbing was but was not about to expose my ignorance yet again.

'For the benefit of our guest,' Rollo went on, 'that's when you take the hounds into the covert to get the scent of the foxes. We let the cubs go but give them the scent of the adult ones. Then, tomorrow when we take the pack out, they have the scent in their nose.' He took a swallow of his coffee, cradling the cup itself, not the handle. I immediately adjusted my own hold on my cup. This was most confusing.

'Ideally we'll put up the old bugger we've been after for a few seasons now. A wily old dog fox with black points who keeps eluding us. Tomorrow we'll put on a proper show for him. Hunting pink, the lot.'

'That'll be a bit of a change for you, eh, Mowgli?' needled Gideon. 'Hunting with horses and hounds? Still chucking bloody spears in India, I'll bet?'

I waited for Rollo to correct this. He knew what an advanced hunting culture India had. I knew his father, Monty, had lived there until Independence in 1947, at which point he'd moved back to England, married and had Rollo. I knew that because I'd actually met Rollo's father. But Rollo didn't stick up for me, or India. He was laughing all over his handsome face.

I will not say it did not hurt. And being used to such insults never seems to make the receiving of them any easier. Once again, I heard my father say, *Don't mention India*. But I had something to say that I didn't think even *they* could look down on. The portrait by the sideboard had reminded me, and I was not strong enough to keep my mouth shut. 'Actually,' I said, 'the queen stayed with us in our *palace*. To go hunting, as a matter of fact.'

That silenced them. I took a prim sip of my tea, enjoying the surprise on their faces.

'When?'

'Eight years ago.'

'*Bollocks.*'

'Not at all,' I said. 'My parents – the Maharajah and Maharani of Jaipur –' I couldn't help myself, even though I knew to boast about your connections was very non-U, according to my mother – 'took Her Majesty and Mr Prince Philip on a tiger hunt.'

Miranda snorted. '*Mr* Prince Philip.'

Everyone ignored her. Rollo looked at me closely. 'Really? *You* took the queen hunting?'

'Yes. I thought you knew.'

'How the bloody hell would *I* know?'

'Because your father was there,' I said simply. 'Mr . . . Colonel Monty.'

Rollo looked taken aback. 'I knew the pater had been tiger hunting with the queen once. He settled here after Independence, but he went back in '61 to accompany the royal party, because he used to be the secretary of the Tiger Club in Jaipur. And that was to *your* family home? I didn't know that.'

I considered the possibility of saying that that was because this was the first real conversation we'd had in seven years. But I did not. For the first time, I felt like I had the upper hand. *I* had been on the hunt. *I* had met the queen and Mr Prince Philip. Rollo hadn't. It had been during the holidays, so I supposed that while I was hunting tigers, Rollo had been here at home with the women and children. My lip curled a little. 'Did he not tell you about it?'

'Of course,' said Rollo, trying to regain the ascendancy. 'In fact,' he said proudly, 'he told me how he saved the queen's life.'

I remembered every detail of the day, but I certainly did not remember that bit. I did not wish to gainsay Rollo, so I said carefully, 'I do not recall Her Majesty's life being in peril that day.'

'That's thanks to the pater,' said Rollo. 'The queen has a distinctive perfume, which she wears every day. Something

French, apparently. They were getting in the jeep to set off from the Tiger Club, and the pater got wind of it. Advised her to wash it off, or she'd be tiger food.'

'Why?' asked Miranda.

I knew this one. 'The tigers love cologne,' I said quietly.

'Correct,' said Rollo, and I felt oddly proud. 'They go crazy for it. They would have attacked her just to be near the smell.'

'Gosh! I hope she thanked him,' said Serena.

'She did,' said Rollo. 'She gave him this.' He got something small and metallic from his pocket. It was a lighter. 'See,' he said. 'It has the queen's own coat of arms on it.' He passed it to me, surprisingly, seemingly anxious that I believe his story. I studied the lighter, with the lion and the unicorn and the royal arms in between. I passed it back, and Rollo flipped the top and spun the wheel with his thumb. A little flame sprang obediently to life.

'Lights first time,' remarked Gideon.

'Always does,' said Rollo. 'It was a gift from the queen of England. Not going to be rubbish, is it?'

Gideon said to me, 'You catch anything on this "royal" hunt, then, Mowgli?'

I raised my chin. 'Yes. A fierce tigress called Melati.'

The girls all giggled. Francesca said, 'She had a *name*?'

Serena picked up on the joke. 'Did she introduce herself before she took the royal bullet?'

'No,' I said. 'I mean, that is, *I* named her.'

Rollo seemed interested. He put his cup down and breathed a single word at me. 'Why?'

'It is a tradition, to name your prey. It helps you focus on their capture. It is also a way to honour them. She was brave and cunning. She gave us a good hunt.'

'It's a mistake to anthropomorphise animals,' said Charles, who never uses a short word where a long word will do. 'It elicits sympathy.'

'Oh, I did not feel sorry for her,' I said hurriedly. That was not true. I remember my father told me to put my foot on Melati's throat so a photographer could take a picture. I remember her fur shifting under my hunting boot over the muscles of her powerful neck, just as it would have if I had been stroking her. That shift had given me an odd feeling of shame. I'd felt, in that moment, that my foot should not be there. I posed for the photograph next to Her Majesty the Queen and Mr Prince Philip, and my parents, and Rollo's father; but the moment the picture was taken I took my foot off her neck. And that was the last time I put the sole of my foot on Melati. I would not stand on her again, even when she was a rug on the floor of our townhouse in Jaipur.

I tried to express this feeling now. 'I respected her. She gave us a good hunt. And if you respect your prey, you are halfway to catching him.'

'What a load of hippy codswallop,' began Gideon. 'Let's all get our sitars out.' But Rollo shushed him with a wave of his hand. And that gesture finally unlocked the dynamic between them. Gideon liked to *think* of himself as a leader, but Rollo, though quieter and less demonstrative, was the boss. And it had nothing to do with this being his house. He was the one with real authority. Now I understood.

Gideon was the Eggman.

We were the Eggmen.

Rollo was the Walrus.

The Walrus buttered his toast with deft flicks of a silver knife. 'What you say is very interesting, old boy. Tell me, how would *you* catch this fox we've been after for years?'

Once again, everyone was looking at me. I swallowed with difficulty, the food bone-dry in my mouth.

I remembered going after Melati with the royal party. I had spotted the tigress first, half hidden in the undergrowth, the tall grass and her stripes becoming one, and in that split second I'd had a decision to make: I could call out or let her go. For that instant, she had looked at me with her amber eyes and I had held her gaze.

I came back to the present and answered Rollo's question. 'I would look him in the eyes,' I said. 'I would let him know me, so that I may know him.'

Gideon let out a splutter of laughter.

I ignored him. Men were talking now.

Their eyes were still on me, but now I did not mind so much. I had once had a tiger's eyes on me. For the split second before I had betrayed her to a queen.

'Well, well, well,' said Rollo, looking at me in a new way. 'This afternoon we will test your methods. Approved by Royal Appointment, eh?'

I knew what this meant. The leather shop where we'd bought my weekend suitcase – and this diary – had a royal crest over the door. My father had pointed to it like it was a shrine to Durga herself. *See?* he had said reverently. *The ueen.* By Royal Appointment meant you could display one of those crests that

I'd seen in the shops in St James's. The royal coat of arms, just like the one on Rollo's lighter. As we finished our breakfast I thought of myself with the warrant painted on me, like the painted warriors of old. It was a pleasing thought.

Stables hold no fear for me. I am as confident in my riding as I am about anything. But even I took a step backwards when I saw the mount they had chosen for me.

He practically blocked out the sun. He was big and jet black and skipped around on the cobbles, jogging sideways. *Bad habits*, I thought, *because everyone is afraid of him*.

'This is Satan,' said Rollo, his eyes fixed on me. The girls giggled, as they always did.

Ignoring them, I put my foot in the stirrup the groom held out to me and vaulted onto the monster's back. He threw his head up, an old trick, and if you are not fast, this manoeuvre will give you a bloody nose.

I was quick. I jerked my head out of the way just in time. I looked down at the groom. 'These his usual antics?'

The groom shot a look at Rollo and gave a surly shrug. Satan started dancing crabwise on the cobbles again, so I gathered the reins into a leather loop and slapped his cheek hard. *Bahen Chod*, I said under my breath. A terrible Hindi word. And Satan quieted down and stood like a statue, with four feet planted on the ground.

Suddenly the Medievals did not seem so cocky. They still had to be mounted. While some of them seemed accomplished riders – Serena, particularly, vaulted up like an Amazon – I enjoyed Charles hopping around with one foot in the stirrup as

135

the big bay he had been allocated circled around, refusing to stand still. Charles did not look so clever then. At length we were ready to ride out to battle, and as we rode under the stable arch I noticed there were red roses climbing prettily over it.

They were the colour of blood.

Midday

Cubbing was not an especially exciting pastime, not if you have hunted a tiger from the back of an elephant. As far as I could tell, our purpose was to stand in a ring around a spinney of twisted trees, the hounds weaving in and out of our horses' legs, and to turn back any mature foxes that peeped from the undergrowth. In a brace of hours I let a couple of cubs slide past me – the hounds put up a frenzied yelping but were not allowed to follow and sulked visibly in the undergrowth. The only thing I liked about the pastime was that we were strung out around the covert so that we were too far away from each other to comfortably hold a conversation. Of all the Medievals Rollo stood nearest to me, still and cold as stone, his blue eyes fixed on the covert.

The cold came for us all. There was a white autumn sky, mizzling with rain; the leaves were sodden underfoot, the branches dripping, and the cold crept into one's bones. I dropped my reins and pushed my hands into my padded jacket. The hoarse crows mocked me from the black branches and I longed for the heat and dust of India. It really was miserable, and many times I wondered why I had yearned for so many years to be invited to a country-house weekend.

We stopped for a lunch of soup and sandwiches in a gamekeeper's hut that had the dimensions of a good-sized skiing chalet. There was a brazier in the centre of the wooden room, which made no impact unless one stood practically on top of it. No one spoke to me at lunch except Ina, serving soup in her uniform. Her eyes met mine over the tureen. 'Hello, Aldrin,' she murmured in greeting.

'Hello, Armstrong,' I said in reply.

Her shy smile was the only warmth I felt this afternoon.

I thought we would go back to the house after lunch, but Rollo seemed determined to keep watch until he found the particular fox he was looking for. It seemed intensely personal to him, and we were all carried forward by his determination. It was his will alone that was keeping us all there, like a string of prayer beads, holding the spirit of the prey he sought within that charmed circle. If one of us broke the chain, his prey would escape. The hounds, as they had a habit of doing, had disappeared, as if they were as bored as I.

Then, when I was about to fall from my horse with the cold, I saw a little triangular face. I knew this was the dog fox Rollo was looking for. He had black points on his ears and snout, and a seasoned, wily look most unlike the cubs I had freed.

I knew I should call out for Rollo, just like I had given up Melati to the Queen of England. But I knew in my heart that I should not have called out then, and that I should not call out now. It had been my fault that Melati's life had ended that day, to spend eternity on the floor of our house in Jaipur. Was I about to end another life? I looked at the fox, and the fox looked at me. Neither of us moved. I didn't speak, but I sent him a message – this will sound foolish – with my eyes. *Go*, I said. *Run. Be free.*

And the dog fox with the black points trotted past me into the open country.

I turned my horse's head to the covert and caught the white blob of a face in the corner of my eye. I turned to see Rollo looking right at me. He had seen the whole thing.

He rode over. 'What the bloody hell d'ye think you're doing?'

'I . . . I . . .'

'That was him! That was *the* fox!' He flung out his arm to the fox's path. 'You were supposed to turn him back. Show him to the hounds.' I was silent.

'Are you an imbecile? What happened?' I could have told him. About the tigress and the queen. But I didn't even know how to begin.

'Cat got your tongue?'

A tiger got it, I thought, and absurdly wanted to laugh. Instead, I said, 'I thought he was a cub. I did not know he was an old fox.' But I did know.

He regarded me with his cold blue eyes. 'Some hunter.' He curled his lip. '*By Royal Appointment.*'

Then he rode away.

And I wanted to cry.

I haven't seen him that angry ever. In all the years he has presided over my humiliation at STAGS, he's always done so with a smile, killing with kindness, cutting with charm. This was not the flash of irritation he'd shown over Ina the night before. This was white-hot anger. I felt it in my middle just under my ribs, right in the very heart of me. His anger, and something else too. Yes – his <u>disappointment</u>.

I didn't know what to do, so I followed. We were a sombre procession riding home. Rollo's mood affected all of us. No one spoke until we had all dismounted in the stable yard. Serena laid a hand on Rollo's arm, but he shrugged it away. 'I'll see you all at dinner.' Then he strode off alone, back to the house, flicking his boot angrily with his riding crop as he walked. I had to endure the scornful glances of the Medievals, but after Rollo's scorn I barely felt them.

In my bathroom I ran the hottest water I could into the claw-footed bath and attempted to boil myself warm again. Largely it worked – the feeling came back into my fingers and toes and limbs. But there was something cold in my core, and I thought I could give a name to it. Rollo's anger – no, his disappointment – still lodged in my chest like a stone. I must have stayed in that bath for hours, almost unmoving, watching the branches wagging about on the brow of the distant hill, watching the sky rot from white to grey to black. I stayed in there until the water was cold, then I heaved myself out and dressed for dinner.

<u>Evening</u>

As if I was not nervous enough, dinner was in the Great Hall, a place I had not yet been. The first thing I saw in the enormous baronial room was a tiger-skin rug, stretched out on the floor. Immediately I was reminded of Melati, reclining forever on our floor in Jaipur, but as I walked closer I could see that this one was a male – an enormous, grizzled old warrior, doubtless laid low by some de Warlencourt blunderbuss many moons ago. I mentally named him Shere Khan, and I skirted him carefully and took my place at the table – a much more formal setting than last night, with a snow-white tablecloth, regiments of steel cutlery and sentinels of crystal glass. Silver candlesticks stood guard in pairs all down the length of the table, and the Medievals sat, boy/girl/boy/girl, in strict rotation. The young men, including myself, were in the evening uniform of white tie and tails. The young ladies were in coloured taffeta of green, amber and red. They reminded me of traffic lights.

They all spoke to each other, over the space of three courses, as if I was not there. They spoke of plans for Christmas, families they all knew. They spoke of the royal family, and Charles, the new Prince of Wales – with whom some of them seemed to have more than a nodding acquaintance – with obvious approval. They spoke of the civil rights movement in America with just as obvious disapproval. Then they moved on to the Stonewall riots. The only issue that seemed to exercise them as much as black people having a voice was homosexuals having a voice. Those who had taken part in the protests over the summer in New York occupied Gideon's particular Seventh Circle of Hell. 'I'd shoot the lot of 'em,' he said. 'Bloody deviants. The scum of the earth.'

Charles agreed. 'The Raj had the right idea. They condemned queers to death. Strung 'em up like rats.'

All of them drank heavily. Not one of them spoke to me or looked at me. I wonder if they had been briefed by Rollo or were merely following his lead. I began to question my own existence. But that was Rollo for you. His charm was palpable. When he smiled at you, the sun shone. When he frowned, the clouds came and you felt the chill of the shade.

As the evening wore on I found that I could not bear it. I *had* to speak to him.

I wanted to wait until the traffic-light girls were gone. I knew, from my mother's tutelage, that it was traditional at the end of the meal for the womenfolk to withdraw to the drawing room to drink coffee, and for the men to stay around the table drinking port. But that did not seem to be happening. Unable to stand it any more, I burst out: 'Can't we hunt him tomorrow?'

There was a silence, and everyone's eyes swivelled to fall on me. I looked at Rollo. Would he pretend he did not know what I was talking about?

He did not pretend. 'We might put up another fox,' he said coldly. 'But not that one. He'll be in Yorkshire by now.' He turned away to talk to Gideon. I had to stop him.

'I could catch him for you,' I blurted rashly. I knew I had let the fox go today. It had been my fault. And I was by no means certain that I could catch that particular fox for Rollo. But I felt I had to try. I had to lay him at his feet as a tribute. Then maybe he would not look at me as he was looking at me then.

'How?' he asked pointedly. 'Look them in the eyes, I suppose.'

'No,' I said. 'Call him by his right name. *Know* him. *That's* how you find him.'

Rollo looked interested. He turned to the ancient butler. 'A bottle of the Veuve Clicquot 1912, Coles.'

The old man bowed. 'Very good, m'lord.'

All the staff filed out behind him, and I wondered why it took five of them to get one bottle of wine. Ina gave me a tiny smile as she passed. Watching them all go gave me a tiny jag of panic under my ribs. When you are being bullied at school, you don't like it when the teacher leaves the room. This was like that.

And then, just to make matters worse, all the electric lights went out.

The girls squealed happily. Rollo said easily, 'Ah. What a nuisance. Bloody power cut. Happens all the time. At least we have the candles. The old ways don't let you down.'

The air was humming with a certain energy. The staff leaving, the lights going down – I felt like I was filling up with foreboding, like a glass of dark wine.

'Let's play a little game,' said Rollo, 'to test your theorem.'

'A parlour game?'

'Let's call it a variant on hide and seek.' He rose and walked over to me, standing just behind my chair. My flesh began to prickle.

'I must call you by your right name.'

I kept my eyes looking dead ahead and listened. In this insane ceremony of his, would he call me Hardy, as he had when I came into his house as his guest?

'I name you Mowgli.' I felt a hand on my head, just as the Abbot blessed the kindergarten children in the chapel at STAGS.

'But we have to christen him properly,' urged Gideon. 'Wet the baby's head.'

'You're absolutely right, Gidders.'

Then, at last, I turned my head, just in time to see Rollo hold his glass of claret high and pour it all over me. Over my carefully combed hair, my dress shirt and my tail coat.

As the wine dripped, I looked imploringly at the door. Surely the butler would be back with the champagne Rollo had asked for, and then this insanity would have to stop? But no one came.

Rollo bent close to my ear. 'We're going to see if we can catch you,' he whispered. 'If you get away, you win. If we catch you, we do.'

'*What* do I win?' I asked, heart thumping.

'Your life,' said Gideon.

'You are joking,' I said nervously.

'Of course he is,' said Rollo smoothly.

'So?' I could barely trust my voice. 'What do I win?'

'What do you want? What do you want most of all?'

He walked around my chair and hopped up nimbly onto the long table, perching right in front of me.

'I know what you want.' He looked directly at me. 'I'll give you what you want most of all.'

I knew now I had nothing to lose. 'And what is that?'

'You want to be like *me*,' he said, clearly now, so that all his minions could hear.

'You want to walk like me. Talk like me. Don't you, Mowgli? Because, you see, even someone like *you* can learn to be human too.'

I recognised the similarity to the *Jungle Book* lyrics a split second before the laughter started.

'So, Mowgli,' said Gideon, over all the vultures crowing, 'here are the Laws of the Jungle.' Once again, he was attempting to assume the role of leader. 'No going outside, including the roof. No bedrooms except your own. And no help from the servants.'

I looked back at Rollo for evidence of a joke. This was insanity. But he only smiled sleepily and quoted, once again, from *The Jungle Book*. This time he was playing Shere Khan, the tiger giving the defenceless man-cub a head start to make the chase more 'interesting'. He leaned very close to me, as close as a kiss. And started counting. 'One . . .'

I looked into his blue eyes, then at all the other Medievals.

He meant it.

They meant it.

I ran.

Night

It is impossible to describe how unnerving it was being in that house in the dark. Outside the Great Hall, and beyond the golden light of the candles, it was hard, at first, to see anything at all. I knew that the Great Hall led into the atrium where the grand staircase was, so I made for that. I galloped up the stairs on all fours like an animal. From the Great Hall I could hear the Medievals baying to me – *Run, Mowgli, run*. I could not tell you how many flights I climbed, or when my instinct told me to stop climbing and run down a passageway, or where I ended up. I paused in my flight and tried to let my eyes get used to the dark. There was no light but the weak silver moonlight, filtering through the

144

diamond-paned windows. I was in a part of the house that I have never been in before. Judging from the dim view through the window over the neat and formal gardens – the green now rendered in silver and grey – I was reasonably high up, perhaps on the third floor. Turning back, I could just make out that I was in a wide passageway, with carpet on the floor and paintings on the walls, and chairs squatting at intervals, arms open in welcome, inviting me to sit down. I knew I could not. I had to keep moving, but also, like any prey, I had to gauge where my pursuers were. I stood very still and listened. The catcalling from the Great Hall had stopped, but the silence was much more frightening. It was so quiet that I could hear the sound of my own heart thumping. Then a sudden sound almost made me jump out of my skin, like the tiger downstairs. It was a regular wheezing, like someone breathing, but almost mechanical. Then the music started: a plinky-plonky guitar arpeggio, filling my veins with ice. Then the voice began to sing – a woman's voice – and I think I will remember the song it sang for the rest of my days.

It was a breathy little-girl voice, and it was spine-chilling. She seemed to be singing to a tiger, asking him to teach her how to kiss him, and to show her what to do. It had a refrain which went *wah wah wah* – half little girl crying, half grown woman kissing. It was deeply disturbing. Almost in a trance, I walked towards the sound, until I could see, in the moonlight, the wide metal bell of the gramophone – the same gramophone that had been transported up to the folly. The device was now sitting on a side table, between two chairs, and black vinyl was turning, turning. Numbly I watched the record revolve, my mind whirring too. I had to deal with two possibilities. Either the gramophone had been set going by an unseen hand, in which case the Medievals were already ahead of me, or there was some supernatural force at work in this dreadful house. Either way, I could no longer stay. Game or not, I abandoned the hunt. I just wanted to get away. The breathy music seemed to enter the very bones of me, poisoning my flesh from within, and the passageway seemed in the darkness to be leaning in, closing down to trap me as I turned and ran.

No bedrooms, except your own. Gideon's words came back to me. The Laws of the Jungle dictated that I could not go into any bedroom except my own. But that meant that I *could* just go to my room and sit this nightmare out. If I was on the third floor now, I had to get back down to the first floor, where my bedroom was. I ran swiftly back down the stairs and turned right into the passageway where I knew my room was located. For a panicked moment I could not remember the name of my room – something to do with a number. I looked at the names lettered in gold on each door. Forster, Fenwick, Musgrave, Raby. Something to do with a number. That was it: Levens.

I turned the handle and then I saw something right in front of my nose that I had not seen earlier – perhaps it was the moonlight that picked it out. It was a pair of deer antlers, drawn in chalk on the wood, just like I'd seen on my leather suitcase. But I did not have time to wonder about the strange rune that marked out my door at that moment. I burst through it, locked it behind me and then leaned on it, breathing hard.

I had not found the room particularly welcoming when I

arrived. It was icy cold, like anywhere in northern England, when you moved more than a yard away from the fire. The leaded windows (now stained dark with night) had no curtains, but the four-poster bed did, and there was a boar's head on the wall over the mantel, but at that moment it seemed like safe harbour in a storm. Nothing was stopping me from staying in here, closing the heavy drapes around the bed until I was in a square of safety, pulling the brocade bedspread over my head and waiting for daylight. It didn't seem very glorious, nor very manly for my newly eighteen-year-old self, but I no longer cared. At least nothing could happen to me in here. I put on every light and lamp in the place to banish the dark corners.

I was not willing to leave the room to visit the bathroom. Luckily my room had a fitted basin, so I was not dependent on the washstand and the brass cans of hot water that poor Ina had to carry up and down. I took off my tail coat and untied my tie; rolled up the sleeves of my wine-stained dress shirt. Before I ran the tap I leaned on the cold porcelain with both hands and regarded myself in the mirror above the basin like I was looking at someone else. All black hair and black eyes and brown skin; tall enough to be a man. I looked at that person like Rollo had looked at me, with that unforgettable stare of utter contempt. But the person in the mirror just looked scared. I despised him.

I looked away from his gaze and ran the hot tap into the basin. The tap gave a gurgle, then a spit, then it began to run.

As I've already written, I'd put on all the lights, so I know that what I saw was real.

What came out of the tap was not water, but <u>blood</u>.

147

For the first fraction of a second I thought it was brown water, which sometimes gushes out of the ancient plumbing at STAGS before it runs clear. But I put a finger below the flow and held it to my nose. It even had the sickly meat-and-metal smell I remember from tiger hunts.

I jumped away in horror before it could splash me and caught my reflection in the mirror once again. The room was arctic; the blood was warm and so the mirror steamed up at once. My terrified face blurred with condensation, but a few lines stayed clear. Lines that made up letters, written on the mirror by an unseen hand.

RUN

I started backwards. Who was doing this? I turned frantically, expecting to see someone in the room, but there were only blank windows, a dying fire and the empty bed. The only presence was the boar's head on the wall. As I looked – and I swear to all the gods this is true – the head <u>moved</u>. It swivelled on its mount, neck straining, snout snuffling, little tusks curled like an elephant's, to look straight at me.

That's when I took the mirror's advice. I unlocked the door, wrenched it open and ran.

As the upstairs held no sanctuary for me, I went all the way down the grand staircase again, to the ground floor. No longer caring for Gideon's Laws of the Jungle, I rattled at the great doors to the outside but they were, of course, locked. I pelted down a passageway, right to the end, and pulled open a door into the dark. Once inside, I looked around, eyes adjusting, but I could hardly have found a less friendly haven. The hunter's moon – my only ally tonight – described the filigree of chainmail and the wicked blades of a thousand swords and spears mounted on the walls.

An armoury.

The room was flanked with suits of armour and it was chilling walking between them, my bare feet soundless on the parquet flooring. At every instant I expected the faceless knights to turn and look at me, as I was convinced the boar had done. It occurred to me that I could hide among these metal ghosts. Could I even put on that suit and stand, sleeping on my feet, until morning? As I put out a hand to touch the nearest breastplate, a voice spoke out of the blackness.

'I am Gian Maria Visconti, Renaissance prince.'

I froze to the spot as the hollow tones boomed out of the metal helm. 'This is my armour. For sport I set my hunting hounds to course and dismember men.' The knight raised one creaking arm and pointed his jointed finger at me.

Heart still pounding, I reversed out of the room as fast as I could and ran the other way, doubling back on myself towards the stairs. I raced through the cavernous atrium, past the grand staircase, with the statue standing at the top.

I stopped in my tracks. There had not been a statue there before.

'I am Diana, goddess of the hunt.'

It was, of course, the statue that spoke. She pivoted on her plinth, looked down and addressed me, her blank eyes as black as a shark's. 'When Actaeon looked upon my nakedness, he had to be killed.' The voice was Francesca's. The moonlight had leached her hair of its fiery red colour and lent a luminous sheen to her already-white skin. If Francesca was the statue, that meant she was standing there naked.

'Are you looking upon *my* nakedness?'

I was. Of course I was. She was the first naked girl I had ever seen. I told the truth. 'Yes.'

'Do you think I'm beautiful?'

I told a lie. 'Yes.'

She seemed satisfied with this answer, and I counselled myself. This was only Francesca. The voice of the knight, though distorted by the metal helm, I now knew to be Charles. I tried to slow my heartbeats with this knowledge. And it worked, until something truly incredible happened. Francesca raised her bow, pulled the string back to its fullest extent with a creak of the wood and pointed the wicked arrow right at me.

'Well, now you've seen me, Mowgli, you'd better keep moving,' she said, her voice thrumming on the taut bowstring like the song of a sitar. 'We don't want any accidents.'

Then she actually loosed the arrow. It sheared through the air and thumped into the great door behind me, just inches from my head.

I sprang to the side, but if she'd wanted to hit me, it would have been too late. I skidded down the passageway in the other direction from the armoury and went through another pair of great doors. This was a vast room, the floor as polished as ice, with a chandelier hanging above, capturing the moonlight in its brilliants. The walls were covered in something, floor to ceiling, and a curving iron ladder offered the sanctuary of a gallery above. I scrambled up it and lay down, heart nearly bursting out of my chest. I was still for some moments, trying to calm myself. Until that arrow, I could believe it was only a game. Now I knew it was much more serious.

Minutes ticked by and I began to take in my surroundings. A row of shapes beside my face resolved into being. Books. The walls were covered in books. This was a library. The friendly moonlight helped me read the lettering on the spines next to my head – dates. Black books with no titles, just dates – decades stretching back in time; perhaps encyclopaedias or something of that sort.

I heard a muffling, shuffling sound from below and froze again, listening. A soft thud; footsteps approaching; footsteps retreating. I was confident that where I lay I could not be seen by any pursuers below, but I was also trapped. I wished then, very hard, for some secret passage that could take me from this place. But it was no good wishing. I would have to go down eventually. I waited for utter silence and then made my move.

As I descended I could see very clearly and unmistakably, by the light of the big double doors, a body, lying prone on the parquet. I trod closer.

It was Gideon, lying dead with an arrow in his chest.

Someone was shouting. It was me. My screams echoed through the malignant house.

Better keep moving. We don't want any . . . accidents. Had Gideon been an accident? Now giving myself away didn't matter. Now was not a time for games. Now was the time for grown-ups – for the servants, for the police, for the coroner.

But no one came to my aid. Once I'd stopped howling, there was waiting and darkness and silence. The silence told me something.

They were not going to stop.

They were going to carry on with this twisted game of hide and seek.

My one hope was the servants. Ina said she lived in. But I did not know where her quarters were, and I knew that, however great the emergency, I could not burst into a young woman's room in the dead of night. Discovery would result in the dismissal she so feared. As for the footmen and the housekeeper and the butler – who was to say they wouldn't be on Rollo's side? Who was to say this was unusual? The de Warlencourts needed prey, and I was it. For all I knew, the order for champagne was the signal to the servants to get out of the way. This might be quite a commonplace weekend at Longcross Hall. Gideon had been caught in the crossfire, but if they had no qualms about killing one of their own, what had they got saved up for me?

I had no choice but to run again. I burst through the heavy doors into the Great Hall and scanned the room to make sure there was no one in there. There were the antlers on the wall, frosted with moonlight. There was the polished table, littered with the detritus of dinner; the servants had indeed disappeared. But there was *someone* in the room.

The tiger-skin rug. Eyes and mouth wide, snout ridged in a snarl. His eye teeth were almost luminous. Earlier I'd dubbed him Shere Khan, and in the *Jungle Book* film he would have been my enemy. Now he meant home, and with the servants gone he was the nearest thing to a friend in this devilish house. I genuinely did not know what to do next, or where to run. So I did the only thing that seemed to make sense to me. I lay on him, face down, and rested my cheek on his massive skull. 'Shere Khan,' I said, 'help me.' Then I said it again in Hindi, in case he didn't understand. But he was silent. 'Say something,' I said. 'Cat got your tongue?'

Then a phrase of my father's came back to me.

Sometimes you have to put your hand in the tiger's mouth.

He didn't, of course, mean it literally – in India, that was the quickest way to lose a hand. But I was safe with this tiger. I curled my hand round Shere Khan's jaws and put my fingers between his teeth. The tongue was a solid dry mass – desiccated flesh, rough as sandpaper. It had no answers for me. I took out my hand and rolled onto my back, defeated.

The moon looked on, remote and heartless, through the diamond-paned windows. But suddenly something, caught in a stray moonbeam, gleamed at me from the wall. I jumped up and walked over to the panelling. There, crossed and mounted on the wall, were a pair of ancient long-nosed guns.

Duelling pistols.

They were beautiful things. The stocks were made of polished wood inset with a decorative silver scroll. On the right-hand gun, the curlicues on the scroll wreathed about the central design of a little Christian cross. On the left-hand gun, the cross was upside down.

I touched one silver barrel. It was cold. I grasped the left-hand gun of the pair and wrenched it down. It was surprisingly heavy as I tested it in my hand. I checked the powder and the musket ball – it was loaded. I raised it level with my shoulder, aimed it squarely at Shere Khan's head and closed one eye. I felt better already.

You see, when my father said that sometimes you had to put your hand in the tiger's mouth, he didn't mean in the way I just had. He meant sometimes you have to face your troubles head on, be brave, take action. 'Thank you,' I said to Shere Khan, still pointing the pistol dead between his eyes.

I did not leave the room in the same way I entered it. I did not run. I walked. I was clothed in the confidence – the warmth, the overcoat of false courage, that man has worn ever since the age of firearms dawned.

I was no longer alone.

I had a gun.

Back in the atrium I sniffed the air and listened. My father had taught me well and I knew I was a dead shot. Even with an old flintlock like this, I reckoned I could do some damage. Now I was not trying to *escape* my pursuers. I was trying to *track* them. The painted queen had been right. *Either a hunter or the hunted be.*

On silent feet I went back to the armoury to find Gian Maria Visconti. I put the gun barrel into the black space between helmet and visor, but the suit was empty. I banged on the breastplate with the stock of the gun. 'Hello!' I shouted, making myself laugh, giddy with courage. The armour sounded as hollow as an old tin can. Very well then. Charles was somewhere else.

Back to the hallway again and I looked to the head of the stairs, but Francesca the archer had gone too. Not that I

154

would have cared, now, if she had been there – I had my gun.

I climbed the stairs and kicked open the chalk-marked door to my own room like a cowboy. There was no one there. The letters had gone from my mirror, and there was a tidemark of blood around my basin but the flow had stopped. The boar was still once more, staring glassily down the barrel of my gun when I pointed it at him.

I went back to the place I had started: the passageway with the gramophone in it. The Louis XIV chairs squatted still, the bell of the gramophone emitted no sound and the glossy black disc sat as still as a pool of ink. In fact, there was no sound at all in the house. Almost by tacit consent we had exchanged places – *they* were now hiding from *me*. My heart swelled with the power.

In the cavernous stairwell once more I heard something at last – faint noises from the very top of the house. I climbed again, this time all the way up until the stairs ran out. I moved soundlessly, gun held low, into a place I'd never seen – an enormously long room with moonlight streaming in at intervals. There were portraits all the way along the walls. In the dim light I could only make out the nearest one – apart from the clothes, the man in it looked exactly like Rollo. The room was so long I could not see the end of it – it disappeared into blackness.

And then I heard it. The whispering.

Mowgli, Mowgli, Mowgli.

I forgot how to be brave. What was it, at the foot of the stairs, that had made me feel less afraid? Ah, yes. That was it. The gun.

I raised the thing to shoulder height and pointed it into the dark, towards the whispering. *Mowgli, Mowgli.* I was convinced, then, that I was going to die.

They'd already killed Gideon, and he was one of their own. *Be the hunter or the hunted*, the painted queen had said.

I made my choice.

I squeezed the trigger and fired into the dark at my unseen adversary.

The ancient gun backfired and there was a flash and a firework smell. The blast knocked me off my feet and there was a searing pain at my left earlobe. I put my hand to my ear and it came away wet. My shoulder was sticky with blood. I think I blacked out for a moment and as I came to, Rollo skidded over to me and knelt by my head. Someone struck a match and I thought I must still be unconscious because Gideon stood with them, grinning all over his face, an arrow sticking out of his bloody chest. Closest of all was Rollo's face, a portrait of concern.

'Wake up, Mowgli. I say, it was only a rag. What possessed you to get hold of that bloody hand cannon? You could have shot your bally head off!' I could have sworn he sounded relieved. He picked up the pistol very carefully by the stock and handed it to Charles, who wrapped it reverently in his tail coat. I got a very strong sense that the gun was worth far more than I was. Francesca, now fully clothed, took a couple of candles from the sconces and lit them from Rollo's match, holding them high like beacons of justice.

Charles was peering at my ear. 'Just a flesh wound,' he pronounced, as if he were a doctor.

'All right,' said Rollo. 'Show's over. Charlie, go and switch the electrics back on. All you others, time to go to bed. Come on, Hardy.' He hauled me to my feet and plonked me on one of the Chippendale chairs that lined the Long Gallery. He took a handkerchief from his pocket and pressed it to my ear. 'Hold this tight,' he said, not unkindly. But I thought, even then, that one could not tell if he was more concerned for my ear or for the gold silk of the Chippendale.

I'm writing this back in my room with Rollo's handkerchief pressed to my ear. When I take it away the bleeding has stopped, but there is a large stain on the cloth that looks like a red map. A map of a country where this sort of behaviour is normal.

Postscript

I cannot sleep anyway, but I have just remembered something else. As I was sitting on that chair in the Long Gallery with my left ear pouring blood, my right ear heard Gideon and Rollo talking. I am going to record it like the scene of a play, such as Mr Orton might have written.

Gideon: Shall we write him up?
Rollo: Write him up?
Gideon: In the game book.
Rollo: Not exactly a kill, was it? Strictly speaking, he shot himself.
Gideon: Still a scalp for the Order though . . .
Rollo: (reluctantly) I don't know. It doesn't feel right somehow.

Gideon: Why ever not?

Rollo: Well, *he* chose the Judas pistol. So something about it feels like . . . it's not exactly . . . cricket.

Gideon: If he'd got hold of the Jesus one instead you wouldn't be standing here. *(Pause)* We always write 'em down, even if we only wing 'em. *(Another pause)* I am Grand Master, old boy.

Rollo: What you mean is, you don't want your first weekend as Grand Master to pass without a scalp. *(Pause again)* All right. What day is it?

Gideon: Technically Sunday.

Rollo: We can't just write *him* up. Bit of a giveaway.

Gideon: Just write some birds down as well. Then it looks like it happened on a shoot.

Rollo: All right. I'll get the book.

I have no idea what this exchange meant, but I write it here in case it becomes important later.

<u>In case I never get out of here.</u>

'My God,' I said, giving Shafeen such an enormous shove he nearly rolled off the divan. 'That's the *game book*. They're talking about the game book.'

'Yes,' he said soberly. 'What they wrote is the very page we read when we were in the library the first time we went to Longcross. That's the game book I stole and brought back to STAGS.'

'And d'you remember all that palaver about the *Grand Master, Rollo de Warlencourt*? Whether or not he and the Grand Master were two different people?'

'Only separated by a comma,' said Shafeen. 'Yes, I remember.'

'Well, now we know for sure. Gideon – the Old Abbot – *was* the Grand Master that weekend.'

Shafeen looked down at the diary where it lay on the silken cushions. 'That doesn't let Rollo off the hook though,' he said, his mouth set in a hard line. 'He's still complicit in all this.'

'Oh, totally,' I said, but my voice sounded, even to myself, a little bit doubtful. Was I starting to . . . not feel *sorry* for Rollo – that would be ridiculous – but to *understand* him a little? 'Let's keep reading.'

But Shafeen was already turning the page.

Sunday, 26th October 1969

<u>Morning</u>

When I woke the basin and the tap were back to normal. The mirror was clean. I examined myself in it. My ear had scabbed over during the night. It hurt to the touch and the edge was slightly ragged. I wondered if it would always be a slightly different shape to the other one. It is lucky that I wear my hair fairly long.

I washed and dressed and went to breakfast in the morning room. I eyed the queen's portrait again. I had taken her advice, and for what?

But something was different. The Medievals all greeted me when I entered and took my seat. Their triumph of the night before, where they had tasted first blood, made them almost amicable. They seemed quite content for me to question them about their 'jape'; in fact, they seemed rather proud of themselves.

'How did you change the water in the basin?' I asked as I applied marmalade to my toast with a silver spoon.

'That room has its own cistern. We just filled it with pigs' blood. Or rather, young Perfect, the keeper's boy – he did it,' said Rollo amiably.

'Didn't want to get your hands dirty?' I asked acidly. I think I had a right to be annoyed.

'Absolutely not, old boy.'

I took a swallow of my tea. 'Just that room? Just Levens?'

'Levens is the room for japes, dear chap,' he replied. 'The cistern. The boar's head . . .'

'That was me,' crowed Miranda. 'You operate him from the next room.'

'I did the mirror,' said Serena proudly. 'I wrote *RUN* in Vaseline when you were in the bath. It doesn't show until it gets steamy.'

It was like that old story of the Brahmin, the Tiger and the Fox, where the fox shows the workings of the cage to the foolish cat. Now it all made sense. The deer's antlers chalked on my suitcase; the same antlers chalked on the door of my room. I was a marked man from the very start. I wasn't invited in the spirit of friendship at all. Whatever the painted queen said, *I* was prey, and the unhappiness squeezed my heart into a stone. And since I have been caught, whether by my own hand or theirs, I will not now be taught to be a gentleman. I know as I write this that it sounds naive in the <u>extreme</u> to have

160

ever expected Rollo to keep his word in this regard. But he did promise to teach me to be like him. And I had thought that, whatever else he was, he was a man of his word.

For now, he was still explaining the mechanisms of his trap. 'Charlie was Gian Maria Visconti, hiding in that old tin can. Francesca was the statue of Diana, but you know that, of course.'

I could feel myself blushing. Everyone at that breakfast table knew I'd seen Francesca naked. The lady herself seemed unconcerned – calmly munching toast.

'But that arrow was real,' I said, not quite meeting her eyes.

'Bless you, Mowgli,' she said. 'If I'd wanted to hit you, you wouldn't be talking to me now. I could split an apple off your head.'

'Gidders was a corpse, as you know,' Rollo went on.

'Bloody tricky holding my breath while you were howling, old boy,' put in Gideon. 'Thought you were never going to leave.'

'Then I was waiting for you in the Long Gallery,' finished Rollo. 'I had a rather good jape planned, using the portraits. But of course we never got that far.'

'Always prowling the gallery, is old Rollo,' teased Gideon. 'Favourite room of the house, eh?'

'That's perfectly true,' Rollo replied calmly. 'I like communing with the ancestors.'

'Ancestors, my arse!' exclaimed Gideon. He turned to the collective. 'It's his hunting ground for the birds. Here's his MO.' He waved his coffee cup to encompass the entire table. 'Takes a girl up there. Shows her all the lineage, all the ghosts of de Warlencourts past. Then takes her on the roof and gets his

161

end away. Works every time, eh, Rolls?' He put on a dreadful parody of Rollo's voice. *'One day, this could all be yours. Please let me put my tongue down your throat.'* He laughed loudly. 'Man's an absolute legend.'

'Shut up, Gidders,' said Rollo, not entirely displeased.

I could not focus on Gideon's bawdy nonsense right then. I wanted to focus on what had happened to *me* in the Long Gallery. This had been no courtship. This had been a carefully coordinated plan to scare me to death. In fact, if that ancient pistol had backfired a little to the left, I *would* be dead. And all for what? A game to amuse these privileged young sprigs of English nobility? I had been an innocent, a greenhorn, a rube.

'How long have you been doing this? This hunting of the guests?'

'How long has the family been doing it? Centuries, old boy,' admitted Rollo brazenly.

'And has it ever . . . gone really wrong?'

'Right, you mean?' Gideon sniggered. 'Couldn't possibly say, old chap.'

It was then I began to feel an emotion I had not yet felt at that house.

Anger.

The anger helped me decide. Last night I had turned from the hunted into the hunter, and I was not going back. Today I was going to be a hunter again. I would no longer be a willing victim. 'So,' I said coldly to Rollo, 'what is on the agenda today?'

'Well, I thought about what you said. I think we *will* have a spot of foxhunting after all. Not a proper meet. No master,

162

no hunt servants – just the seven of us, and we'll take the gamekeeper's boy to do the wet work.'

He reached for a second piece of toast and buttered it lavishly. 'Might as well give it a bash. I'm feeling rather optimistic.' He bit into his toast with even, white teeth. 'According to your methods, we just have to call him by his right name, correct? We just have to christen him, as we did with you. I had a flash of inspiration for your foxy friend.' He gathered the glances of the Medievals. '*Reynard*.'

'Of *course*,' said Gideon. 'Like that bloody endless poem.'

'The Masefield,' said Charles.

I knew what they were talking about. The poem that was on the syllabus for our English literature Probitiones, entitled *Reynard the Fox*, by the English writer Mr John Masefield. It was the story of a hunt, and it was extremely long, but rather good.

'Reynard,' repeated Charles, echoing his betters as he always did. 'That's a jolly good name.'

'It is a mistake to anthropomorphise animals,' I murmured. 'It elicits sympathy.'

Gideon got to his feet. 'But it worked last night, didn't it?' He ruffled my hair as he walked past me with his plate. 'We named our little savage, and we caught him.'

I swallowed. So this was how they saw me – a brown savage, more animal than man. They had no intention of teaching me their ways. So there was no point in being nice any more. 'But you didn't catch me,' I said. 'I caught myself. Maybe because you *didn't* call me by my right name.'

They all looked at me as if the tiger-skin rug had got up

and talked. Then they all started hooting and laughing in mock-shock.

'*Someone* grew some balls overnight, didn't they?' said Gideon from the sideboard as he harvested more scrambled egg.

'Someone got ideas beyond their station, more like,' said Miranda in a superior voice.

'Oh, I *like* this new Mowgli,' said Rollo in admiration. 'Yes. This could be a rather interesting day.' He dabbed his mouth with his napkin and got to his feet. 'Leave that, Gidders. Let's go and get Reynard.'

Midday

The hunt was a very different proposition to the casual cubbing of yesterday.

After breakfast I found a full suit of clothes on my bed, including the famous jacket of (according to my mother) hunting pink. I examined myself in the looking glass and even I could see that I looked well in the shiny black boots, the white breeches, the red jacket and white tie. If it were not for the colour of my skin, I could have been one of <u>them</u>.

We mounted our horses at the grand front entrance – I had my old friend Satan. He rolled his eye at me as the groom held my stirrup, but once I mounted he stood stock still. He knew better, after yesterday, than to cross me. Now I had the more difficult task of teaching the Medievals to respect me likewise.

We waited while the kennelmen brought the hounds, in a white-and-tan mass, tails wagging with joy. Ina came round with a tray loaded with small silver goblets. She held them up to each of the seven riders, beginning with the ladies and ending with me. I might have been lowest in rank, but I was the only one favoured with a smile.

'Stirrup cup, Aldrin?' she murmured.

'Why thank you, Armstrong,' I said. My mind was on the hunt ahead, but I did think, rather distractedly, that she looked remarkably pretty that morning. The winter wind blew a few brown curls from under her cap, and the low sun turned her green eyes to jade. Her earthy prettiness was the daytime antidote to the poisonous moonlit nakedness of Francesca.

I shifted my gaze to Rollo. It was hard to break the habit of a lifetime and I still watched him almost constantly. It looked as though the hunting pink was made for him, which I imagine it was. He sat easily in his saddle, supremely confident, like a king. I had pledged to be his champion today: to bring him Reynard and lay him at his feet like a trophy. As I watched Rollo take a golden horn from his saddle and raise it to his lips, as the procession of death moved off down the drive, the hounds baying in competition with the horn, I thought what a fool I had been to make such a promise. I had no power to bring Reynard to account, and I dreaded to think what Rollo would do if I failed him again.

And failure came almost at once. Not far from the house, in open country, Rollo reined in his horse to a stop. The other Medievals circled him as if he were their general, as he shouted over the heads and tails of the hounds, to me.

'Well, Mowgli?' he said. 'Which way?'

I swallowed. It was a cold day, but my reins slipped between sweaty fingers. Everyone looked at me, from the riders to the hunt servants to the hounds. It was time to make good on my promise.

I closed my eyes, making them all go away. I thought only of the pointy, bright-eyed face of the fox. 'Reynard,' I whispered, calling to him. Yesterday I spared him, as I wish I'd spared Melati. I cared about him. But I cared about pleasing Rollo more. Shutting out the sound of the snickering Medievals, the grumbling servants and the whimpering dogs, I concentrated on the fox and only the fox. Where would he go?

I thought about myself last night. The sweaty, dry-mouthed panic and heart-pounding fear of the pursued. Where does someone go when they feel in danger? Somewhere they feel safe. Where had I instinctively gone? To my room. Where would Reynard go? To where we'd first found him when cubbing. To the spinney that was his lair.

'This way,' I said, spurring Satan. And this time I took the lead.

Now I was at the vanguard, leading the field. We'd been doing *The Charge of the Light Brigade* in English lit., and the lines marched in my head with the drum of the hoofbeats. *Half a league, half a league, / Half a league onward.* I put Satan over every five-bar gate like a maniac, and he popped over them like they were nothing. And I was always one step ahead of Reynard. Reynard was to discover, as I had done, that his room was no haven. Incredibly, he was there, and the riot the hounds made put him up. He emerged from the undergrowth, took more than a glance at us this time, and ran.

I cut him off at every covert, every spinney, every ditch. It was as if we were playing chess and I was always one move ahead. Then, finally, we cornered him in a valley on the far side of Longwood.

Into the valley of the shadow of death, I thought.

There was one last check, when he looked me in the eye. It was different, this time, to when we looked at each other yesterday. Then I was going to let him go, and today I wasn't going to do that. He knew it too. He knew he was finished. He was a brave soldier – he snarled at me right at the end. And after that last moment of defiance, Perfect, the gamekeeper's boy, called on the dogs.

The hounds, in a frenzy, tore him limb from limb. I watched them, feeling nothing. I never stopped, even then, to ask myself why it was so important to me. Why I had to take this life for Rollo.

The keeper's boy waded in with a stick and beat the hounds away from the corpse. Red-mouthed and rabid, some of them growled at him, but he did not flinch. He took the fox, now a blur of meat, from the grass and it dangled from his hand. The body was a thing abominable – limbless, tailless – but the head was intact, still open-eyed, still staring.

Surely the winter sun shouldn't be this bright? Surely the day shouldn't be this beautiful? Where was the pathetic fallacy of driving rain that we'd also learned about in English lit.? But it was beautiful; the sun of Rollo's smile shone upon me and the horrible thing in the hand of the gamekeeper's boy. I was Lancelot to Rollo's Arthur, and all was well with the world.

Then the dreadful child Perfect drew a hunting knife and sheared off the head. Unbelievably, he held it out to me.

'Sir, you want the mask?'

This lunk of a boy was holding out the fox's head to me in his massive hand. I looked at the others nervously. But all of them, all, for the first time, were smiling at me. Not with malice or agenda, but with congratulation and admiration. Perhaps this boy was weak in his wits?

Rollo said, 'It's your right to have the head as a trophy. It was your kill.'

Only then, looking at the pathetic bloody thing in the baby giant's hand, did I realise what I had done. Then I was sorry, and the golden glory of Rollo's approval dimmed a little. 'No,' I said. 'No. Take it away.'

Perfect, not understanding, looked at his master.

'That's all right, Perfect,' said Rollo. 'Stick it in the ice cellar.'

'Very good, m'lud,' said the man-child, and he retreated with the horrid thing.

'I'll get it mounted for my room,' said Rollo. He looked at me with the same look of admiration with which the other Medievals had regarded me. 'It's quite the trophy. I shan't want to forget this day.'

Then he did a frankly incredible thing. Commanding Perfect to come closer, he dabbled his finger in the neck hole of the fox's head and then placed the finger between my eyes, in a strange twist on the bindi that marks the Hindu people. The blood was warm and stinking – the metallic smell of last night. I recoiled. 'What are you doing?'

'It's called blooding,' said Rollo. 'It's a tradition on your first hunt. You are one of us now.'

And suddenly, just like that, I was in.

Afternoon

Late in the afternoon I had the house to myself. The Medievals had retired – no doubt to wash and dress for dinner – but I could not relax. My victory made me restless, and I prowled the house like a tiger. I left my boots in the boot room and my jacket in my own room, but otherwise I stayed as I was. Like a knight returning from battle who couldn't bear to relinquish his armour, I strode those ancient rooms in my muddy breeches and shirt. In the armoury, as I regarded myself in a shiny shield, I loosened the stock at my throat. I liked what I saw. My hair was ruffled, my colour was high, but there was a new look in my eyes. I was no longer a child to be bamboozled by tricks. I was a battle-hardened man.

I stalked about the house as if it were my own. It was important to me to revisit all those places from the night before, in the daylight, as a victor. I had to adjust to my new status. Places like this had to be home to me. If I was to fulfil my father's dream of Oxford and Sandhurst, then I had to be an English gentleman not just for this weekend, but underline forever underline.

Aadhish was no more.

Mowgli was no more.

This was the age of Hardy.

There was one more place I had to go. The Long Gallery, where I'd managed to ignominiously injure myself with a backfiring duelling pistol. And it wasn't until I reached that long, gilded room that I saw another living soul.

Rollo was wandering the gallery in the twilight, under the

169

eye of his ancestors. He too was in his riding breeches and shirt, and as we walked towards each other we could have been mirror images, through a glass darkly.

He looked wary. 'What are you doing here?'

'Walking off the saddle-sore,' I said. 'You?'

'I like to come up here and think sometimes,' he said. 'It makes me feel like I belong.'

My eye ranged along the rows of portraits. 'Because they all look like you?'

'Something like that. All those centuries of blond hair and blue eyes.'

I thought of the pictures in our summer palace in the Aravalli Hills. Of all those pictures of the ancestors. Of the centuries of black hair and brown eyes that made me. Of how different Rollo and I were. And how similar.

I pointed to the portrait nearest to us. 'Who is this one?'

'The rebel. Nazereth de Warlencourt. He turned his back on the family, changed his name and went to London to become an actor.'

I looked at the man with Rollo's face. 'And did he come to a terrible end?'

'Yes and no,' said Rollo, smiling a little as if at a private joke. He wandered down the gallery and I kept pace with him. I no longer felt like a courtier who had to walk several paces behind the king. Now we were equals.

He stopped in front of another portrait; another man with the de Warlencourt face, but moustachioed and wearing the uniform of the Scots Guards.

'And this one?'

'The conformist,' he replied. 'STAGS and the army. Duly produced his son and heir.'

'Who?' I asked, expecting another portrait.

'Me,' he said.

Of course.

'This is Colonel Monty. My father.'

Indeed.

Now I recognised him. In the portrait he would be not much older than Rollo. I'd seen him more recently, filled out and grey at the temples, but now I looked more closely, it was unmistakably the same man. 'If it wasn't for him, I wouldn't be here.'

'Me neither,' joked Rollo. 'How come you?'

'He told my father about STAGS. Recommended that he send me there.' I didn't tell Rollo the rest, not yet. That my father had asked Monty how to make me into an English gentleman. 'He said it was the right sort of school.'

'Well, he was correct,' said Rollo. He ran a finger along the gilded frame, almost with affection. 'He was right to tell your father that.'

That was a matter for debate. 'Where is he this weekend?'

'In London with the mater. They have a little boy.' It was interesting that he did not say *my brother*. 'I'm the heir, and now they have a spare.' He gave a short laugh, which was almost like a bark and totally without humour. He looked back at the picture. 'He's a good sort, the pater. But he expects a lot.'

'Mine too.'

'Fathers, eh?' Rollo said. Then he looked away from his own and down the long room. 'One day there'll be a portrait of me here.' We began to walk again, more slowly now. He was silent for a time, then he suddenly burst out, 'Do you ever feel that your life is mapped out for you?'

'How do you mean?'

'Well, you know. STAGS. Oxford. Sandhurst. The army. Then I'll take over here. Marry the right sort of girl – some deadly debutante the mater's found by sticking a pin in *Debrett's*. Pop out an heir or two. There'll be decades of good estate management and being a jolly good squire, reading the lesson in Longcross church at Christmas, opening the grounds once a year for the county show. And a spot of huntin' shootin' and fishin' whenever I want a little excitement. My face will get redder, my waistline rounder. People will describe me as *florid* or *well preserved*.' He crammed his hands into his pockets as he walked, and I mirrored him again. 'I mean, I even know how I'll die. Here in this house, in my four-poster bed that kings have slept in, with the eminently suitable wife I haven't met yet by my side. Longcross will pass seamlessly to my son and heir. Then it will all begin again.' He sighed. 'It's all so *fucking* boring.'

The word pulled me up short. The Medievals did not tend to swear – it was all *bloody* this, *bloody* that. That word, that powerful word, was a clue to the strength of his feelings.

'Do you know what I mean?' he appealed. 'Is everything planned for you?'

I thought of Ritu. 'Yes.' I pictured the future he'd outlined, but with Ritu and me in the Aravalli Palace, and I didn't like one bit of it.

He nodded, slowly. 'You *see*, don't you? I see you see.' And he took a step closer, until I could almost feel his breath.

'And we can't . . . deviate from the path,' he murmured. 'To do so would be to risk so much.'

'Risk,' I echoed, almost in a trance. I felt like Mowgli talking to Kaa the python. I was lost in Rollo's blue gaze. 'Risk . . . what?'

'Disapproval.'

'Whose?'

'Society's. The family's and, most of all, my father's.'

'And mine.'

He put his hand on my shoulder. 'Well, he would have been proud today.' He let the hand lie there for a moment while he studied me with his blue eyes. Numerous other pairs of blue eyes, ranged along the gallery, watched me too.

I felt I couldn't move. 'I . . . I'd better dress for dinner,' I said at last.

Looking back as I write this, I now think his face fell a little when I mentioned dinner. He removed his hand and dropped his python's gaze – the spell was broken. 'Dinner,' he said. He didn't meet my eyes again. 'Ah yes. Dinner. Of course.' He cleared his throat. 'Better go and change.'

He went, and my shoulder burned where he'd touched it.

I was so happy then.

But not for long.

Evening

Tonight's dinner could not have been more different from last night's.

Yesterday, after I had let Reynard go, Rollo was tetchy and coldly furious. The Medievals took their lead from him and studiously ignored me. Tonight, with Reynard dead, they were witty and urbane and friendly. The champagne flowed – they drank a toast to me as champion hunter and I felt like I walked on the moon. Then we drank to everything and everyone we could think of. We even drank a toast to Reynard the ex-fox – very funny; everybody laughed. I was courteously drawn into the conversation. They went on a charm offensive and I had no defence in the face of it.

I would hazard a guess that I knew more about the new books and the new plays, the new films and the new music, than they did. It was odd to think that I could probably teach them about the swinging culture of our decade. But what they could teach me were the rules that no one outside this charmed circle knew. The unchanging, unwritten ways that had not altered for centuries. That's why I am here. And tonight I found all the right things to say – the right questions; the right answers. I laughed with others; others laughed with me.

This feeling of rightness lasted for exactly one and a half courses. We had the champagne toasts, and the prawn cocktail passed without incident. Then the second course came and I was so busy talking happily to Serena about tiger hunting in Ranthambore that I ate without thinking. The meat was delicious, and it was only by chance that I glanced down at my plate. Circles of some sort of dark meat in a wine sauce. I put down my fork with a clang.

'What meat is this?'

They all looked at each other and started to laugh. Gideon said with relish, 'Finest medallions of beef.'

174

No longer caring for table manners, I spat into my napkin. I rinsed out my mouth and spat that too, then used the damp napkin to wipe the inside of my mouth. But it was no use. I'd swallowed some. I looked straight at Rollo and, in contrast to our conversation earlier, he would not meet my eyes. Of *course* he had known about it. He was master here. He had ordered the menu. This was why he had looked so sheepish when I had mentioned dinner in the Long Gallery.

I stood. 'I thought we were friends.'

For a moment the mask slipped and he looked genuinely sorry. But then, sensing the eyes of the other Medievals upon him, the supercilious look was back and he played, once again, to the gallery. 'Whatever gave you that idea?'

That turned my stomach almost more than the beef.

I pushed back my chair and ran.

I didn't know where the kitchen was, but I knew there must be one and I knew it would have what I needed.

I knew from my mother that kitchens were always at the bottom of a great house, so I headed down the back stairs until I found a flagged passage. Pushing my way past a couple of startled maids, I headed towards the cooking smells that made my nausea worse and burst through a pair of swing doors.

There, a tableau of industry froze before my eyes, like a roomful of waxworks. A plump, red-faced cook paused with a ladle above a steaming pan. The kitchen maids, holding pottery bowls steady, stopped mid-whisk. Ina, knife in hand, looked up from the scrubbed wooden table and a pile of chopped herbs. No one spoke until Ina burst out: 'Aldrin!'

Her words, like abracadabra, magically galvanised the room.

The cook dropped her ladle and a curtsy at the same time. She shot Ina a look that made the girl chop assiduously, dropping her head to hide her scarlet cheeks.

'Mr Aldrin, is it? A pleasure to have you in my kitchens, I'm sure, sir. Is there anything we can assist you with?'

Her astonishment was palpable, but I could not, just then, trouble myself with the etiquette of a guest bursting into the kitchens. 'Carbolic soap, if you have some.'

'Of course, sir. Spillage on the dress shirt, is it? If you'd care to change it and give the soiled one to your valet, the laundress will make sure to clean it before the stain sets.' She thought I didn't know how things worked in a great house.

'I would rather take care of it myself,' I said sharply.

The cook's obsequious manner deflated a touch. 'Very good, sir. Ina.'

Ina jumped a little.

'If you've finished with that parsley, take Mr Aldrin to the pantry and show him the carbolic soap.'

Ina got to her feet. 'Follow me, sir.'

It was cool in the pantry and we were alone.

'What's wrong?' Her face was full of concern.

I could not answer her fully yet. 'Get me the soap, please,' I said. 'And a large basin.'

Bemused, she located the soap from one shelf, a basin from another, and wordlessly handed both to me.

Steeling myself, I did what I had to do. I took a big bite of the soap and swallowed it down. A moment later, the inevitable happened and I heaved my insides out into the basin. Luckily the workers in the kitchen were making such a row resuming their labours that my exertions could not be heard.

I took out my handkerchief and wiped my mouth. Sweating, I loosened my tie and sat back in the chair, head resting on the cool wall. When I could speak I said, 'I'm sorry you had to see that.'

'Me too,' she said.

I tipped my head forward and looked at her. She started to smile. I smiled too. Then we both laughed. I stopped first – it hurt.

'Are you all right now?' she asked.

'I would not say no to a glass of water.'

She went away with the basin and came back holding a full glass of water. I drank it down, beginning to feel better. She'd brought a tinderbox and lit another lamp. The cold room felt warmer with Ina in it, and now I could see shelves of dry ingredients, tins, copper pans and plates. The place was no bigger than a large cupboard. She pulled up the only other chair.

'What in the name of all the saints was that all about, man?'

'It was the beef.'

She bristled a bit. 'The medallions? I helped cook those myself. Nice bit of beef from the butcher – fresh this morning, they were.'

'I did not mean they were "off".'

'Oh. Doesn't beef agree with you?'

'No,' I said. 'It's forbidden. I can't eat it.'

'Why ever not?'

'Because in my religion we believe that cows are sacred.'

'*Cows*?' She sounded incredulous.

'Yes. We worship them. They wander round the streets and no one can hinder them.'

'What, in all the traffic?'

'Yes. The cars just have to go around them.'

'That's . . . that's fairly odd.'

I was not having that.

'Is it odder than feeding five thousand people with a few loaves and fishes?'

She shrugged. 'I s'pose not.' She picked at the frill on her apron. 'Do you think they knew?'

'Of *course* they knew. I have been at STAGS – that is our school – for seven years. Every time there is beef I just have the potatoes or the vegetables, or plain bread and butter. They know all right.'

She said nothing.

'Let me ask you a question. Who orders the menu?'

'Lord de Warlencourt. He always does – he sees cook after breakfast every day.'

Rollo. I had suspected it, but knowing for sure was worse. 'So it was just another prank. All of a piece with last night.'

She pulled her chair an inch closer. 'What happened last night?'

I told her.

'Sounds right enough,' she said, and I wondered then what other humiliations had been visited upon her during her employment here. Anger rose in my throat, just as the vomit had done, burning with acid rage. '*Oh.*' I spat. 'Oh, it is no good.'

'What's no good?'

'Trying,' I said. 'Trying to play their game. Trying to say the right things. Do the right things. I even killed Reynard for them.'

She looked shocked. 'Who's Reynard?'

'The fox. The hunt, today. We found it, and killed it.'

'*You* killed a fox?' Her face was a mask of shock.

'Yes.'

'*Why?*'

'I thought it would make me like him.' I registered the slip. 'I thought it would make me like *them.*'

Her eyes were full of sympathy. 'And did it work?'

I shook my head.

'The problem is,' she said, 'killing a fox *does* make you like them. It makes you a shit.'

I looked up, shaken from my self-pity.

She laid a hand on my arm. 'Why try to copy their worst traits? Why kill a defenceless animal to be like them? Why strive to become something that's . . .' She searched for the word. 'Rubbish.'

I was interested. 'What would you do?'

'What would *I* do? Or what would I do if I were you?'

I think I knew the answer to the former. She would have to keep quiet, or else lose her job. 'The second one.'

It might have been the lamp, but it looked as if the light of battle flared in her eyes. 'Fight back. Let them know who you really are.'

I slumped. 'I'll always just be Mowgli to them.'

'Then embrace that.'

'What do you mean?'

She pulled her chair closer still. 'Embrace the spirit of Mowgli, man.' She waved a V sign at me with both hands, like the hippies did. 'Instead of trying to prove you're not him, prove you *are* him.'

'I am afraid I do not know what you are talking about.'

'What was his power over everyone else in the jungle?' she asked. 'Even the tiger?'

'Man's red flower,' I said. 'Fire.'

'Hmm,' she said, thinking.

'You are surely not suggesting I burn down this whole house?' I said. I had a sudden fantasy of setting Longcross, and everyone in it, aflame with the royal lighter that always lit first time. But the moment of madness passed. 'Because if Longcross is razed to the ground, I think you would be out of a job. And I would be in prison.'

'Haway. I didn't mean *that*. I just think you need to take the fight to them. Burn them as they burned you.'

And then I had it.

The bhut jolokia.

I leaned forward and took Ina's cold hands in both of my own. 'What is next on the menu?'

'They'll be eating the vichyssoise now,' she calculated.

'The what?'

'The soup. You'll have missed that.'

I was not thinking about my own belly. 'Then what is the main course?'

'Venison mess.'

Deer stew. That could not be more apt for my STAGS compatriots. 'Perfect. Can you do something for me?'

'I'll try.'

'Come with me and just follow my lead.'

'All right. What's going on?'

'You will see.'

I strode back out through the kitchen, which was once again a hive of activity. 'I have instructed this girl to collect my soiled shirt,' I said haughtily. 'Send her to my room in a moment or two.'

The cook bobbed her head. 'Yes, sir. She'll be up directly.'

I left the kitchen sedately, then ran up the back stairs. In the atrium I could hear the sounds of the Medievals making merry from the Great Hall, but I ignored them. Soon enough the laughter would stop.

I dashed up the grand staircase to my room. Ignoring the boar's head and the trick basin, I went straight for the top of my wardrobe and my lovely caramel-leather weekend suitcase. I placed it on the bed and flipped the catches.

It had taken me just one short term at STAGS to realise that the food there needed to be significantly spiced up. At the very first Christmas holidays, when I returned to India, I collected some chillies from the kitchen to take back with me. I have used them to cheer up the dreary cottage pies and hotpots ever since, and keep them topped up on each visit home. Over the years I have learned that, in order not to run out of chillies and have to endure a bland and beige end to my term, I have to bring the strongest, hottest chillies my continent can provide. And that means the bhut jolokia.

Bhut jolokia, also known as ghost pepper – because they are so hot they can kill you. The bhut jolokia measures over a *million* units on the Scoville scale, which measures the heat of chillies.

One bhut jolokia pepper keeps me going through the entire term and beyond. But I always bring three in my case, just to be sure. The tiniest sliver, curled in my palm and carried down to Commons, is enough to cheer up the grey cuisine and give me a much-missed taste of home. I just have to remember to carry the tiny slice in my left hand, because if you touch your eyes after touching a bhut jolokia, however fleetingly, your eyes will burn so agonisingly that you will want to tear them out of your head.

I found the bundle I was looking for and unwrapped the rough canvas square. The chillies lay there, red and glossy as blood, ridged and shrivelled as if desiccated by their own heat.

There was a soft knock at the door and Ina slipped into the room. I was tempted to give *all* of the chillies to her, but that would be too much. I did not <u>actually</u> want the Medievals to die, just to suffer as I had suffered. In the end I picked up just one of the chillies and handed it carefully to my new friend as if I was carrying a grenade.

'Take this,' I said. 'Chop it up small, small, small and put it in the venison stew. Mix it in well. All right?'

'Yes,' she said.

'Then – and this is really important – wash your hands. Take that carbolic soap you gave me and wash them once, twice, three times. Have you got that?'

She nodded, eyes bright. 'Yes,' she said again.

I had a moment of misgiving for what I was asking her to

do. 'I am responsible for this,' I said. 'Not you. I will see you don't get into trouble.'

I could see that, in all the excitement, she had not thought of the danger to herself. Now it dawned. 'How will you do that?'

'Because I will confess. Do you not see? I *want* them to know it is me.'

She nodded. 'I get it.'

'Very well. Quickly then.'

She headed for the door.

'Wait,' I said, remembering. 'I need to give you my shirt. It is our alibi.'

'Shall I turn my back?' she asked.

'Better wait outside,' I said. I wanted to protect her reputation. It was the most precious thing she had.

She looked at me like she had been given a present. 'You're so sweet,' she said.

That was the first time a girl had ever called me so, but there was no time to reflect. When the door closed I quickly pulled off my dress shirt and took a new one from the wardrobe. Decent again, I opened the door. I kept hold of the shirt for a moment so she had to meet my eyes. 'Thank you, Armstrong,' I said. 'Really. Thank you.'

She smiled. 'Good luck, Aldrin,' she said. 'See you on the other side.' Then she wrapped the chilli in the shirt and bounded down the stairs.

I went back into my room and retied my bow tie. My hands seemed to be shaking. When I'd finished and smoothed my hair I went back downstairs. Inhaling deeply as if I was going to take a dive, I opened the double doors to the Great Hall and walked back in.

The Medievals had all clearly been drinking heavily, because I was hit by a wall of noise – talking and laughing and singing. There even seemed to be a food fight starting – at least one bread roll flew across the table. Gideon and Charles had their trousers down and were showing their bottoms to each other like monkeys, singing 'Blue Moon' tunelessly and collapsing with laughter. Rollo was the first to spot me and actually got unsteadily to his feet. 'My dear chap,' he said, feigning – or feeling – concern. 'Are you all right? You've been an age.'

'I just had to take some air,' I said pleasantly. At which they all began to make realistic vomiting noises.

'*Mea culpa*,' said Gideon. 'My idea. I have to take the credit.'

I might have known. Despite Rollo being the host, Gideon seemed to have some sort of leadership role in the various methods of torture being practised upon me this weekend. Perhaps I'd been wrong about him. Maybe Gideon was the Walrus after all.

'Beef disagreed with you, did it?' he said as I sat down, unsuccessfully attempting to hide his grin.

'You know it didn't.'

I glared at Rollo. He would not look at me but poured me a glass of wine with his own hands, waving away the footman who jumped forward to help.

I said to the room at large: 'You know why I've been avoiding beef at school for the last seven years.'

Gideon blinked, his pale blue eyes blank. 'Not the foggiest, old bean.'

One eye on the door, I took a drink of the wine to settle my nerves. 'Well, let me enlighten you. I consider the cow to be sacred. I consider the cow to be a nurturing and providing being who gives me milk. I consider a cow to be a member of my own family. Would you eat a member of your own family?' I looked at all of them in turn. 'Silly question; you probably would. Do you hold *anything* sacred, Gideon?'

Now no one would meet my eyes except Gideon, still arrogantly defiant.

He sketched a salute. 'Queen and country, old boy. Queen and country. And God. But the *actual* God, you know, not your fairy-tale ones.'

'Fairy-tale?' I said quietly, just as, at the same time, Rollo said, 'Steady on, Gidders.'

'Still not clear?' Gideon asked pleasantly. 'I mean, not your damn silly superstitions. *Sacred cows*, indeed.' He laughed. 'Winston Churchill said Indians were a beastly people with a beastly religion. I didn't know he meant it literally.'

Sickened, I thought of Father. He revered Churchill. Did he know this? My pity for him seemed to rise in my throat. I washed the bile down with the wine and spun my glass, which was somehow already empty, between my fingertips. 'Oh, it gets better than that,' I said lightly, pretending it didn't matter, pretending I didn't care. 'There are all sorts of "funny" beasts in this fairy-tale.' The glass fell over and I left it lying where it was. 'Our god Brahma, the creator of the world, has four heads. Vishnu, the preserver of the world, has four arms. And

185

blue skin. Oh, and you'll like this.' I was warming to my theme. 'Shiva, the destroyer of the universe, has blue skin too. She <u>also</u> has a third eye and carries a trident. And then there's Ganesh.' My voice was getting louder and louder. 'The god of prosperity and wisdom.'

'Does he have blue skin too?' hooted Miranda.

'No, but he has the head of an elephant. And he travels with a rat.'

'Stop it.' Gideon wiped his eyes. 'You're killing me.'

Just as he said that, the door opened and Ina entered the room, holding a plate of food in each hand. She was followed by three footmen, also holding plates.

The main course.

'Of course, my favourite goddess,' I said to no one in particular, 'my *favourite* goddess is Durga.' I was sure they had stopped listening, distracted by the arrival of the delicious-smelling food, but I ploughed on. 'She has ten arms and wields ten swords. She rides on the back of a tiger and she sweeps down on her enemies seeking furious vengeance, leaving them helpless before her.'

I gave Ina a small, tight smile as she put the venison stew in front of me. She winked and I had to drop my eyes quickly before I gave the game away. I studied the plate in front of me instead. Here and there in the steaming dark brown mass I could see little red fragments of chilli, gleaming like rubies in a dung heap. I took up my silver knife and fork. They felt heavy and cool in my sweaty fingers. I had no intention of using them. Ina had done her job well – eating that deer stew would be like forking up dynamite.

The especially evil thing about bhut jolokia is that it takes a good few seconds for the body to recognise what it has ingested. All the Medievals – drunk enough to be peckish – had taken quite a few good, hearty bites. Overcome by a sudden feeling of calm, I stretched out my hand for the wine bottle, set my glass upright and poured in the remainder of the wine.

Then I waited.

I did not have to wait long.

'My *God*!'

'He won't help you now, *Gidders*,' I said drily.

As they all began to gasp and choke, I announced, 'You have just had a dose of bhut jolokia, otherwise known as ghost pepper. It is the hottest chilli in the world.' I took a leisurely sip from my glass and, I must say, wine has never tasted better. With some pleasure I recalled the dreadful symptoms of eating bhut jolokia. The agonising, burning pain in the mouth and throat. The stomach cramps, the vomiting. The involuntary tears that spring from the eyes. The increased heart rate until you think your chest will burst. The tongue that feels like a hot coal. The breath that feels like you are a fire eater. The liquids that your helpless body produces to try to repel the invader – the snot, tears and sweat that pour from your facial orifices until you are a blubbering mess. And the beautiful thing was, the symptoms lasted for at least twenty agonising minutes. I watched them dispassionately, all the Medievals, as they began to disintegrate in front of my eyes, almost scientifically assessing their differing reactions. Francesca began frantically wiping the inside of her mouth with her napkin. Charles took off his glasses as they actually began to steam up before his eyes. Miranda wailed like a cat, and Gideon began to repeatedly bash his fist on the table. Serena jumped up from her chair, as if she could escape her own burning throat, and then vomited helplessly all down her satin gown. And Rollo? He began to sweat profusely, his blue eyes more striking than ever in his reddening face. They all began to fight over the water jug and I let them for a moment before saying kindly, 'I would not do that. It only makes it worse.'

It was true. I had once looked into the science of it and water only spreads the capsaicin – the hot molecules of the chilli – around the soft tissues of your mouth, making them burn more.

I enjoyed the show, calmly drinking my wine.

'*Get me cook*,' choked Rollo. As he leaped for the bell I moved like a cat. I knew if he pressed it that the little bell down in the kitchen that said *Great Hall* would be clanging like mad, and help would come. I put my hand over his. He was so weak it was easy to wrest his fingers away from the bell.

'There is no point laying blame,' I said coldly. '*I* did this.'

He clutched his throat, eyes streaming. 'You?'

'Yes. Just a *jape*, old boy, don't you know?'

Gideon staggered towards me, his face puce. '*Help* us.'

'Well, let us see,' I said. 'Let's find out who in the class has been paying attention.' I strode over to the tiger-skin rug and stood on Shere Khan's stripes. 'How many swords does Durga have?'

They looked at each other, choking and gagging.

'*How many?*' I repeated.

Charles was the first to speak. He always paid attention in lessons. 'Ten.'

'And which animal does she ride?'

'A tiger.' This time Miranda spoke. 'A tiger.'

'And what does she want?'

No one answered.

'What does she *want*?'

'Vengeance,' said Francesca. 'She wants vengeance.'

'That's right,' I said. I wandered leisurely to the duelling pistols, where they hung back on the wall. I caressed one pewter barrel, taking my time. Fascinating really – except for those two tiny crosses, you couldn't tell which was which. 'Now, one more question. Then I'll help you.' I walked back to the rug and put my foot on Shere Khan's head, all-powerful now.

'What is my name?'

They looked at each other again, wiping eyes and clutching throats. 'M-Mowgli.'

'*Wrong*,' I said. 'That is *not* my name. What is it?' I decided to prompt them. 'Not what *you* call me. What I call *myself*.'

None of them knew. They'd been calling me Mowgli for so long they'd forgotten.

'We are sorry, Mowgli,' said Serena. 'Help us.'

I turned to the archvillain. 'Are *you* sorry, Gidders?'

'Yes,' he gasped. '*Yes*.'

'Then call me by my name and I'll help you.'

They looked to each other in their suffering, all crying real tears, their mouths working like fishes, for what seemed like an age.

'Hardy!' It was Rollo who shouted. Then, softer, like a sob,

'Hardy.' He fell to his knees before me on the rug, as if paying homage. 'Your name is Hardy.'

I went right up to him and petted him like a dog. His golden hair was soft under my hand. 'That is right,' I said benignly. I turned to the rest. 'Will you all remember that?'

'Yes, Hardy,' they chorused as best they could, and the power swelled in my heart so much that it frightened me. 'Good,' I said, softer now, icily calm.

I went to the bell and pressed it once, hard. I walked past my vanquished enemies without another glance but tossed the help they needed over my shoulder as I went.

'Tell them to bring milk. It is the only thing that helps.'

And with that, I stalked out of the room.

Night

I had to tell someone of my triumph. I had to tell Ina.

As I leaped up the grand staircase, three steps at a time, I wanted to laugh and scream and cry and shout all at once. I felt all powerful, felt fire burning through my veins, as if it was I who had eaten the bhut jolokia. **BJ**, I thought – and it seemed suddenly perfect that the instrument of my vengeance had those initials. So then I did laugh.

But, of course, I had a while to wait before I could talk to her. Although I was fairly certain that dessert and coffee and port would now not be required in the Great Hall, the Medievals would require the more prosaic fare of glasses of milk and Alka-Seltzer before they could lay their evil little heads to rest. Poor Ina would be running back and forth at their beck and call. I needed occupation until I could talk to her, and, as the servants would be otherwise engaged and I was returning to school tomorrow, I went to my room and packed my suitcase myself.

In my room my triumph dissipated into a flat feeling of disappointment. Although I did not think the Medievals would bully and belittle me any more, and I certainly did not think they would call me anything but Hardy from now on, the price was high. I would never be invited anywhere again, never be allowed to cross the threshold into that exclusive inner sanctum. I could watch Rollo de Warlencourt all I liked, at school, at Oxford, at Sandhurst, but I would never be like him now. Never would I be an English gentleman. I'd packed this very suitcase so full of hope, and now I was repacking it, the hope was quite, quite gone.

Still, I'd had my victory, and the victory must be shared. I had made one friend this weekend, and not at all the one I thought I would make. So once I was sure the Medievals were all settled I went to wait by the back stairs. I knew enough about stately homes by now to know that, while the greatest slept, the least were the last to rest.

Again, I felt I could not risk Ina's reputation by seeking out her room, but I had thought that I might be able to waylay her on her way up to bed from the kitchens. As it turned out, I was quite wrong. I saw her on the stairs all right. But it was quite a different Ina from the one I had come to know.

She was wearing a tiny miniskirt that looked like it was made of silver foil, and her legs, encased in fishnet tights, seemed to go on forever. She had on a sleeveless white top with a polo neck and an imitation fur, dyed baby pink, slung across her shoulders. Her lips were painted the same very pale pink; her eyelids were painted silver and over each eye she'd drawn a heavy black line, which flicked out at the edges, so that her green eyes resembled a cat's. She looked incredible and entirely unknowable, like an alien from the moon.

I stepped from the shadows. 'Armstrong!' I whispered.

She jumped a mile in the air, then put a hand to her chest. 'Aldrin! Why, man, y'almost gave me a heart attack.'

'Where are you going?'

'Who are you? Me da?' She stuck her tongue out at me, pink as her lips. Then she smiled. 'There's a hop in the village.'

'A what?'

'A hop. A dance. A disco. In the institute. The village hall.'

'On a Sunday?'

'Bank Holiday Monday tomorrow, isn't it? Isn't that why you lot are here? Long weekend?'

She was right. I'd be going back to STAGS tomorrow, but classes would not start until Tuesday.

She grabbed my arm, a mischievous sparkle in her cat's eyes. 'Come with me.'

I looked down at my dinner jacket. 'Can I go like this?'

'Smart suits didn't do the Beatles any harm,' she said. 'Here.' She rolled up the sleeves of my jacket and ruffled my hair with both hands. 'There. You look like a rock star.'

'Like a Beatle?' I said, amused.

'Yes,' she said, 'just like a Beatle.' She smiled, and I smiled back, and suddenly my heart lifted again.

'Come on,' she said, taking my hand. 'And stay quiet, mind.'

We sneaked out of the tradesman's door and walked round the side onto the drive. As we got further and further away from the house my mood continued to lift. I had well and truly burned my bridges at Longcross Hall. It didn't matter what I did now, and it felt good to get away.

For Ina, though, the stakes were considerably higher.

'I take it you are not supposed to be out of the house?'

'Not on your nelly,' she said – a strange expression, which I took to mean the negative. 'Us maids get one afternoon off a week; no followers; no dances. Mrs Nicky – that's Mrs Nicholson, the housekeeper – she's a right tartar and I'll be in forty kinds of trouble if I'm caught.'

'Where are we going?'

'The institute in Longcross village. That's where the hop is. It'll be jumping by now – we're a bit late to the party.'

On the way we talked about her family. She had two brothers and a sister. 'And are they in service too?'

'No,' she said. 'Our Peggy, the little'un, she's at the village school. Our Billy's at the grammar school. Our Tom, the eldest, he's a slater and tiler.'

'Shouldn't you be in school too?'

'I passed the exam to go. But me mam and dad couldn't afford to send me.'

I didn't see the problem. 'But a grammar school is free of charge, is it not?'

'They couldn't afford the uniform to send a girl. They could barely afford the boys' ones. Our Peggy won't be able to go either. She'll go into service too.' She looked at me sideways. 'There's no work in the North East. No money for fancy clothes.'

I did not know what to say to this, walking along in my Savile Row evening suit. 'Your outfit tonight is wonderful.'

'I made this with me own fair hands.'

'You look like a spacegirl. Like Barbarella.' I was not practised at talking to girls, but I thought Ina would like this. And she did. I could see her teeth gleaming in the moonlight as she smiled.

At length we saw the lights of the village, and the village hall lit up brightest of all. Before we even got near I could hear the heavy beat and twanging guitars of pop music.

We had to get a ticket on the door from a woman sitting at a trestle table. She gave us each a number from a book of pink raffle tickets (to my great shame I had no pocket change, so Ina had to pay a sixpence for me). The heat of the interior hit me like a wall and I had a moment of misgiving. All the revellers were dressed like Ina, in a thoroughly modern and up-to-date fashion. Now I was the alien. How would these white spacemen take to me? But then the disc jockey began to play the Beatles' 'Here Comes the Sun'. Ina and I looked at each other and grinned delightedly. It was a sign.

Someone pressed a beer into my hand, and then the bright young things dragged me off to dance.

It was such a contrast to my weekend at the Hall. No one in this tiny northern village seemed to mind the colour of my skin. So many of the young people called me <u>cool</u>, or <u>rad</u>, or <u>groovy</u>, or other words that I had never heard applied to me. It sounds crazy, but I belonged. When I wasn't dancing, these familiar strangers talked to me about George Harrison and

Ravi Shankar – the Beatles have made India cool, so I have more to thank them for than my dress sense. There was no formality. I have no idea where my dinner jacket went. I was offered drink, cigarettes; there were hands on my person at all times, flung around my shoulders, in my hair, round my waist. It was egalitarian, and insolent, and beautiful. That night, after being stuck in the aspic of the 1920s, I was a child of the sixties.

The music took hold of me and I sang along to songs I knew and songs I didn't. The words, the wonderful nonsensical words, were a jumble of psychedelic happiness – yellow submarines and octopus's gardens and honky tonk women. I danced like a savage with anyone and everyone, boys and girls, but kept coming back to Ina.

'Let's get some air,' she said eventually.

We went outside to cool down and sat on a low wall, drinking punch from plastic cups. The music hummed through the walls and windows, the mawkish lyrics reaching our ringing ears even where we sat.

'All the songs are about love,' I said. 'Every single one of them.'

'What else is there to sing about?' she said. 'What else is there to think about? What's more important than who you're going to end up with?'

Even after all my years at an English public school, some colloquial phrases confused me. 'End up with?'

'Who you're going to marry.'

'Ah. Well, that I already know.'

That surprised her. '*Really?*' She opened her eyes very wide.

'Her name is Ritu Rathor. She is of a good Rajput family.'

'Do you like her?'

'From what I know of her, she seems very pleasant.'

'Hold on. You have *met* her, surely?'

'Once.'

'But you'll start walking out with her? When you go home, I mean.'

'Walking out?'

'Courting.'

'Well,' I said, 'since I'm at school over here, the next time I see her will probably be at our wedding.'

She shook her head. 'So *strange*,' she said. 'How can you build a life with someone you barely know?'

'Because her parents and mine have determined that we would get along well together. The plan is that we learn to love each other.' It was hard to defend a scheme for which I had so little enthusiasm, but I gave it a try. 'And it seems to work. The divorce rate is higher in England than in India.'

Ina thought for a moment, looking out across the village green. 'I'm not sure that love can be learned,' she said, now looking into my eyes. 'I think it just happens.'

I held her gaze. 'I think so too.'

Just then the disc jockey took to the microphone, interrupting what was becoming a most interesting conversation. 'All right, all you cats and kittens,' we could hear him saying, in a strange hybrid of Ina's accent and an American one. 'We're getting ready to slooooooow things down.' He dragged out the word.

I looked at Ina, not sure what this meant. She took hold of my hand and dragged me back inside to the heat and the dance floor. She wound her arms about my neck and we danced like that, cheek to cheek. I was so surprised that it took me a second to recognise the song that was playing – the plinky-plonky guitar arpeggio, the breathy little-girl voice, begging the tiger to show her how to kiss him.

'What is this song?' I asked Ina, as we swayed to the beat.

'It's called *Teach Me Tiger*, by April Stevens,' she said in my ear. 'Don't you love it?'

'I'm not sure,' I replied, listening to the *wah wah* chorus.

The last time I'd heard that song, I'd been scared out of my skin, in that dark passageway of Longcross Hall, with the gramophone playing on its own. Now it had no power to frighten me. It had all been a trick, and I had been the hunted then. Now I was the hunter.

Or was I? It took me just a few revolutions of the dance floor to realise I was still being pursued, but in a very different way. Ina's hands moved to caress my back, my hair, then she took her cheek from mine and put her lips on mine instead.

They were soft and warm, and she used them skilfully with barely a clash of teeth.

And I felt nothing.

I was kissing the prettiest girl in the room, but despite the music and the moonlight I felt . . . nothing. And it wasn't to do with Ina, or even with Ritu.

It was to do with me.

Then the lights flickered and came on, showing the ruin of the room – paper streamers and plastic cups on the floor; cigarette butts and even false eyelashes among the detritus. All the revellers, including, I am sure, myself, looked very different. But something else had changed too. Ina and I held onto each other's hands but stood far apart now. She squeezed my fingers. 'Come on,' she said, smiling a little sadly. 'Let's go.'

Outside, the freezing air was welcome. My jacket was long gone, but I needed to cool down anyway. As we got away from the crowds, replying cordially to all the farewells, we were at last alone, wending our way through Longwood to the house. We made the fateful decision that, since it was so late, we could risk going in through the front door. As we walked down the drive I felt the need to make an apology. 'I'm sorry.'

'What for?' she said. '*I* kissed *you*.'

'You know what for.' For feeling nothing. For not reciprocating. For not being in love with her.

'Yes,' she said. 'I do.' She gave herself a little shake. 'It's fine. It's just . . . I've never been kissed before –'

'Ever?' I interrupted. 'I would have thought . . . I mean, someone as beautiful as you . . .'

'Haway with you!' she exclaimed. 'I've been snogged *loads* of times. Do you not think I look cool in me best togs?' she teased. 'No. I was going to say I've never been kissed before by someone who's in love with someone else.'

'I am not in love with Ritu,' I said truthfully.

'I didn't mean Ritu.'

There was a small silence. Then she took my hand again; not the whole thing – we were not in that place now; she linked my little finger in hers and then shook it a bit.

I carried her hand to my lips and kissed it.

That would have been a better goodbye with Ina than the one I was destined to have. Our actual farewell was not nearly this neat.

As we approached the house we saw two figures seated on the front steps. It was impossible, in the dark, to tell who they were. But then there was the familiar metallic *snick* of the queen's lighter, and the thing struck first time to illuminate two blond young men lighting cigarettes from the same flame.

Gideon – and Rollo.

It was too late to avoid them. I moved Ina behind me.

'Let me handle this,' I said.

In the moonlight the boys could almost have been twins. Both in evening dress, both with bow ties undone, both smoking in a mirror image of each other. But in a panicked flash of inspiration, I knew then that they were nothing at all alike.

It was Gideon, not our Lord of the Manor Rollo, who spoke first. Once again, I got the odd impression that he had some sort of authority this weekend. That he was some sort of Master of Ceremonies. Maybe that's what that fragment of conversation meant, overheard and forgotten: *Grand Master*. 'Where have you been?'

'To a dance,' I said. 'I invited Ina.'

'A likely story. How would you know what's going on in Longcross village? She must have told you.'

'I meant that she had no choice but to *take* me,' I said hurriedly. 'It was an order.'

'Bet she didn't put up much of a fight,' said Gideon. Now he addressed Ina. 'You dirty little *bitch*. I knew you liked me copping a feel the other night. Can't get enough, can you?' He sauntered down the steps and stopped in front of her. 'You look damned tasty tonight.' He did a little mime with his forefinger, as if he were stirring tea with it. 'Turn around. Give us a twirl.'

Ina looked at me.

'Don't,' I said. I put myself in between him and her. 'I thought I had demonstrated my power to you once tonight. Don't make me do it again.' Then I got right up close to him. 'We are jungle creatures, Gideon. And the dark is all around us.'

I locked eyes with him, holding his gaze, willing him not to look at Ina. 'Go to bed.' It was as if I were speaking to a dog. Gideon, amazingly, dropped his eyes, turned and slunk inside.

We had almost forgotten Rollo was there. He had not spoken until then, but now he got to his feet. In the moonlight he was absolutely white with fury. 'Where have you *really* been?' he said to me, just as he'd done on the very first night, when I'd followed Ina from the folly. And he looked at me with such utter disdain that my heart shrivelled within me. I could not be sure that his eyes were not wet with tears – the moonlight had turned them to mirror. 'I thought you were different.'

All at once I was back in yesterday's bath, letting the water go cold around me, as his disappointment seeped into my soul.

Rollo threw his cigarette on the steps and crushed it out savagely with the glossy toe of his evening shoe. When the fire was completely extinguished, he turned on his heel and crossed his threshold, leaving Ina and me on the outside.

Suddenly I felt the cold, the bitter wind whipping through the thin cotton of my evening shirt. Ina, deflated, looked up at me, her eye make-up smudged, her eyes enormous. 'Don't worry,' I said. 'It will be all right. You go first – we shouldn't be seen together. Go right up to bed.'

She ducked her head and ran inside.

And I was alone.

I entered the house where I was no longer welcome, and walked slowly up the grand staircase, my thoughts racing. I couldn't go to bed, not yet. A strange, unsettled feeling twisted my stomach. There was only one person I wanted to see. I felt the compulsion to explain to Rollo how it had been. I was still angry with him, with all of them, over the dreadful weekend of fun and games they had planned for the brown boy, and who knows how many other misfits before me. But I still had a ridiculous yearning to follow that unspoken code of the gentleman. Rollo, the host, might not have behaved in a way that was due to *me* as his guest, but I wanted to be clear that *I*, as his guest, had not abused his trust as my host. I wanted him to know that I had not importuned Ina in any way, not abused a young girl in his employ, as Gideon had so readily done. It was suddenly the most important thing in the world to let him know that nothing had happened between Ina and me. I wanted him to know I was better than that.

And I thought I knew where to find him.

I heard Gideon's voice in my head. *Always prowling the gallery, is old Rollo.* And Rollo himself had said, *I like communing with the ancestors.*

I climbed the stairs to the Long Gallery.

But when I got there, there was no one in the long room. Nazereth and Monty and all the other de Warlencourts stared at me from the walls, and the moonlight flooded in through the windows, silvering the polished floor. I walked the length of the room, downcast. I had already turned to retrace my steps and return to my room when I heard the cry.

Whether in fear or pleasure I could not tell. But one thing I knew for sure.

It was Ina.

I heard Gideon's voice again. *Then he takes her on the roof and gets his end away*...

There had to be a stairway to the roof. I skidded back down the gallery to the far wall and began to push and press the pictures, the skirting board, the beams – anything I could think of. It seemed hopeless, but in fact a little panel swung inwards to reveal a stone flight of stairs. I dashed up it into the freezing night air and emerged onto a strange silvery moonscape – tiles and chimneys and acres of slate as far as the eye could see. I was on the roof of Longcross Hall.

I forced myself to stand absolutely still and listen. There was the sound again: half cry, half sob; air being pressed out of lungs. I ran lightly in the direction of the sound and there, behind a chimney stack towards the front of the house, I saw them.

Ina splayed out like a silver spider, crying out the word *no*, her bright foil skirt all but extinguished by a shadow. A dark shape twisting and writhing on top of her.

And a head of bright blond hair.

'Rollo!'

I think I roared his name in a rage. The dark shape stilled. Blind with fury, I grasped two handfuls of his tail coat and pulled him off Ina's prone body.

An enraged voice spluttered, 'What the *hell*?' It was Gideon's voice.

I turned him to face me. 'You animal,' I spat. 'You utter *Savage!*' Ina sat up and straightened her clothes, dazed. I took no more than a second to make sure she was all right, and then began to pull Gideon with me. The rage lent me superhuman strength and I dragged him to the edge of the roof. 'All your breeding,' I said, 'and no one taught you how to treat a lady.'

He struggled, but I had him up against the parapet. 'She's not a lady,' he spat. 'She's just a common *slut.*'

I really believe I hadn't decided what I was going to do until that moment. In a trice I had him dangling off the edge of the roof, leaning out into space, holding him only by the lapels of his tail coat. He grabbed and clawed at me. 'All I have to do,' I hissed, 'is let go.'

His eyes widened. 'No . . . please. *Please,* Hardy.'

I leaned him out further, drunk with rage and power. Not the nursery power of feeding someone a chilli, but real, grown-up power over life or death. *I* was the Raj now.

He was crying, his feet scrabbling on the lip of the roof, desperately trying to find a footing. 'I beg of you. I'm *begging.*'

I don't know what I would have done if Ina hadn't touched me on the shoulder. 'Don't, Aldrin,' she said. 'Let him go.'

For a second Gideon and I were locked in that deadly embrace. Then I felt something warm at my leg. He'd wet himself, his urine falling onto the leads and down the ancient drains. My anger drained away too, to be replaced by a cold contempt. I pulled him back onto the roof and threw him down on the tiles.

I glanced at Ina. Her skirt, the one she'd made so lovingly, scraping together pennies from her wages for fabric, hung off her in shreds. Oddly, of all the sights I'd seen that evening, the ruin of the silver skirt made me want to cry. I said to Gideon, 'Apologise.'

'I'm sorry, Hardy. I'm sorry . . .'

'Not to me! To *her*.' His mouth worked like a fish and I realised then he didn't even know her name.

'*Ina*.'

'I'm sorry, Ina.'

'Now get out of my sight.'

Without meeting my eyes, he scuttled to the stairwell and disappeared.

I went to Ina, not sure what to do. My instinct was to embrace her, but I thought she might not welcome the male touch right then.

But she stumbled into my arms and I held her tightly.

'Are you all right?'

'Yes.'

'Did he . . .' I could not think of the words. <u>Penetrate</u> was too medical, <u>rape</u> too brutal. But what I wanted to know – *had* to know – was whether Gideon had . . . had . . . 'Did he hurt you?'

She understood. 'No,' she said. 'Not in *that* way. But if you hadn't arrived when you did . . .'

I looked at her face, the tear tracks silver too. I could feel the rage rising again. 'How the hell did he get you up here?'

'He was waiting for me on the nursery corridor and wouldn't let me past. He said he wanted to show me something and it wouldn't take a minute. Said if I didn't come with him, he'd tell Mrs Nicky where I'd been tonight, and I'd be dismissed.'

I thought again of how little power she had. The ultimate threat of dismissal hung over her head like a sword and made her everyone's creature. 'What can I do?'

She smiled through the tears. 'I feel like I want a bath. Actually, I feel like I want about ten baths.'

'Then have one.'

'Haway,' she said – that strange word again. 'You think we've got a bath in the servants' quarters? We get one once a week, man.' She sounded much more like her old self.

Suddenly I was certain. 'Use mine.'

Her eyes brightened a little. 'Can I?'

'Of course. Take as long as you like. I'll stay away. I don't think I'll sleep tonight anyway.' It was true. There was too much going on in my head for sleep.

She kissed my cheek. 'Why don't you go and find him?'

'Find who?'

'*You* know.'

I did.

Aldrin and Armstrong embraced under the light of the moon.

I let her go first. Just as she was about to disappear down the hatch to the little stairwell, she turned back. Her silver space-skirt caught the moonlight.

'*Good luck, Mr Gorsky*,' she said.

Midnight

I am about to write the reason why no one must <u>ever</u> find this diary. I don't think I have ever been so happy. Nor so afraid.

When Ina had gone I sat on the roof, shivering, but not from cold. Why had I been so angry?

Because I had felt protective of Ina, yes. But did that explain my rage? No. I had not felt the same white heat of anger that first night when Gideon had put his hand up her skirt. I had felt pity and empathy, but not anger.

So why?

The moon, staring kindly down, let me work it out for myself.

I had been angry because I thought Gideon was Rollo.

I didn't want Rollo making love to anyone.

Anyone *else*.

Ina had known.

You're in love with someone . . .

Why don't you go and find him . . . ?

<u>*Good luck, Mr Gorsky.*</u>

I got to my feet and walked, as if in a trance, down the little staircase, along the Long Gallery and to the door of Rollo's room. I lifted my hand to knock, but before I could do so Rollo opened the door. He was dressed only in his evening trousers, and his chest and feet were bare. In the moonlight he looked like a silver angel.

'I know,' he said, as if we were already in the middle of a conversation. 'I *know*.'

'What do I do?' I asked helplessly.

The tiger song from the gramophone, and from the disco, was singing in my head. *Teach me, tiger, how to kiss you. Teach me what to do.*

Can someone else hear your thoughts? If they and you are bound together somehow? Only that would explain what he said next.

'I'll teach you.' He drew me into the room and the door closed behind us. Then he put his hands in my hair and kissed me on and on.

And then everything was all right.

'*Oh. My. God.*'

I didn't mean to be Janice from *FRIENDS* but that last entry in Aadhish's diary really was a record-scratch moment.

I let Shafeen say it.

And, in a daze, he did. 'He *loved* him. My father was in love with Rollo de Warlencourt.'

I looked up at the Indian night, and the same moon that had watched Aadhish and Rollo in 1969 watched us now. Even I needed a moment for it all to sink in, so God only knew what Shafeen was feeling – Aadhish was his *dad*.

I took his hand. 'Do you want to stop?'

'Are you kidding?' he said, incredulous. 'No way. I want to see how their story ends.'

Monday, 27th October 1969

<u>Morning</u>

I woke with my head on Rollo's chest, supremely happy for the first time in my life. He was awake. The moon had gone and the early-morning sun turned him to gold. He smiled, his blue eyes for the first time soft and kind, and my heart failed. He stroked my hair, unhurriedly, but then said, 'No one can ever see us like this.'

A cloud came. 'I know.'

'No one can ever know.'

'I know that too,' I said.

'It would be over for us. Our lives would be over.'

I looked away. 'Yes.'

'You know what they'll call us.'

Now I looked back at him. 'Yes.' I did know. I was not so sheltered. *Faggot. Queer. Bender. Poof. Queen.* Brutal names to add to the roll call I already had. 'I'm used to names.' Now it was his turn to look away. 'Mowgli. Hardy. Aldrin.' I didn't explain that last one. 'And none of them my own.'

'I'm sorry,' he said. 'I'm so, *so* sorry.'

It was time. I held out my hand, as if we'd just met. And in a way, we just had. 'My name is Aadhish. My *real* name, I mean. Aadhish Bharmal Kachwaha Jadeja.'

He took the hand and shook it seriously. 'Delighted to make your acquaintance, Aadhish Jadeja. But you'd better go before the girl comes to do the fire.'

'Ina,' I said. 'While we are calling people by their proper names, her name is Ina.'

'Ina then,' he said. He propped himself up on his elbow. 'You know Admiral Lord Nelson?'

'Of course. The column in Trafalgar Square?'

'The very same. He had a dear friend called Captain Hardy. They were devoted to each other, soulmates, and fought side by side on many campaigns. Hardy was with Nelson when he died. Nelson's last words were "Kiss me, Hardy".' He traced my profile with one finger. 'So when we're in public I'll call you whatever you want. But when we are together like this, just you and I . . . well, with your permission, you'll be my Hardy. And I'll be your Horatio. Would that be all right?'

'Yes. That's different.'

'How is it different?'

'Because it *means* something. It's not a nickname, or a racial slur. And –' I smiled – 'because you asked me.'

I threw back the covers, but now it was Rollo who pulled me back. He wrapped his strong arms around me from behind, tight, tight. 'I don't want you to go.'

I put my hand on the arm that was across my chest. 'We'll be together,' I said. 'At school. At Oxford. At Sandhurst.'

'And then?' he asked, turning me around. He put his hands on either side of my face. 'Me here. You in India. Both of us taking over the family firm. We'll have to marry. We'll have to have sons. All the things we talked about in the Long Gallery. There's no future for us.'

I took his wrists and pushed him back on the bed, holding

both his hands above his head until we were both shaking with silent laughter.

I looked down at his golden beauty, breathing hard. We were both suddenly deadly serious. 'There's no future,' I said. 'But there is a now.'

'Then what do you suggest we do?' he said, his voice ragged.

'Well, for a start, let's go to breakfast. I am *starving*.'

He smiled and the sun was back. 'And then?'

'Then we catch the train to school.'

'And then?' Softer now.

'Then tonight,' I said, softly too, 'tonight, you will come to my rooms.'

He nodded.

'Are you afraid?' I asked.

'Yes,' he said.

'Me too.'

'Then kiss me, Hardy,'

And I did.

PART 5
Colonel Hathi's March (reprise)

19

It was the dead of night.

We'd been reading for hours, stretched out together on the divans under the bright lanterns, with the brazier burning beside us.

I struggled to find something to say and, as always, found the answer at the movies. 'It was a lion all along, not a tiger, that was the key.'

'How d'you mean?'

'Rollo quoted this film called *The Lion in Winter* to me. Then your dad did too, in this diary. He told Gideon that they were jungle creatures, and the dark was all around them.'

'So?'

'So, in the film, Richard of England and Philip of France, the heirs of two enemy kingdoms, were secret lovers.'

Shafeen put his head in his hands. 'Greer,' he said, his voice muffled, 'could you *just*, for *once*, not see everything through the prism of film. Not everything is a movie.'

I was struck. 'That's just what *he* said.'

'Who?' Shafeen looked up.

'Henry. He said exactly that at the top of the waterfall before he fell. Maybe you have more in common than you think.'

'Well,' he deflected, 'this is not about us. This is about Our Fathers, Who Art In . . . well, one in the hospital, one in the morgue.'

I resisted the temptation to make an *Untouchables* reference. I must be growing. I sat up and looked out at the city. 'Whatever happened to them?'

Shafeen sat up too, mirroring me. He wrapped the leather tie around the diary, reverently, as if it were a holy text, and made a clear space for it on the low table among the remains of the evening meal we'd devoured while reading. 'We know what happened. Exactly what Rollo said. They couldn't be together – not at that time. You heard the diary. The Stonewall riots had only just happened, so the gay rights movement was in its infancy. Homosexuality had been illegal until 1967, only two years before they got together at Longcross. And it was only legal between two men who were twenty-one, so they'd still have been breaking the law. Plus, my father was brought up at the very end of the Raj, when gays faced the death penalty.'

I thought of what Gideon had said in the diary. *The Raj had it right*. 'Is that true?'

'Yes, of course it was true,' said Shafeen. 'The Raj wasn't just some Merchant Ivory fantasy of parasols and pavilions. The British imported their racism and homophobia along with their governance. Both of those boys were raised in times and places where their love would have been unacceptable. If they'd lived in a different age, in different societies, maybe they would have been together.'

'But then *you* wouldn't exist. And neither would Henry. So

I'm sad for them. But glad for me.' I took his hand. 'God. If they'd met later . . . in a . . . *kinder* age . . .'

'We'll never know. But not then. I guess the world wasn't ready.'

'It explains a lot,' I said. 'About your father's love for English things.'

'Yes,' said Shafeen softly. 'After that tiger hunt with the queen, my grandfather sent my father to an English public school with the express instruction to become an English gentleman. I'd always thought that he'd taken that instruction to heart, that he'd somehow never been able to shake off the Raj. Now I know he didn't love the Raj. He loved Rollo. And he spent the rest of his life emulating the lover he'd lost.'

'Just like *The Jungle Book*,' I murmured. '"I Wan'na Be Like You".' I sat up on the divan. 'Speaking of resemblance, no wonder Rollo got such a shock when you turned up at Cumberland Place, looking exactly like your dad did in 1969. You even wear your hair the same – that long, layered 1960s look.'

'Yes,' he said soberly. 'Yes, I see that now. And why he wanted me to join the STAGS Club.'

'Also why,' I said slowly, 'he saved you from the hounds. At the Red Mass, he said you were not to be touched.' Shafeen hadn't believed me then. But I could see he believed me now.

'And at the very end of his life, he thought I *was* my father. That's why he said, *Kiss me, Hardy*.'

The kiss of death – from the boy he had once loved. It was so *sad*. 'At least we now know what they did together. And that he wasn't sorry. Whatever sort of monster Rollo became, I'm glad he got to say that at the end.'

Shafeen's face was sombre. 'Me too.'

'Will you tell your mum?'

'No, of *course* not. I'd hate her to think that he ... that he ...'

'Never loved her?'

'Yes. And he did, Greer. He does. I'm sure he does, in his way.' He was quiet again and we sat for a moment, looking at the light of Jaipur, the floodlit palaces and the moon above.

'Shall we go back down?' I suggested.

He turned to me. 'No,' he said. 'Not just yet.'

He kissed me, hungrily. And, for once, everything was right. Where we were, and what we'd read. The moonlight, the night breeze, the lanterns, the divans. And most of all, the right boy. Suddenly we were lying back in the soft cushions. 'Is this all right?' he said between kisses. 'Are you ready now?'

'Yes,' I said. '*Yes.*'

20

In the morning, the Princess Himani was at breakfast, looking tired and dejected. We both kissed her, and I caught again that faint scent of Guerlain L'Heure Bleue – her signature perfume. The perfume the Queen of England wore every day of her life except one – when she'd gone on a tiger hunt. Once again, I was struck by the sweetness of the scent, and also that Himani wore perfume to visit her comatose husband.

'Any change?' asked Shafeen.

Himani smiled slightly but shook her head. 'No. No change.'

It was a strange meal. I don't think I'd ever been so happy, nor so sad. I'd turned a page in the night. A new chapter of my life had begun, but Aadhish still lay in a hospital bed, his story, quite possibly, behind him. Shafeen and I had spent what little of the night there was left on the roof, twined around each other on the divan beneath the stars, and had woken with the dawn to sneak down to our rooms to wash and change. Now we sat opposite each other, not touching, but cradling two enormous, life-changing secrets: what we'd read in the diary, and what we'd done together. And we could not reveal either one of them to the exhausted woman who sat between us.

We all sat in silence, going through the pantomime of eating when none of us had any appetite, all of us in our different ways consumed by love.

But after just a few mouthfuls the princess said, 'My dears, I think I shall have to go to bed. Enjoy your day. Hari will be at your disposal.' And Shafeen had to help her up the stairs into the house.

When he came back we sat in silence for a moment, as if she was still with us. But then Shafeen wound his little finger round mine and we both smiled – a delicious secret smile. We didn't talk about the night before. There was nothing to say. We'd said it all on that divan on the roof.

Prem, dressed in his customary white robe and turban, brought some little pastries. Thinking of Ina, I said sincerely, 'Thank you, Prem,' when he set them down.

He looked slightly surprised and then said, 'Thank *you*, memsahib. It is truly an honour. Yes.' And he saluted me, as he always did – that strange hangover from the Raj.

Shafeen said nothing and as Prem left I asked, 'How long has Prem been with your family?'

'Since forever,' he said. 'Long as I can remember. And his father before him.'

'Does he have a wife and family?'

'I *think* so.'

'Only think? You've never met them?'

'No. I think they live in the suburbs.'

'How often do you think he sees them? If he's here waiting on you, I mean?'

'Really, Greer, I've no idea.'

I straightened my cup and plate virtuously. 'You know, I'm sure, what I'm thinking.'

'Yes,' he said, shifting a little. 'You're thinking of Ina.'

'Your father's only ally at Longcross.' A thought struck me. 'That explains why he was so understanding about you going to Longcross on Boxing Day. You remember? He only agreed when you told him you were going to help a damsel in distress – in your case Ty. That was the language he understood. It was right out of his playbook, his chivalric code.'

He thought about this. 'I suppose so, yes.'

'Your father considered her a true friend.' I hammered the point home. 'Even though she was a servant. Forced into service and seeing her family twice a year.'

'But Prem is hardly the same.'

'Really?' I said. 'Because apart from their gender and ages, the scenarios seem pretty similar to me.'

'Prem is a Dalit.'

'The lowest caste. An untouchable. I know. But I don't think you're making the point you think you are. He's still a person.'

Prem came back with the tea and went to move *The Times* to make room for it. The old newspaper that had started this whole goose chase – or rather tiger chase – still lay on the table.

'No,' Shafeen said sharply. 'Leave it.'

I shot him another stern look.

'I mean, that's all right, Prem. I'll keep hold of this for now. You can go.'

'Yes, sahib,' said Prem, smiling and nodding as he always did. 'Would you like me to get the latest one for you? Yes? I know the very fellow, the newsagent, where I get it for the prince. Yes? It is the agent of news on the road to . . .'

'For God's *sake*, Prem,' Shafeen exploded. 'Stop being so bloody *helpful*. Just go away.'

Prem jumped back at once, wearing a look of unbelievable hurt on his face, like a puppy who had just been kicked. He forgot his customary salute and scuttled back into the house. I turned to let Shafeen have it with both barrels for being so shitty to him, then I saw his face. He'd been under enormous strain, these past few days.

He saw me looking. 'I just wanted to keep the bloody paper,' he snapped. 'Is that so hard to understand?' Then he relented and put his hand on mine. 'I'm sorry.'

'You should be apologising to Prem, not me,' I said stiffly.

'You're right. You're right. And I will.' He turned to Rollo's obituary page again. 'I just think Father would like to have this when . . . if . . . he wakes up. This was the man he loved, after all.'

'May I?' I took the paper from him and read the obituary once more. I remembered the Rollo I'd known – the white supremacist, the bad hangover from the British Empire, the monster who chased children of colour. But then I thought of the young Rollo. The one who had, however briefly, allowed himself to love.

'What are you thinking, with that face?' asked Shafeen, sounding much more like himself.

'That if Rollo'd been allowed to be with your father, that if they'd both been able to step outside of their rigid societies, he might not have become what he became. He was thwarted. He must have been really unhappy.'

'Not being able to live your truth is hardly an excuse for behaving like he did. On all those fun little weekends at Longcross. Even to his own *son*.'

'Not an excuse, of course. But maybe . . . an explanation?' I handed the paper back.

Shafeen looked at the photo one last time before he folded the paper away. He half smiled. 'He looks *just* like Henry.'

I sat up very straight. 'Say it again.'

He looked at me quizzically. 'Rollo looks exactly like Henry.'

'Yes.'

'So?'

'So it follows,' I said slowly, 'that Henry looks exactly like Rollo.'

'Greer,' he said, teasing once more, 'are you having a breakdown?'

'No . . .' I said, feeling my way. 'It's just . . . why don't we get *Henry* to come to the hospital?'

Shafeen threw the newspaper on the table among all the breakfast mess and sat back. 'What are you talking about?'

'Well,' I said, warming to my theme, 'you know those films where people get a bang on the head and they lose their memory, and then they get another bang on the head and they feel fine again? This could be like that. He's heard your mother's voice and he's heard yours. Beloved, familiar voices. And if Henry looks so like a young Rollo, mightn't he sound like him too? Henry could be just the shock he needs to wake up.'

Shafeen looked doubtful. 'Henry'll never do it.'

'Why not? You did it for Rollo. You pretended to be your father so he could have a happy death.'

'You don't think . . . You think Father's going to *die*?'

'No, no . . .' Although I privately thought things did not look good for Aadhish. Himani had already said that he was still unresponsive. 'I bet we could persuade Henry. He's changed.' Shafeen still looked massively dubious, so I played my ace. 'He saved Ty,' I said quietly. 'I suppose . . . I suppose . . . if there's a lesson to this – all of this, from 1969 *and* today – it's that no one is totally good and no one is totally bad. There is always greyscale. There is always nuance.'

'How d'you mean?'

'Look at Rollo,' I said. 'On the surface, completely evil. But he must have been good once. Then there's Henry: nice little boy, screwed up by a father who by then was bitter and twisted, maybe because of having to live a life he didn't want to live. Henry was a truly shitty teenager, and now . . .'

'Now?'

'Well, maybe he's changing. Maybe he's coming back from the dark side of the moon. He must have been brave in the fire to get Ty out of Longcross. Remember his hands when we saw them at the Tiger Club . . .' I stopped. 'That's it!'

'That's what?'

'*Your father*,' I exclaimed, eyes wide. 'Think about it. He reads at breakfast of Rollo's death – a man who, we now know, he loved in his youth.' I grabbed *The Times* from the table. 'There's a big picture of Rollo in his STAGS gear, when he was eighteen (because, look, he has his Medieval stockings on). Then your dad goes chasing off to the Tiger Club, because it was where he met Colonel Monty, Rollo's dad, and it was always a de Warlencourt enclave. Maybe he wanted to feel closer to Rollo. And when he gets there, what's the first thing he sees?'

'Henry de Warlencourt,' supplied Shafeen.

'*Exactly*. Secretary of the Tiger Club. Looking *just* like Rollo when Aadhish got together with him. He must have thought he was *seeing* Rollo, alive again and standing in front of him. I think the shock was too much for him.'

'It *literally* broke his heart,' breathed Shafeen.

'Yes. Henry *was* the bang on the head. We just need another one to bring him back.'

Shafeen looked at me, his eyes on fire. 'It's worth a try.'

'Yes, but listen. Henry said there's a tiger safari today, Saturday. And after that he goes back to England.'

Shafeen hesitated for maybe half a second. Then he tore the obituary page out of the paper in one decisive motion and stood up. 'Then we'd better get going.'

21

It was an anxious journey into the hills.

We'd been slowed down by having to get changed into club-friendly stuff, then Prem couldn't be found to call Hari, then Hari couldn't be found to drive us. When he turned up, presumably from some errand for the princess, it was already ten o'clock. Smiling, smooth and silent, Hari drove as fast as usual, but it still wasn't quick enough for me.

'God, I hope we get there in time for the safari,' I said as the car wound upwards into the Ranthambore hills.

'Greer,' said Shafeen, 'let's call it what it is. It's a hunt.' His voice was brutal. 'This is their MO. It's just like the trail hunts, remember? You gather with all your privileged buddies, you pretend you're following a trail of foxes' urine, but really the hounds are going after *real* foxes and tearing them apart. It's the same here. They *say* it's a safari, that they are going to observe these wonderful creatures in their natural habitat. But really it'll be all bankers and dentists and ex-army types getting out their blunderbusses and shooting the tigers dead for trophies. Just like the bad old days.'

'Well, whatever it is,' I said, 'let's hope we get to Henry before he sets off.'

Shafeen checked his watch. 'I've got to tell you, I don't like our chances. Tiger hunts go pretty early. It's usually a whole day.'

I looked out of the window anxiously at the sunrise scenery and willed the miles away. The car smelled strongly of the Princess Himani's perfume. It brought to mind something I'd forgotten. A fragment of conversation never followed up; a riddle never solved. 'Shaf?'

'Yes?'

'What did Henry mean yesterday at the Tiger Club? About your mother?'

'Which bit?' he asked guardedly.

'He said, *Did you tell Greer what would have happened to your mother if your father died, if we hadn't come along?* "We" meaning the Raj, I suppose. He had a word for it. A word beginning with S that I can't remember.'

There was a pause. Then Shafeen said, like a sigh, 'Suttee. He said suttee.'

'What's suttee?'

'When a Hindu man dies, his body is burned. Suttee, or Sati, was the practice of his widow throwing herself on the fire.'

I didn't understand. 'But . . . but . . . she'd die.'

'Yes,' he said soberly.

'So what Henry meant,' I said, feeling my way, 'was that if it wasn't for the Raj, if your father died, your mother would burn too?'

'To be fair,' he said, 'by the time of British rule, Hindu groups were already campaigning against it.'

'But it was the British who banned it?'

He didn't seem to want to admit it. 'Yes.'

Everything seemed to combine – all the little fires. Mowgli and *The Jungle Book* and the ultimate power of man's red flower. The bhut jolokia chilli. Rollo's foot grinding out the cherry of his cigarette when he thought he had no chance with Aadhish. The fire at Longcross fifty years later, turning each window into an eye of bright fire. St Aidan, the guardian against fire who could not extinguish the white heat of a widow's funeral pyre. The little fires kindled into one huge conflagration in my mind.

Shafeen was the first to speak. 'She'll still burn. Even now.'

'What do you mean?'

'How many times have you heard her say, *Your father says this*, or *Your father says that*? Or mention his name or one of his opinions? She's lived her life in his anglicised fantasy, not because *she* wants it, but because *he* does. She *loves* him, Greer. She truly loves him. I realise now that nothing in his diary is going to change that. We *have* to bring him back. If we don't, desolation and loss will burn her up and there'll be nothing but ashes left.'

Numb, I dropped my head back against the headrest and breathed in the princess's perfume. What was it – Guerlain L'Heure Bleue? The perfume of England's queen. Odd, because at breakfast she'd only smelled very faintly of it, and she hadn't been in this car today. I wondered if the smooth, smiling Hari was using it himself on the quiet. The thought made me smile to myself, and God knows I needed to smile.

22

When we got to the Tiger Club there was no sign of Henry.

Shafeen instructed Hari to wait, then we went up the white stairs together. Colonel Moran, the bluff and British undersecretary person, was waiting at the top of the steps, greeting his safari-goers. A bearer, dressed much like the absent Prem, carried gin and tonics around on a tray, even though it was only about eleven in the morning. As we explained that we needed to join the tiger safari, the colonel listened politely. But then he said, 'Look here. This is awfully sticky. But as you are – neither one of you – officially members of the club, it's really against regulations to let you come along. Your father, Mr Jadeja, is, of course, a member, but you are not. And Miss Greer is *your* guest, not his. I would ask Lord de Warlencourt, but he's gone ahead to check the bait and the hides, just to see that everything's tickety-boo.' I remembered from our previous visit that the colonel's slang was about a hundred years old. 'Of course, outside guests are sometimes invited, but that's not the case here.'

'Oh, but we were invited,' I said, perfectly truthfully. 'Didn't Henry say?'

'No,' said the colonel. 'Regrettably he did not.' You could see him struggling between being polite to his boss's chums and following the club rules by which he lived. 'I don't think . . . that is, it's quite irregular. If only there was a way to . . . confirm . . . with Lord de Warlencourt.'

What you need right now, buddy, I thought, *is a mobile phone.* But I didn't say anything.

'Let me offer you a drink at the very least,' he said, beckoning the bearer. 'I would certainly urge you to linger for a moment and see the . . . safari . . . off. It's quite the parade.'

'We don't want –' began Shafeen hotly, but I grasped his arm to shut him up.

I suddenly had a thought as I took my glass from the tray. I raised my drink to the colonel and said, very deliberately, *'I like to drink to the Siege of Gibraltar.'*

The colonel stopped with his glass halfway to his lips. He looked at me and then at Shafeen. He never drank that drink, but set his glass carefully down on the tray. 'If you come with me, I'll have the houseboy find you some suitable clothes.'

23

You could obviously stay at the Tiger Club, because the room I was given to change in was as nice as the nicest hotel, with rattan furniture and a ceiling fan and a lovely private veranda opening out onto the plain.

With a massive feeling of déjà vu, I put on the clothes that had been left on the bed. Odd, really, that the outfit I'd been given was not very different to the huntin' shootin' and fishin' gear we'd been given at Longcross. A light shirt, breeches, boots and a jacket in army green with plenty of pockets, one of which was fitted with a wicked little hunting knife – I could have been heading into Longwood. But this wasn't Longwood. This was the jungle.

When Shafeen knocked on my door he was wearing much the same, except that around his neck he wore the stripy orange-and-black tie of the Tiger Club, just like the one belonging to his father, which he'd worn as a belt at dinner the other night. 'Ready?'

'I think so,' I said. My stomach felt extremely weird. 'Is it dangerous?'

'No,' said Shafeen. 'In the bad old days, they even drugged

and baited the tigers so that the participants would see "good sport". Then they'd make out that the tigers were all fierce and deadly, even though they were really half asleep. It made the hunters feel braver. I imagine it's the same today. When have you ever known the de Warlencourts to play with a straight bat? The tigers won't get near us.'

'That attitude isn't helping,' I said. 'Remember, you need to ask Henry for a favour.' But at the same time, I suspected he was right.

We went out onto the steps just in time to hear the sound of a purring engine. Hari, no longer needed, was driving away, and Colonel Moran pulled into the space he'd left in an ancient jeep – which seemed a bit Savage for this antiquated club.

As we got in he said, 'Awfully sorry about the old banger. We're playing catch-up, as the others rode out while you were changing.'

'On horses?'

I envisaged the day going a little bit like the Boxing Day hunt at Longcross – that now we'd been given things to wear, we'd be given things to ride.

'No horses,' bellowed the colonel as politely as he could over the noise of the engine, the jeep bouncing over the terrain. 'Lord de Warlencourt's orders. His family don't have much luck with horseflesh.'

Shafeen and I exchanged a knowing glance. 'Is that right?' he yelled back. But, as it turned out, Colonel Moran wasn't only talking about Rollo on Boxing Day.

'Oh, yes,' the colonel hollered back. 'His grandfather Monty rode every day of his life – well into his nineties. We all tried to stop him, but he insisted that he would carry on until it killed him, which of course it did.'

'It did?' I yelled.

'Yes. Went out for his morning ride from the clubhouse, on this very route, aged ninety-two, if you please. Horse got spooked by something, reared and chucked him off. And then, damn me if the very same thing didn't happen to his son the Earl of Longcross this Boxing Day just gone. Dashed bad luck.' Shafeen and I couldn't look at each other. 'So Lord Longcross – young Henry, that is – doesn't ride any more. He's a bit superstitious, and I can't say I blame him.'

I remembered Henry once galloping up the drive of Longcross Hall on a black stallion, and couldn't help thinking that was rather a shame.

'Not that it matters anyway,' Colonel Moran went on, 'because we don't ride horses on the safari. Horses don't like big cats.'

'So what *do* you ride?'

It was the earth, not the colonel, which seemed to answer me. As the undersecretary stopped the jeep, the ground seemed to continue to move.

The earth shook beneath my feet; my ribs shuddered in my chest. Through the trees – enormous, grey, long of trunk and baggy of knee – came a herd of elephants.

24

The muster of the elephants for the tiger hunt was one of the most surreal things I'd ever seen.

The huge grey beasts were picturesquely decorated, as if someone very skilled had gone crazy with a pack of felt tips. They all had caste marks on their foreheads. 'That's the red of the goddess Kali,' said Shafeen. But all I could think of was the fox's blood dabbed on Aadhish's forehead when he was blooded at Longcross after his first kill. There would be more blood today.

I wasn't the only one who thought so. The vultures we'd spotted in the distance on our last visit circled in the skies above – much closer now – and a jackal slunk by, side-eyeing us hopefully, his chops drooling in anticipation of a carcass later.

'I don't see Henry,' I said to the colonel as we decanted ourselves from the jeep.

'He'll have gone ahead to make sure everything is in place,' said the colonel. 'Don't worry, we'll catch him up.'

The poor elephants were being loaded with gear – some stuff recognisable, some less so. There were bottles and hampers, as if we were going on a glorified picnic, but also long poles and leafy branches. 'What's that stuff for?'

'That's for building a machan – a kind of platform in the trees,' said the colonel. 'Sometimes there's quite a wait for a tiger to come along. Machans can be quite sophisticated, with roofs to keep off the sun and cushioned seats. In the old days they used to take gramophones up there.'

'Is it safe though?'

'Not *entirely*,' he said thoughtfully. 'Tigers aren't great tree climbers, but other big cats are. A panther might easily get you.'

We were directed to our elephant – bizarre though that sounds – by the colonel. 'We don't have to drive it, do we?' I said to Shafeen in an undertone.

'God, no. Each elephant has a mahout. The mahout has often been with the elephant all its life. They have a unique bond.'

We clambered up onto a platform on the back of our elephant, which had obligingly gone down on its knees. I thought we would be lifted up on its trunk like in *Indiana Jones and the Temple of Doom*, but in fact we used a sort of bamboo ladder. The platform looked very uncomfortable for the poor elephant but was very comfortable for us, with padded seats and siderails. Apparently Shafeen and I were the only passengers for this ride, for Colonel Moran raised his hand to us in farewell. 'Happy landings,' he said cryptically, before heading off to find his own ride.

The mahout sat astride the neck, I guess you would call it, between the flapping ears. He smiled at us and nudged the elephant with his toes, at which it gave a sickening lurch as it got to its feet. I had to cling to Shafeen to stay on.

We set off at a rolling gait, which reminded me of being

at sea in very choppy waters. It was the oddest Uber in the world. As we went, I noticed that some elephants carried only a single rifleman. 'Those are the shikars,' said Shafeen. 'They are experienced hunters who run the hunt at different "beats" and direct operations.'

'They're *armed*.'

'Yes,' he said. 'Just in case.'

Despite the heat, this pronouncement made me shiver.

The way was draped with fabric, hung at intervals in the trees. That, and the fact that many local men on foot lined the route, chanting and pounding the trees with hollow bamboo, gave the hunt the air of a carnival. I could see why the colonel had wanted us to see this spectacle. 'Those men are the beaters,' supplied Shafeen. 'They drape turbans and body cloths along the route to direct the tiger to the machans.' I watched the beaters shout and clap and wave branches. 'I'm amazed the tigers come anywhere near that noise.'

'They don't mind noise so much. It annoys them rather than frightens them, so it's a way to drive them where you want them to go. But it's a fine line,' said Shafeen. 'If they make too much noise, the tiger might charge them directly.'

'A risky job,' I said.

'Yes,' he agreed grimly. 'You'll notice the shikars keep the lines properly regimented. Beaters are placed in gaps in the trees as "stops" to prevent the tiger getting through. They are human barriers.' He squinted at me. 'It's almost as if the Tiger Club doesn't care about Jaipur's indigenous population.'

I noticed that the elephants ahead of us, bearing all those dentists and ex-army servicemen and British noblemen, were creating their own path through the jungle and trumpeting as they went, exactly like Colonel Hathi and his troops in *The Jungle Book*. All we were missing was the marching music.

'We're heading to the nala,' said Shafeen. 'The watering hole. It's a hot day, so the tiger will go to drink, and the elephants know where the water is. The beaters crush down underbrush and drive them in the right direction to keep the tiger moving along the tiger beat.'

'You seem to know a lot about it,' I said. Then I remembered the very first time we'd been hunting together, pursuing the stag at Longcross on our first ever morning there. He'd told me he knew how to shoot from hunting tigers. Then I wondered if he'd been joking. Now I knew he hadn't been. 'You've been before, haven't you?'

'Yes, I've been before. With my father.'

Before I could get into this, there was a shout ahead and the whole procession stopped. We didn't quite all pile into the back of each other like Colonel Hathi's brigade, but it was close enough. Ahead, one of the mahouts was pointing and shouting, and all the others took up the cry.

At length the procession moved off again, and I said, 'What's going on?' Shafeen relayed this question to the mahout in Hindi and he turned and addressed me directly.

'*Padachihn*, memsahib,' he said. 'Footprint.'

And he jabbed his finger at the ground as we passed.

I followed the pointing finger and I saw it. I'm not kidding when I say that the print in the soft mud – quite distinct, with five toes and the gouge marks of claws – was as big as a bin lid.

It was both beautiful and absolutely terrifying.

25

We emerged from the lip of the jungle to see a watering hole fringed by trees.

'This is the nala,' said Shafeen as our elephant lurched forward into the strong sunlight.

I took in the scene. Each of the shady trees that stood by the watering hole had a white goat tied to the trunk, with just enough rope to let the creatures wander temptingly. The unwitting goats bleated wretchedly, only making themselves more obvious. They were the cheese in the mousetrap.

The stage was set. And into the scene, sitting atop an elephant behind his mahout, rifle in hand like the shikars, rode the main character.

Henry de Warlencourt.

When he caught sight of us he jumped so high I thought he was going to fall off his elephant. 'What the hell are you doing here?'

A series of expressions was marching across his face. Shock, fear and then . . . something like relief.

'We need to talk to you!' Shafeen called out.

'I'm a bit busy to be honest, old chap,' Henry called back

drily, recovering his self-possession. He gestured around at his honoured guests on elephant-back. 'Could we do this later?'

Then there was a shout from the beaters. *'Baagh, baagh.'*

We turned as one. I didn't need a translation – I remembered that Shafeen had called himself the son of a *baagh* at that long-ago dinner at Longcross.

Baagh meant 'tiger'.

She came out of the jungle, low and slow like a wraith. Her belly was close to the ground and her tail, trailing low behind, was lashing back and forth. Every muscle was tense, and you just knew she could have jumped many feet instantly, in any direction. The beaters wisely retreated as fast and discreetly as they could into the undergrowth, running for their lives as soon as they were clear. To be on foot around this mountain of bunched muscle bound in orange fur would be madness.

Her veins stood out like whipcords. She was big enough to carry a goddess and moved on silent feet as big as the beaters' drums, now pounding even more wildly.

In contrast to the cacophony of the beat, every soul was silent apart from the mournful goats, still singing their own requiem.

The tiger gave out a low, murmuring growl, which I could feel in my ribs, and then ominously began to sniff the air.

Subconsciously I began to inhale too. Then, on the breeze, I caught it: a breath of the Princess Himani's scent: the Guerlain L'Heure Bleue. Faint, but quite distinctive.

'Can you smell that?'

Shafeen, without taking his eyes off the tiger, whispered, 'What?'

'Your mother's perfume.'

'Greer,' he said from the side of his mouth, 'what the hell are you talking about?'

'Can't you smell it?'

'Actually yes. But now is not the time.'

'Where's it coming from?' I persisted.

'It must have been on us from the car,' he hissed. 'But don't worry, we're quite safe up here.'

'I don't see how we can still smell of it – we've completely changed clothes.'

'Greer. *Not now*.'

Then, in the distance, I saw a man in white sheltering under a tree, just like one of the stupid goats. He was the only one on foot in the entire hunt now the beaters had dispersed. Added to his brazen foolishness, he was keening in a long, piteous note, just like the sacrificial goats – a strange, mournful song that was sure to attract the attention of the tiger. I wondered what the hell he thought he was doing. That tree wouldn't protect him. I had to break that terrible silence or he would be killed.

'Get out!' I shouted to him. 'Get away! *There's a tiger*.'

At the sight of me, the sound of me, the man ran forward, then was snapped back cruelly as he came to the extent of his rope.

His *rope*.

He was tied to the tree like the goats.

'Memsahib!'

It was the Tiger, the Fox and the Brahmin again. Except this time it was a Dalit, not a Brahmin.

'Shafeen . . . it's . . . it's *Prem*.'

'He's soaked in my mother's cologne,' said Shafeen slowly.

Then, more urgently as he came to the same dreadful conclusion as me, 'That's why we're smelling it . . . The tiger'll ignore the goats and go for him.'

We'd thought ourselves so clever, working out that the Tiger Club 'safari' was all a cover for them hunting real tigers. But, of course, this was the Order of the Stag we were dealing with. They were not interested in hunting tigers any more than they were interested in hunting foxes. It was humans they were after all along: anyone they saw as inferior. Today they were hunting the lowest caste, because they thought they didn't matter. They'd been doing this for years – centuries.

'So much for Henry changing,' spat Shafeen furiously. 'So much for any of them changing. For God's sake, this has to *stop*.'

He unsheathed his hunting knife and began to rise from his seat. The platform rocked perilously on our elephant's back, and the great beast shifted his weight.

I grabbed Shafeen's arm. 'But you need Henry's help. Let *me* go. If you go up against him, he'll never wake your father for you.'

'I know,' he said. 'But think of Ina. I know this is what Father would want me to do. This is what *he* would do.' And he swung his legs over the basket and slid down the elephant to the ground.

Ignoring the shouts of the hunters, he ran for Prem and began sawing at the rope that bound him. The tiger's head snapped round, caught by the flash of movement, and she began to prowl towards the tree, tail switching back and forth. Shafeen's hands were bloody from where he had missed with the knife – Prem was babbling in horror and clinging to him, impeding his efforts, and the rope was still intact. There wasn't enough time.

I didn't give myself a moment to think, or I would have been too terrified to do what I did. I slid off the elephant too and down to the ground. As swiftly and silently as I could I ran for Henry's elephant, the dry grass whispering at my calves. All I knew was that he was the nearest to Prem's tree and he had a rifle. He yanked me up to his platform and to safety.

'Greer, are you *crazy*?' he began.

'No time,' I said. 'You have to shoot her.' I got right behind him. I remembered Shafeen's dad and Melati, and how he wished she had been saved, but this was different. This was his son and a different tiger, and if it was between the tiger and Shafeen . . . I put my arms around Henry and raised the gun, in a dreadful reversal of the time we'd been at Longcross and he'd made me shoot the stag. I wrestled the firearm to aim it at the tiger, my heart against his heart, my hands on his hands.

Beyond the pewter barrel of the gun, I could see that Shafeen had abandoned his plan to cut the rope and had desperately picked up a dry branch from the ground and was jabbing it helplessly towards the tiger, holding her at bay. I thought again, out of nowhere, of the lie he'd told at Longcross, about him being the tiger's son – I wished it were true that he'd suckled tiger milk, and that he was one of them, and that the tigress would feel some connection to him, would protect him. But I knew that was just – what had Shafeen called it? – mystical bullshit. He was just a man-cub with a branch standing in front of a tiger.

'Shoot her,' I urged Henry. 'Just *shoot* her.'

Henry lowered the rifle. 'I *can't*.'

'Listen to me.' I grabbed handfuls of his jacket and spoke right into his face. 'You have to save them. I know they don't matter to you. I know to you they are only Indians – some sort of inferior brown race in your white-supremacist bullshit world view. But there's something you should know. Your father was in *love* with an Indian. He loved Shafeen's father. They were *lovers*.' It was brutal, but I had to somehow shock Henry into action.

He shoved me off him. 'I can't shoot her because I might shoot *them*,' he said impatiently. 'I can't take the risk. She's too close.'

Then I understood. The tigress was in front of Prem and Shafeen, prowling back and forth like you see in the zoo – there was no clean shot. Henry was *protecting* the two men.

'But we have to do *something*.'

'We will,' he said determinedly. He scrabbled at his jacket and got something from his pocket. I just saw the gunmetal-grey flash in his hand as he threw the object, fast and accurately, towards Prem's tree. I thought he was throwing something to scare the tiger, but then I heard him shout Shafeen's name. Shafeen reacted instantly, throwing out one hand, as he had so often for a cricket ball at STAGS, and catching the object. He cocked the top of the lighter with his thumb, spun the little wheel once. His eyes flared just as the flame did, and in the next second the dry branch he held kindled into a sword of fire.

Man's red flower, I thought – the only thing a tiger feared.

Shafeen waved the burning branch right in the tiger's face.

She shrank down until the grass touched her white belly, the muscles in all four legs bunched as if to strike. It seemed as if that instant stretched out for eternity, then seconds or minutes or hours later time started again, and the tigress fell back on her haunches, checked, turned and ran.

'Quick, Henry!' I cried.

'Mine!' he shouted to the other guns. But then he swung the barrel skywards, as if he were shooting pheasant. He squeezed the trigger at the searing blue sky and the shot rang out harmlessly, kicking both of us backwards and nearly sending us tumbling off the elephant.

No one else saw what Henry had done, so intent were they on the fleeing tiger. They fired too, but the tiger was long gone. As the thunder died away, I said to Henry, low-voiced and wondering, 'You *meant* to miss.'

He put a finger to his smiling lips. 'Shhh,' he said. 'Don't tell. Everyone will think I've gone soft.'

26

Shafeen half dragged, half carried Prem over to us.

Prem's wrists were bleeding where they had chafed against the rope, and he was babbling and sobbing, almost unable to walk, his knees buckling with terror. 'We have to get Prem back to the clubhouse,' gasped Shafeen. 'He needs medical treatment.'

'Who the hell is *Prem?*' said Henry.

'*This* is Prem,' Shafeen snapped. 'He's our houseboy. How did he come to be here?'

Henry had the grace to look guilty. 'One of our scouts brought him. Smooth chap, wearing sunglasses and stinking of cologne.'

Hari. The Jadejas' suave and smiling driver. *He'd* supplied Prem to the Tiger Club as bait, covered in his mistress's cologne, as a worthless, expendable low-life. Hari, the faithful retainer, had turned on his masters as surely as Bates the butler had turned on his.

'God,' said Shafeen. 'You really are a first-class *shit*. You knew about this? And you let it play out?'

'Not that he was tied to the tree, of *course* not. I just thought he was one of the beaters.'

'A likely story,' scoffed Shafeen.

I shot him a warning look. We still needed Henry's help. 'Look,' I said, 'let's leave the inquest until later, shall we? Can we just get Prem some help?'

This seemed to cut through. Shafeen and Henry lifted Prem into the jeep, and Henry himself climbed into the driving seat.

'No,' said Shafeen. 'Not you.'

'Don't be an ass,' said Henry, not unkindly. 'How will he get help at the club if I'm not with you?'

Back at the club, Henry parked the jeep at the foot of the white steps in a swirl of dust. 'Brigadier Charteris will see to your man. He was an army medic. Come on.'

We made an odd appearance in the refined, rattan-furnitured dining room. We were all dusty and dishevelled, Shafeen was bloodstained and covered in ash, and Prem's white gown was soiled with dirt.

The moustachioed brigadier's face went puce over his club tie when he learned the identity of his patient.

'For God's sake, Longcross,' he sputtered, expelling a shower of whisky and soda. 'He's a bloody untouchable.'

Henry's face went dangerously still. 'You'll treat him as if he were your own son, or I'll know the reason why.'

The medic stiffened. Then, miraculously, he gave up his chair for Prem and we left him checking his vital signs.

'I need a drink,' said Henry to Shafeen, 'so I'm damned sure you must.'

We wandered out to the veranda, which was now in the

afternoon shade. No one spoke until we were seated with the inevitable burra pegs of gin and tonic in front of us. Henry took a huge gulp. 'Now,' he said to Shafeen, setting his glass down, 'what's all this about your father and mine?'

There was so much to say. Shafeen and I talked and talked until the sun began to set. The disappointed vultures circled home to be replaced by kinder birds whose job seemed to be to sing greetings to the night.

With the fading light I saw Henry's face blurring, the angles softening. Was I mistaken, or did his expression soften too? The moon came out and sailed above us; the moon that turned men into tigers and tigers into men. Had it worked its magic on Henry?

The story of Longcross in 1969 was a long one to tell properly. The moon party, the cubbing, the evening of beasting, the hunt, the chillies, the village hop, the assault of Ina on the rooftop. And the final, poignant coming together of Aadhish and Rollo – two boys from entirely different but in some ways very similar worlds, in which their love was equally forbidden.

I kept my eyes on Henry as Shafeen told this part. I don't know what I expected from Henry – surprise? Pity? Even disgust? But his expression was unreadable.

When Shafeen finished there was a long silence, only broken by the benevolent birds. Eventually Henry said, brokenly, 'I never knew.'

'I suppose,' I said hesitantly, 'it's not the sort of thing you just . . . bring up.'

'Yes,' said Henry drily. 'It's something that requires exquisite timing. On a deathbed, for example.' Henry stretched out his long legs and his haughty demeanour returned. 'You see, I wasn't there when he died.'

Shafeen was silent. There was nothing he could say to that.

'He didn't ask for me. He asked for *you*,' Henry continued coldly.

Shafeen smiled sadly at Henry. 'And now you know why.'

For a moment there was silence. We all looked up at the moon, and the moon looked down at us.

Then Henry spoke. 'Shafeen.' I don't know if I'd ever consciously heard Henry use the name before. 'As you say, I'm nothing but a first-class shit. So what do you want from me?'

Shafeen took a breath. 'My father knew about the fire at Longcross, but I never told him that your father had died. But then we saw your father's obituary in *The Times*. It had been at my father's breakfast table on the day he collapsed. He'd read that obituary and then come straight to the Tiger Club – a place he associated with your family. His own father, my grandfather, had been a member of the club – the first Indian member. Your grandfather Monty had been tiger hunting with him and the queen. So my father's first instinct when he read about Rollo's death was to come to the club to feel closer to him. And as soon as he got here, what did he see? Or rather, *who* did he see? You.' He unfolded the obituary from his pocket. 'Look.' He stabbed his finger at the picture of Rollo at STAGS. 'He's the absolute image of you. We think,' Shafeen continued, 'that when he saw you, he thought you *were* your father – young again, just as he was when my father fell in love with him. He literally saw a ghost. Tell me,' he said to Henry, 'did he meet your eyes?'

'Yes,' said Henry quietly. 'Just before he collapsed.'

'Well, there you go,' concluded Shafeen.

Henry returned the page of newsprint. 'Suppose what you say is true,' he said guardedly, 'what can I possibly do about it now?'

I took a breath. This was my crazy theory; I'd better be the one to expound it. 'OK. Have you ever seen a film called *Overboard*?'

Henry smiled tightly. 'A Medieval like me? No.'

'Long shot, I know,' I admitted. 'Well, Goldie Hawn plays this rich woman who gets a blow on the head and ends up in hospital with amnesia. When she sees her husband again, that's the prompt she needs to jog her memory, and she's cured of her amnesia and becomes her old self again.'

'Your point?'

'*You* are the husband in *Overboard*,' I said. 'Aadhish needs a reason to come back, and you're it.'

Henry was silent for a moment. His lip was curling, the softness of earlier gone. 'Why should I come? He's nothing to me.'

Shafeen leaned forward in his chair. 'He may be nothing to you. But he was something to your father. And he's everything to me. Look, Henry . . .' The naming thing was obviously catching on. 'This might be goodbye for me. And I love my father. It's not like you with yours. I *truly* love him.'

'Oh, I did love mine,' said Henry. 'He just didn't love *me*.'

And there it was. The bitterness, the rawness, the humiliation, revealed for us to see. Despite everything he'd done, I felt sorry for Henry de Warlencourt.

'Then I'll trade you,' said Shafeen, his voice unsteady. 'It could be that my father will never come back. It could be that this is the end.' I looked at him in shock. This was the first time he'd admitted this out loud, and I suspected it was the first time he'd admitted it to himself. 'So I'll cut you a deal, Henry. I'll exchange you your father's deathbed for mine.' He was deadly serious, his eyes shining with unshed tears. '*You* can be the one to say goodbye. Say ciao, say cheers, say sayonara. So long as – dear God – so long as you say *something*.'

I could see Henry wavering, but he still wasn't convinced.

I waded into the breach. 'Henry,' I said, putting my hand on his wrist, 'this is your chance to *not* be like your father.' The ruined flesh under my hand reminded me. 'Look what you did for Ty on the day he died. You saved her life. You're *not him*. He could have been a good man, a happy man. He loved once. He laughed once. But something warped him. Don't let that happen to you. *You* can *change*. Will you come? Please?'

The moon had risen fully and it was night. I could barely see Henry, but I could hear him still.

'Yes.'

PART 6

That's What
Friends Are For

27

While the Tiger Club members noisily consoled themselves at dinner for the loss of a magnificent trophy, Shafeen, Henry and I, with the bandaged Prem in tow, climbed into one of the club's Rolls-Royces.

Shafeen had dismissed Hari on the spot and told him that if he gave any trouble, he, Shafeen, would involve the police. Of course, that meant we were without a lift, so one of the Tiger Club's chauffeurs took us into the city.

Prem, usually so chatty, was struck dumb, but it was hard to tell whether this was due to the honour of the car or the horror of the day. Henry, in the front, and Shafeen and I in the back were likewise quiet, silenced by the presence of the driver. But as the lights of the city grew closer Shafeen leaned forward with a question in Hindi, and Prem, with much bowing and gratitude, replied.

'What's going on?' I said.

'We're driving him home.'

'To your home?'

'No. To his.'

I smiled and squeezed his hand, but he snatched it away.

'Don't.' He hung his head. 'I don't deserve anything. I had to *ask* him where he lived, Greer. You were right. I didn't even know.'

We drove to a part of Jaipur I'd never been to before, where the houses were more like shacks than dwellings. Sheets of corrugated iron served as roofs; swathes of fabric stood in for doors. It felt utterly wrong sweeping up to Prem's home in the Silver Ghost Rolls-Royce, which probably cost more than every house in this district put together. Every kid in the street came out to gawp, and we were soon surrounded. Shafeen helped Prem out of the car and, at the sight of him, the residents urged forward a young woman and four children on a wave of chatter and benevolent pushing hands. This, then, was his family: the mouths he fed on what the Jadeja family gave him.

Shafeen greeted the wife with a namaste, and spent some time talking with her and the eldest child – a good-looking boy probably not much younger than Shafeen – who seemed to be taking charge of the situation. The smallest child – a little girl with plaits to her knees – had her round eyes fixed on the silver ghost ornament on the car bonnet. She reached out a little hand to touch it. The chauffeur tsked loudly and made to shoo her away, but to my delight Henry stopped him with a word.

Once Prem had been claimed by his family, Shafeen said his goodbyes. Prem, still a little shaky, lifted his hand to his forehead, giving his traditional Britisher salute. In place of his usual mockery, Shafeen stood up straight and, quite seriously, saluted him back.

As the driver nosed the car away gradually, careful not to run down any of the shoal of kids, I said, 'What did you say to the son?'

'I said, *Your father is one of our family. And you are our family too.*'

This time, when I took his hand he didn't take it away.

'I also told Prem that if he comes to work tomorrow, he's fired.' He smiled. 'He needs a paid holiday, and that's what he's going to get.'

28

When we reached the hospital and hurried down the clean, shiny corridors, the first thing we saw was the Princess Himani, dressed in bright coral and gold, in a huddle with two white-coated doctors.

As we approached, the doctors nodded and left, leaving the princess pressing her beringed hands to her mouth. It was an ominous sign.

Shafeen ran the last few feet. 'Is he . . . ?'

'No,' she said. 'No, he's still alive. But he has worsened. They don't think he will come back now. They asked me . . . They asked me . . .' Her face crumpled.

'If you'd like to turn off life support?'

She couldn't reply but just nodded. Shafeen held her tight in his arms, her head at his throat. Then he set her away from him, holding both of her shoulders. 'Mother,' he said. 'Let Henry try.'

I'd almost forgotten about Henry, who was hovering awkwardly at the edges of this intensely intimate little scene. It was one of the few times I'd seen him look as if he didn't belong somewhere.

Himani looked dazed. 'Who's this?'

Henry hesitated, then said, 'An old friend.'

She clasped his hand with hers, and Henry looked strangely moved. 'If you think it might do some good . . . and what harm can it do?' she said, her voice wavering between puzzlement and desperation.

Shafeen opened the door of his father's room and nodded at Henry. I knew this was no casual gesture, but an enormously meaningful moment. This was part of the deal agreed at the Tiger Club. He was giving Henry his own place at his father's bedside, just as Shafeen had taken Henry's place at Rollo's deathbed. Henry hesitated. 'What should I say?'

Shafeen and I looked at each other. There was only one answer. 'Call him Horatio,' Shafeen said.

Then he stood out of the way and Henry went past him into the room.

As Shafeen shut the door, I helped the princess sit down on the bench in the hospital corridor and then took my place beside Shafeen, peering through the square window in the door, as if watching a scene in a movie. We saw Henry walk into frame and take a seat in the chair by the bed. We saw him take Aadhish's hand, just as Shafeen had done to Rollo at Longcross. And, as clearly as if there was not a door between us, we could see his lips form the word 'Horatio'.

Then, 'Horatio, it's me.'

Did I mistake it, or did the eyelids start to flicker, as they do in REM sleep?

Holding my breath and Shafeen's hand equally tightly, I watched as Henry de Warlencourt leaned forward in the hospital chair and gave Aadhish Jadeja a tender kiss on the cheek.

Silence.

The steady green line on the monitor by the bed gave a leap, then plummeted again like a stone.

It was a dreadful moment. I thought we'd made – literally – a fatal mistake. The princess had been wrong. There *might* be harm in it. The shock of waking to see the love of his youth there might kill him. What if he gave up, in order to join Rollo in the afterlife? What had we done?

But then the line recovered, soared and peaked again, and began to undulate at a steady rate as Aadhish Jadeja opened his eyes, looked at Henry and gave him a beatific smile. The monitor began to shriek persistently, sounding the alarm that life had returned.

At that point we piled into the room, followed by the princess. Shafeen and his mother sank down by the bed and Henry stepped back, his work done. I retreated with him to the corner of the room and squeezed his ruined hand. His face had taken on a new look – one that he'd worn perhaps only a handful of times before. When he'd carried a girl from a burning building. When he'd instructed an army medic to treat an untouchable. When he'd squashed a snooty chauffeur who wanted to shoo a little girl away from his car. If I were to define it, I would call it *goodness*. It enhanced his already considerable beauty, like a golden varnish on an old master. It made it hard to look away from him.

Of course, we were soon elbowed aside by the medical professionals, who crowded into the room and began dealing with tubes and drips and monitors and calling out incomprehensible orders. One orderly turned to us and barked at us in English, 'There are too many people in this room. One only, please.'

Henry and I, Shafeen and his mother retreated to the door, looking at one another, not knowing who should stay.

Then came a voice from the bed, weak but still commanding. We turned as one to see Aadhish pointing with a wavering hand. The dread returned. If he chose Henry to be by his side above the princess, she would burn indeed. Hoarsely but quite clearly, in a voice that had not been used for days, Aadhish said, 'Himani.'

Then, 'My *wife*.'

29

In the corridor, Shafeen, Henry and I sank down on the bench, exhausted and happy to be on the sidelines.

We were silent for a while, watching nurses and doctors bustling in and out of the room – serious, professional but joyful at the vindication of their learning and their science and their clever ideas. They didn't know that what had woken Aadhish had nothing to do with the head. It had to do with the heart.

Henry took out a cigarette, put it between his lips and began to pat his pockets for his lighter. Shafeen, who on any other day would be scandalised at the prospect of someone smoking in a hospital, got Henry's lighter out of his own pocket and lit the cigarette for him. He then put the lighter in Henry's scarred palm. We looked at it where it lay. 'The Queen of England gave it to my father,' said Henry.

That was when it clicked. This was the lighter Rollo had had in the diary – he'd told the same story.

Henry went on: 'But I think he would want *your* father to have it.'

He handed it back, and now Shafeen looked at the lighter in *his* palm: gunmetal grey, with the royal coat of arms etched on the side. The totem that had saved two lives. He closed his brown hand around it and put it in his pocket. 'Thank you,' he said sincerely. 'I'll make sure he gets it.'

Henry got precisely three drags of his cigarette before someone in scrubs told him to put it out, at which he smiled and complied. The same someone took Shafeen away to sign some forms, and it was then that I turned to Henry and said something that had been on my mind for a while. 'I hope you know that Rollo didn't choose *Shafeen* over you at the end. He thought he *was* Aadhish. The young man he'd loved and lost. I don't know if that makes it easier.'

Henry let his head fall back against the wall, his tanned throat oddly exposed. 'I don't know either.'

I had something else to say and I didn't know how I was going to put it. But I felt that Henry was kind of owed something for what he'd done. 'Rollo . . . your father . . . did love you, you know. When he talked of you to me he had tears in his eyes. I know it's not much, but . . .'

He stopped me. 'It's enough.' He closed his eyes, and I thought for a moment he might sleep. So the next thing I said I murmured into his ear, so softly, like a whisper. 'You did a good thing today. For Shafeen.'

He lifted his head off the wall and turned to look at me.

'I didn't just do it for Shafeen, Greer. I did it because you asked me to. I did it because I love you.'

PART 7
My Own Home

30

The Tiger Club's Rolls-Royce drove us back to Shafeen's house, then the driver was to take Henry back to the club to pack up his luggage.

He was staying the night with us as Shafeen's guest and would fly back to England in the morning. Part of me was relieved that we had only one night to get through – one final episode of the particular soap opera in which I'd found myself. Shafeen and I would return the following weekend in time for the start of our Trinity term. Our final term at STAGS.

The emotion of the hospital – what had happened to Aadhish, what had happened to all of us in our different ways – rendered Shafeen and Henry and me silent in the car. I watched the fat moon sailing high in the sky, keeping pace with us as we drove. A trite sixth-form film-studies phrase floated into my head and stuck there.

Love triangle.

Shafeen and I had just taken things to the next level. I'd been happy – happier than I'd ever been. And then Henry had to go and say what he'd said. I looked at Shafeen's dark head next to me, and Henry's blond head in the front seat. Then I looked to the heavens. *Genuine question*, I asked the moon silently. *What the hell am I going to do now?* The secret I was now keeping sat in between me and Shafeen like a buffer.

Back at the house, Shafeen and I got no further than the atrium, collapsing on the divan just inside the doors, for a time too exhausted to speak, just listening to the plashing of the peacock fountain. I actually think we went to sleep for a bit, because when we woke it was pretty late.

Groggily, I turned my head on the cushions to address Shafeen. 'Did they say when your father would be discharged?'

He turned his head to match mine, our foreheads almost touching. 'Next week,' he said sleepily. 'They're going to keep him in for a few days for observation. I can't believe he'll be back here, Greer.'

I took his hand.

'And I owe it all to Henry. You were right about him. He did come back from the dark side of the moon.' He picked at the tassels on the divan, pulling them through his long fingers, as if it cost him something to say that. I was silent. I couldn't tell him *why* Henry had changed.

'That's why he asked us on the tiger hunt. He wanted us to witness it. He *wanted* us to stop him because he knew that it was wrong.'

'So you think he *did* know?' I asked. 'He did know there was to be a man tied there, along with the goats?'

'Yes, I think so. Don't you?'

I couldn't answer this. 'All I know is, when we came he was glad,' I said. 'I could see he was. He was surprised but relieved. You're right. He wanted us to stop it. But why couldn't he just stop it himself?'

Shafeen stretched his arms above his head. 'Perhaps he himself feels coerced.'

'Explain.'

'Well, you read my father's diary. Father thought that Rollo was the Grand Master. So did we when we first read the game book, the first time we went to Longcross. Remember, it was only that tell-tale comma that gave it away that the Grand Master and Rollo de Warlencourt were not one and the same person. My father had it wrong. Rollo was an Eggman. The Medievals were the Eggmen. *Gideon* was the Walrus.'

'You're making zero sense right now.'

'You know – that really trippy Beatles song called "I Am the Walrus". My father referenced it in the diary. The Walrus is the leader. The Eggmen are the followers.'

'Oooooh,' I said – a long, drawn-out sound.

'What I mean is, Henry is an Eggman too. He might be one of the Grand Stags, but he isn't the master of his own fate. Someone else is controlling him in turn.'

It suited me to believe that. It suited me not to have to think badly of Henry at that moment. 'So who is the Walrus now?'

'Same guy as it ever was,' said Shafeen. 'Gideon Villiers. The Old Abbot.'

'So,' I said slowly, figuring it out, 'you think that the Old Abbot is making sure that the death hunts carry on. If they are prevented at Longcross – like the Boxing Day meet was – they'll just carry on somewhere else. Here. Maybe in other countries too.'

'Maybe. But maybe Henry wants to stop now. He's been running away from his true nature – or his new nature, if you believe his fall changed him. He's known this was all wrong for a long time. He wanted to change, but he didn't know how. I think you showed him how.'

He looked at me intently. Almost *too* intently. Had he guessed? I had to deflect from this dangerous subject.

'And you?' I asked. 'He once said you were running away too. What does he think you're running away from?' I thought of something pretty profound, for me. 'From India?'

'No,' he said. 'Quite the reverse. England. Great Britain. And the Raj. Whatever my feelings about India's history, and the past, they were things that were important to my father, and like it or not they are important to me.'

He went to the bureau by the front door and opened the top drawer. He slid out something framed and rectangular.

The photograph of the tiger hunt.

He placed it reverently on the wall, carefully hanging it back on the redundant hook, neatly obscuring the white rectangle that had been protected from fading all those years.

I hauled myself off the divan and went to stand at Shafeen's shoulder, looking past him to that exclusive group of people, both men and women, standing together with Melati the tiger stretched on the ground in front of them. Shafeen's father, a boy of eleven, with his foot on the tigress's neck. His parents: the smiling maharajah, the glamorous maharani. Prince Philip, tall and beaky as a heron. And there, in the middle of the picture, Elizabeth, Queen of England.

It was a troubling image, but if Shafeen had made his peace with it, then so must I – these elite predators, this private club. This *club*.

I shifted my gaze to the tall, blond, moustachioed guy next to the queen, wearing the striped tie of the Tiger Club.

Monty.

Monty de Warlencourt, all medals and moustaches, posing with the queen. *That family don't have much luck with horseflesh,* was what Colonel Moran had said. And it was true. Henry's grandfather Monty had been killed in a riding accident when something knocked him off his horse. And Henry's father Rollo had fallen from his horse when it had been spooked by a tall man rearing up from the undergrowth. I'd witnessed it myself.

Something nudged at me then – the echo of a memory. I'd stood somewhere, in some ancient establishment, looking at a photo in a frame just like this one, of someone in a stripy tie. At the Tiger Club? No. somewhere else.

STAGS.

Where it had all begun.

My eyes still on the photograph, I said to Shafeen, 'What time is it in England?'

He checked his watch. 'Morning. Why?'

I didn't reply but flipped out my phone and texted Nel:

Humour me on this one. Go into Abbot Ridley's study. Find the picture of him in a stripy tie. It's on the wall behind his desk. Send me a photo.

I was so used to all those times I'd texted Ty and not got a reply that I wasn't expecting one now. But this was Nel, the Queen of Tech, we were dealing with.

First, she texted:

. . .

Then:

OK then

I blessed her in the name of God and Krishna and any other deity I could think of. She was such a good soldier, never asking unnecessary questions, always cutting straight to the chase.

'What's going on?' asked Shafeen.

'Just a hunch,' I said, trying to order my thoughts. 'Give me a minute.'

I settled back on the divan for a long wait, but it took Nel less than five minutes to get back to me. She was so quick that it made me wonder whether she was already in 'Nathaniel's' study, but I couldn't think about that now.

She'd sent a good picture from her state-of-the-art Saros phone to mine. I pinched it wider with my fingers and stared.

There was Abbot Ridley, probably in his late twenties. He looked as handsome as ever, curls ruffled by the wind and one eye half closed against the fierce Indian sun. I knew where he was because of the edge of a white veranda over his right shoulder and a set of sweeping white stairs.

I expanded the photo. The date on the frame said 2015. And, even more damning, around his neck hung a stripy orange-and-black tie.

The tie of the Tiger Club.

My vision seemed to lurch and my head felt like it was spinning.

I placed the phone in Shafeen's hands. 'Look,' I said. 'He's a Manslayer.'

'Ridley?' he said.

'I mean, we've known it for a while, since we discovered that he has a brand like mine, but it's different knowing *what* he did – *who* he killed. I thought he might have been tried and branded by mistake, like I was. I mean, I'm damned sure I've never killed anybody. But now we know different about Abbot Ridley.'

'Greer,' said Shafeen, 'what the hell are you talking about?'

I took a breath. 'It was Abbot Ridley.'

'*What* was Abbot Ridley?'

'Who caused Monty's death. In his role as one of the FOXES. He came to Jaipur in 2015, infiltrated the Tiger Club somehow, got himself a tie. Don't you remember that line from Reynard's letter? *If they don't know who we are, they never see us coming.* Monty never saw Ridley coming.'

I could see the scene play in my head like a movie – Monty setting out from the Tiger Club on his customary morning ride, always the same horse, always the same route. A figure rising out of the undergrowth, Monty's horse rearing, the old man falling. It was a dreadful end.

But then I thought of another scene – just one of the many

that prompted this revenge killing. A small black boy by the name of Leon Morgan, newly arrived in England on the *Empire Windrush*, being chased by hounds and, even worse, by his *hosts* at a country house called Longcross. Goodness knows how many Dalit victims over the centuries had been tied to trees like goats on the plains of the Tiger Club . . . Aadhish Jadeja pursued through the haunted halls of Longcross. When you thought about it like that, Nathaniel Ridley was a hero.

I was yanked from my cinematic visions by another text from Nel. The sharp, tinny tone and the vibration of the phone brought us back to ourselves, the text banner neatly obscuring the Abbot's face in the photo.

What's up?

There was no way I could articulate the brainstorm of the last two minutes in a couple of lines of text. 'We'll tell her in person,' said Shafeen. He was right. Telling Nel that the man she was so thirsty for had Manslayed Monty de Warlencourt didn't feel like something you should do in a text. We both huddled over the phone as I typed.

Nothing. Explain later. Coming home soon.

She replied straight away:

Both of you?

At that moment the front door opened and we looked up.

Henry de Warlencourt walked into the atrium and dropped a heavy holdall at his feet. He clocked us both staring at him.

'What?' he said.

I looked at Shafeen and he gave me a single nod. I texted to Nel:

All three of us. Henry's coming too.

Her response was entirely natural:

Henry???!! WTF . . .

I couldn't express in a text the enormity of what had happened here. The diary, the Tiger Club and the hunt. I couldn't convey in little pixelated characters that declaration of love at the hospital, and the triangle, and the dark side of the moon. That would all have to be done in person. So instead I just texted by way of explanation something that was true, but that was intimately connected with Aadhish and Rollo and *The Jungle Book* and the whole mess of past and present and future.

He wants to be like us.

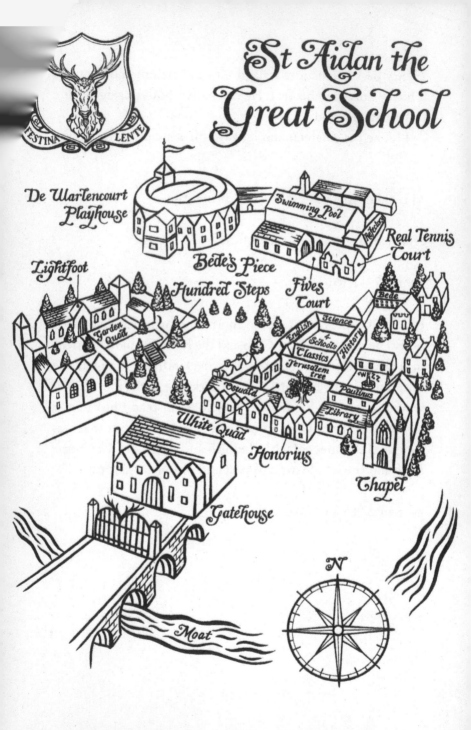

DE WARLENCOURT PLAYHOUSE – built in 1969, the theatre is an exact replica of the sixteenth-century Swan Theatre which used to stand on London's bankside.

BEDE LIBRARY (incorporating the Scriptorium) – named after the Venerable Bede, the library has several notable architectural features, including the medieval Scriptorium, a remnant of the original monastery school, and the Tudor Reading Room.

GATEHOUSE – the gatehouse forms the entrance to the school, reached by crossing the medieval moat. In the days of the monastery school, the drawbridge was raised at night to keep marauding Scots away from the treasures of the chapel.

BEDE'S PIECE – STAGS boasts extensive playing fields, named for a piece of common land enclosed by the school during the eighteenth century.

CHAPEL – Founded in 683, the chapel is the oldest surviving building of the first monastery school. The stained-glass window of Aidan and the stag is original.

REFECTORY – This long building with vaulted ceilings was rebuilt at the time of the Civil War after a fire. The wooden benches and tables on which the students dine are the original ones from the monastery, on which the monks ate their breakfast of bread and beer.

ENGLISH SCHOOLS – In the reign of Edward VI, New Quad –a quadrangle of exquisite Tudor buildings – was built at STAGS to represent the four pillars of learning. The first of the schools (always referred to in the plural) is the English Schools, and the original sign still remains carved above the door.

HISTORY SCHOOLS – The second side of the quad, the History Schools houses the original copy of Bede's work.

CLASSICS SCHOOLS – The third side of the quad, the Classics Schools still fulfills its function of teaching Latin, the language of law and learning.

SCIENCE LABS – Originally the Theology Schools, the fourth side of the quad, despite its Tudor appearance and theological sign carved in stone, now houses STAGS' extensive science laboratories.

THE HUNDRED STEPS – this ancient stone stairway connects the upper and lower schools. Legend has it that in 1348 Edmund de Warlencourt rode up the hundred steps on his horse for a wager.

POOL – The STAGS swimming pool is Olympic-sized and fully compliant with the regulations of the Fédération Internationale de Natation. It is 164 feet long, 82 feet wide and 6 feet deep, with eight swimming lanes marked with rope and buoys.

FIVES AND REAL TENNIS COURTS – Both courts are fully enclosed, and constructed of their original timbers. The Real Tennis court is fashioned after Charles II's court at Hampton Court Palace. The Fives court is designed to replicate one of the exterior bays of the chapel, where the game was first played after Mass.

Acknowledgements

Firstly my apologies to Rudyard Kipling for bastardising the first line of *The Jungle Book* to begin this book.

I'm indebted as always to my friend and agent – Fragent™ – Teresa Chris for her expert guidance.

Thank you as ever to the triple threat of Emma Matthewson, Holly Kyte and Talya Baker for editing, copy-editing and proofreading *T.I.G.E.R.S.* This time I must add Tia Albertson, who heroically went through the whole series to create an invaluable S.T.A.G.S. bible.

I'm grateful to the whole team at Hot Key Books for their hard work and support for the S.T.A.G.S. series.

I'm indebted to Sally Taylor for making STAGS school a reality with her beautiful artwork.

Thank you to ace literary scout Drew Reed, who was the first proper grown-up to like the idea of going back in time to tell Aadhish's story.

Some of this book comes from my own heritage. Ina Forrester was my grandmother, who went into service at the age of fifteen. Much of this is her story.

But some of this history is not my own, and therefore

required a lot of research. I won't bore you with endless titles but must stress that any mistakes made about the people or culture of India are my own. One resource I will mention is Sathnam Sanghera's excellent documentary on Amritsar for Channel 4 (*The Massacre That Shook the Empire*, 2019). I studied history at two schools and four universities but was never once taught about that dreadful day.

I highly recommend watching the film *Junoon* (1992, dir. Mahesh Bhatt). It's a fantastically campy horror.

Once again the film *The Lion in Winter* (1968, dir. Anthony Harvey) is referenced throughout – definitely worth a watch if you are at all into power and kingship.

The photograph of the Queen's Tiger Hunt, which is pivotal to this story, is real. It shows the queen and the late Prince Philip, and a number of other hunters, standing over the corpse of a tiger in Jaipur in 1961. It's a difficult image, and probably not the one that the royal family would wish to promote, but if you want to see it, it can be found online with the most cursory Google search.

Lastly but not leastly, thank you to Sacha, Conrad and Ruby. As Bryan Adams once said, everything I do, I do it for you.

M. A. Bennett

M. A. Bennett is half Venetian and was born in Manchester, England, and raised in the Yorkshire Dales. She is a history graduate of Oxford University and the University of Venice, where she specialised in the study of Shakespeare's plays as a historical source. After university she studied art and has since worked as an illustrator, an actress and a film reviewer. She also designed tour visuals for rock bands, including U2 and the Rolling Stones. She was married on the Grand Canal in Venice and lives in north London with her husband, son and daughter. Her first YA novel, *S.T.A.G.S.*, was published in 2017, shortlisted for the YA BOOK PRIZE 2018 and won the Great Reads 'Most Read' 2018 Senior Award. *D.O.G.S.*, the second in the world of STAGS, followed in 2019.

@MABennettAuthor
@mabennettauthor

HOT
KEY
BOOKS

Thank you for choosing a Hot Key book.

If you want to know more about our authors and what we publish, you can find us online.

You can start at our website

www.hotkeybooks.com

And you can also find us on:

We hope to see you soon!